MIKE CHINN

WALKERS IN SHADOW

PRO SE PRESS™

PRO SE PRESS

WALKERS IN SHADOW
A Pro Se Productions Publication

Written by Mike Chinn
Editing by Dave Brzeski & Melissa Brooks

Cover by Larry Nadolsky
Book Design by Antonino Lo Iacono & Marzia Marina
New Pulp Logo Design by Sean E. Ali
New Pulp Seal Design by Cari Reese

Pro Se Productions, LLC
133 1/2 Broad Street
Batesville, AR, 72501
870-834-4022

editorinchief@prose-press.com
www.prose-press.com

WALKERS IN SHADOW

CONTENTS

PART SEVEN: BEYOND THE BLUE HORIZON

PART ONE:
SAILORS OF THE SKIES

I

The clouds came in fast, reducing the ceiling in a nightmarishly short time. Heavy and black, they stretched endlessly into the atmosphere; premature night fell across the countryside. The New York bound Ford Trimotor looked very small and lost.

In the passenger plane's cockpit, pilot and co-pilot craned forward, squinting through the small windows. Somewhere below there had to be a safe place to land before the storm hit.

The co-pilot frowned. "I guess it's too far back to Manchester, John?"

John Theaker slowly shook his head. "Looks like it's coming down from the north; we'd likely be headed straight into it." He glanced at his co-pilot: the man's normally tanned face was gray. "Don't sweat it, Greg. We'll make it."

Greg Howard's smile wasn't convincing. "Just like the good old days, huh?"

The pilot nodded. Both had met up in the Great War: American volunteers in the British Royal Flying Corps. They'd left as experienced pilots, but Greg hadn't fully recovered from the experience: suffering with nerves ever since.

Theaker picked up the microphone and flicked on the radio. His reward was a screech of static: a giant dragging fingernails down a chalkboard.

"This is Empire State Zero Four out of Manchester, New

Hampshire, calling New York. Can you hear me, New York?" The static howled back, rising and falling in waves that made his teeth itch. "Come in New York!" Nothing. He hung up the mic.

"Looks like we're on our own, Greg. Must be one hell of a storm to create so much interference."

Howard licked his lips. "Maybe I should have taken that desk job, after all."

"The only thing you'll ever a fly is a plane." Theaker did his best to sound confident, but he was wondering if maybe they were getting too old for the job. Twenty years ago he'd have relished the danger; the unpredictability. Now all he could do was worry about the ten passengers back in the cabin.

"Check outside, would you, Greg? See how close the blow's gotten."

Howard looked through his side window. "Still coming up fast. Black as hell."

The pilot checked both compass heading and odometer. He did a quick calculation in his head. "Just passing Providence, I reckon."

Howard laughed. "That's what we need: a touch of providence!"

As though his words had summoned a divine intervention, the blackness abruptly thinned. A dissolute light filled the air and, far below, Theaker could see ground again. He dipped the nose: no finesse, he was getting the kite down before the visibility went again. If that panicked the passengers, too bad. They could complain back in New York.

Howard was craning his head forward, squinting through windows and the blur of the Trimotor's central propeller. "This is crazy, John. There's a hole in the clouds, almost perfectly round. Opened up; just like that!"

"Then let's hope it doesn't just close again!" Theaker was searching the approaching earth; looking for somewhere—anywhere—he could land the Tin Goose. "Eyes open, Greg, let me know if the light's about to go again!"

"Looks to me like it's getting bigger." Howard's voice was unsteady. "Like an invisible hand's pushing the clouds apart!"

Theaker muttered through gritted teeth., "There's your providence!" He hoped somewhere in Rhode Island there was a couple acres of unbroken, flat land. That's all he wanted: two flat acres with no trees or fences.

"It's still— Jesus Christ—!"

Startled, Theaker almost took his eyes off the nearing ground. "What? What is it?"

"The hole… it's… Jesus—I don't believe—!"

"What? Is the light going? Greg! For God's sake…!"

"It's going, all right!" Howard's voice was suddenly brittle, likely to crack any moment. "It's gone…" He started to giggle. The sound drenched his friend in an ice-cold sweat. He'd never heard Greg go to pieces this bad before. Never.

The light was still there, but it looked all wrong. Diseased, was how Theaker thought of it: unhealthy. And it was moving: diffracted sunlight flickering like they were under water. He dropped the nose further; he heard the screams from beyond the curtain leading to the cabin. They made a hellish chorus with Howard's sniggering: clawing at the pilot's brain until it was all he could do not to join in.

The Trimotor shuddered, trying to wrench itself free of the pilot's hands. He kept his eyes on the ground, ignoring the light, ignoring the way it wriggled and coiled beyond the windows. Lightning, he told himself. The plane shook again, battered by the storm breaking all around them. It had to be a storm; what else could it be?

Then the Tin Goose was lurching upwards. The ground spun away. The light twisted and writhed through the glass until it was blotted out by something far blacker than storm clouds. Something darker than any shadow. Something that squirmed in time with the diseased light.

II

A Duesenberg Royalton slowly cruised along a road that was just one notch above a dirt track. The limousine took every bump and hollow in its stride, barely shaking its passenger, finally rolling to a halt under a peeling billboard.

An immaculately-dressed chauffeur stepped out of the limo, walked around the cooling hood, and opened the right rear door. A tall, well-built figure in a perfectly-fitted, dark striped suit got out—moving with the grace of a man who knows he owns most of what he looks at. He brushed at an invisible speck on a lapel as the chauffeur handed him a gray hat. The man slipped it on his head, flicking the brim just so. “I don’t expect I’ll be long.”

The chauffeur bowed a little. “Very good, sir.”

The man glanced at the old billboard. It was advertising a trucking company that had likely gone out of business when the Depression hit: half the letters had vanished, leaving any readers to fill in the gaps. Behind it was the skyline of New York City, its angles softened by distance and an early-morning haze. To the right was a run-down airfield, no different from a hundred gimcrack barnstorming outfits which had thrived a few years ago. Except this one still had airplanes, around a dozen; and not so run down. Each one had recently been given a new paint job, in brilliant red and gold. The place was a regular flying circus.

Must be the place, he figured.

There was a gap in the fence that might have held a gate in better days. As he passed through, it seemed to grow quieter. Some accident of geography. The place looked deserted, though, and he began to wonder if he was, after all, in the right spot. Then he spotted two figures working on a small biplane. They had the engine cowling off and their blue coveralls were smeared with oil and grease. He called out: "Hey! Is this Chaykin Field?"

One of the grease-monkeys looked up. With a shock he realized it was a dame. Her peroxided curls and diamond-blue eyes shone against the layer of grime. "It might be." Her voice held a hint of New Jersey, heavy with suspicion.

"Well either it is or it isn't, I'm looking for a Mr. Damian Paladin. Is he here?"

The second grease-monkey peered around the plane. Hair and eyes as black as the oil that coated his coveralls, he looked the kind of guy who'd lead with his fists, keeping the questions till later—if he didn't have a gun handy. "Who wants to know?"

The dame spoke before the visitor could so much as open his mouth. "His name's Garrard Graves, president of the Empire State Lines commercial flight company. You remember them, Damy? They bought out McDonagh Airlines last year, after that banshee business."

Graves belatedly removed his hat. "How did you—?" He tailed off as her meaning sank in. The black-haired guy was wiping his hands on a cloth even oilier than his coveralls. "*You're* Damian Paladin?"

"Got it in one, colonel. I'd shake your hand, but—" He held up grimy hands. "And the princess with the index card memory is named Leigh Oswin, in case you were wondering."

They stood side by side: black-haired Paladin resting a hand on a cylinder, blonde Leigh leaning against the propeller. Graves felt like he was looking at a crazy pair of bookends, positive and negative.

She spoke first: "So, Mr. Graves—?"

Paladin finished with a white grin: "—Exactly what kind of monsters you got?"

III

Once Paladin and Leigh had changed out of their work clothes, all three sat in the tiny wooden shack that served as an office. They drank coffee strong enough to blind, served from a pot on a Dutch stove. Paladin rested his booted legs across a worn table top, listening carefully as Garrard Graves outlined the three disasters Empire State Lines had recently suffered.

"*Three* planes?" He'd seen nothing in the papers about it. Graves obviously had some leverage.

Graves nodded. "Two on the weekly Manchester to New York flight; the other on the Boston hop."

Leigh took a cigarette from her purse. "While I sympathize, I don't see what that has to do with us." She echoed Paladin's thoughts exactly.

Graves was staring at his untouched coffee. "All three went missing at the same spot. Close as we can tell, anyhow. The weather was fine, the planes brand new. None of them left any radio message—" He took a deep breath. "There was no wreckage. Not so much as a doorknob."

Paladin swung his legs off the table, sitting upright. "I don't want to tell you your job, Mr. Graves, but you sure you were looking in the right place?"

Graves lifted gaunt eyes. It was clear he'd wondered the same thing, over and over. "Sure as I can be. All three were spotted near the area we thought… we *guessed* they got lost. At that point they were on course. It's not likely any of the pilots could have drifted so soon—so… so *completely*!"

Paladin stood, crossing the shack to a tiny cupboard. He reached in and produced a quart of bourbon. Returning to Graves' side, he poured a generous slug into his coffee cup. "You know any of the crew?"

Graves sipped at the juiced-up brew and winced. Paladin wondered if it was the heat or cheap booze that got him. "The pilot on the first plane we lost. John Theaker. We'd known each other since the company's early days. Him and his co-pilot, Greg Howard, were on staff practically from the get-go, when we just flew mail in beat-up warplanes…"

Paladin just grunted and sat down. He thought Graves was taking it more seriously than a company president with a cash crisis.

Leigh lit her cigarette. "Whereabouts did all three planes go missing?" Paladin noticed she avoided the word *crash*. They were all tiptoeing on eggshells round that little word.

"Somewhere just north-west of Providence."

"Not so far from the ocean—" She left the rest unsaid.

Paladin pictured the geography. "Pretty flat land; no real hills to speak of. Not the kind of place to get localized pockets of weather."

Graves hunched over his drink. "No…"

"But?" Paladin could hear a sizeable qualification hanging off that *no*. It was probably central to the whole deal.

"Nothing." Graves gulped more coffee, his wince less noticeable this time.

"Except you don't think it's nothing, or you'd tell me."

Graves stared at the low ceiling. "Some locals reckon they saw storm clouds. Massive thunderheads. A couple even claim to have seen lights of some kind…"

Leigh blew out a stream of smoke. "Lightning?" It wasn't an unreasonable suggestion.

"There were no storms!" Graves stared at her. "Each day the weather was fine and clear. There were no storms for miles, in all directions!"

Paladin leaned forward, all attention. "Level with me, Graves.

There *were* no storms?"

The airline president shook his head.

"And your planes were A1?"

"Look—I already told you…!"

Paladin closed his eyes, blotting out Graves' desperate expression. After all these years, had it come back…? Could it be the same…?

"Look here, Paladin." Graves' voice brought him back to the present. "I hear you're good at explaining the inexplicable; that you're discreet…"

Paladin opened his eyes. "Been talking with Julius Eberhard?"

Graves pursed his lips. "We spoke. Nothing of that McDonagh business ever made the papers."

"People's dirty laundry is nothing to do with me. I just investigate and eliminate." Paladin turned to Leigh with a grin. "Hey, princess, maybe we could use that as the company motto…?"

She stared patiently at the ceiling and groaned.

Graves got to his feet, hand reaching inside his suit coat. It came out clutching a thick envelope which he dropped on the table. "That's two grand, Paladin. I'm good for more if you need it."

Leigh smiled. "I'll bet."

"Just get me something that'll keep the stockholders happy."

Paladin eyed the wad of dough. "Well, the P-12 does need a new engine…" He looked up at Graves. "You understand you might not like the answers?"

"Just do it, Paladin!" Graves grabbed his hat and strode out of the shack, leaving Paladin and Leigh staring at the open door.

Leigh whistled softly. "If we find out his planes are haunted, or something—"

Paladin knew what she meant. "He's not doing it for his company, princess. It's about revenge."

IV

Paladin hung up the phone, looking out the shack's only window. Leigh was waiting by the planes, looking suitably impatient. He grinned; a couple more minutes wouldn't hurt her.

He went to the tiny cupboard and opened the door. Pushing the bourbon aside, he reached to the back, pushing gently against the rough plywood. It gave with a soft click. Paladin slid the false back away, reaching deeper inside. Identifying various objects by touch alone, his fingers eventually closed around a wooden box, the size of a table-top cigarette box, and took it out. He glanced at the box, eyes careful to avoid the grotesque relief carved on all sides. Even though he'd seen it many times, the inhuman images still disturbed him. He slipped it into a pocket in his old leather coat, replaced the false cupboard back and shut the door.

As he made for the door, he cinched a gun belt around his battered, sleeveless flying coat. From the belt hung two heavy automatics, along with a mixture of pouches and loops: a variety of tools and weapons he'd found useful over the years.

Outside, Leigh greeted his appearance with derisive relief. "I thought it was us girls who took our time getting ready."

"I wanted to look my best for you."

She flicked a glance at his clothes. "If that's your best…"

Paladin shrugged. So the sleeves from his flying coat were missing, lost in an adventure a year or two earlier, and his riding pants and boots were equally battered: they were comfortable. He felt happy in them. "I thought you liked my hero suit."

"Yeah…" She gave her own getup a significant once over. The one-piece coverall she was swamped by was obviously meant for someone several sizes bigger. It was turned up at wrists and ankles. "Beats this for fashion, I guess…"

"You look cute as a button."

"I feel like a kid in her dad's clothes!" For a moment she pouted—then a grin wiped the sour look away. "Maybe I should get my own hero suit…"

Paladin wasn't really listening. "Maybe." He turned his attention to the two biplanes standing nearby: resplendent in red and gold livery, fully gassed, cranked up and ready to roll. A Curtiss P-6E Hawk and a Boeing P-12E; single-seat pursuit planes still in use with both Air Corps and Navy. Leigh never asked how he'd gotten a couple of current military planes; he wouldn't have told her anyhow. "I'll take the Boeing. The Hawk's faster, but not so maneuverable. If we get in a jam—a serious one—I want you to hightail it. Got that?"

Leigh said nothing for a moment, just giving him a look he knew so well. Eventually she headed for her plane, calling back over a shoulder: "What's the plan?"

"Head up to Rhode Island. Fly a recce, starting at Providence and spiraling out over dry land until fuel gets low. Refuel—I've arranged for gas to be ready at a small airfield just north-west of Providence—and try again. If we don't get lucky before the sun starts going down, well… you ever stayed in New England?"

"Sounds all kinds of vague." She sprang easily into the Curtiss's cockpit. Paladin walked to his own plane and mounted up. Looking back at Leigh's head, just visible above the cockpit sides, he gave her a wide grin and thumbs up. It was a good performance. He'd never let on what he really felt; not even to Leigh. Especially to Leigh.

Both planes roared across the field, lifting into the calm sky. Leigh adjusted her heading to north-east, and Paladin followed suit, content to let her take the lead. In just over an hour, they'd reach Providence.

V

Flying at just over a thousand feet, they began quartering the distant ground in lazy counter-clockwise spirals. Leigh stayed on Paladin's starboard wing, the faster Hawk easily keeping pace. They saw nothing but abandoned textile mills, small towns, panicked livestock—along with their curious owners—and trees. Plenty of trees. If any plane had attempted a landing there, it would have been obvious: scarred tracts of woodland; pieces of airplane scattered throughout burned-out clearings. The place was pristine.

They refueled the planes once, landing on a matchbox-sized airfield where spare gas awaited. As they filled up, they were watched by a bunch of locals straight out of *L'il Abner*. Paladin figured it was the most excitement they'd had in years. Then they were airborne again: crossing and re-crossing the route all three planes should have taken, if they were on course.

Sitting in his cockpit, looking down at the patchwork ground, Paladin thought back to the days, over twenty years ago, when he'd flown Nieuport *Bébés* in much colder skies. High above miles of mud gouged by trenches and craters. Back then he'd felt a flush of guilty pleasure; an abstract shame that he was looking down on endless destruction, untouched by it. A cold angel passing by the horror. Noting it before moving on.

A shadow rolled over Paladin's airplane. He glanced up, thoughts still decades away, expecting to see the predatory silhouette of a German *Albatros*. But it was just a cloud. A huge thunderhead boiling up from the west, masking the sun, a thick layer of purple-black cloud in its wake. From the color, Paladin figured the cloud layer was miles deep. A bad storm was on its way; maybe something a whole lot worse.

He waggled the P-12's wings to attract Leigh's attention. Throttling the Hawk back, she drew in closer. Paladin pointed up into the darkening sky, and then toward the ground. She nodded and raised a thumb. Perfectly choreographed, both planes turned back toward the tiny local airfield.

They weren't outracing the storm: the light was failing, the distant ground growing dim. Paladin glanced back: the clouds were almost overhead. Black and ominous, their edges glowing with an unpleasant, sour yellow light. Worse, they were moving against the prevailing wind.

Paladin's stomach did a slow roll, something bitter rose in the back of his throat. His hunch was on the money, and boy did he regret being right this time.

He opened the throttle and dropped the nose, hoping Leigh took the hint. If they hit a real jam, she could outrace him back to the airfield. But she wouldn't: too damn stubborn.

A high, electric whine lanced through the sky. Paladin could feel it, worse than any toothache: needling, pulsing. He looked around for the field, but it was getting too dark.

The whine grew louder: it was the roar of ten-floor breakers endlessly smashing into a cliff-face. He glanced toward Leigh: she was on his wing, matching speed effortlessly.

The roar surged from a growl to deafening howls: the ravings of a demented giant. It pounded Paladin's skull, blurring his vision. He imagined words in the fury: words in no tongue known on Earth.

He risked another backward glance. The sky was a single, festering bruise. Swirls of green and purple eddied slowly through the mass. The patterns kept time with the booming, almost-words.

A gap opened in the blackness. Perfectly circular, it widened with leisurely grace. Inside that gap it was bright and clear. Paladin saw movement. He pulled off his goggles and blinked tears away. He looked again: no mistake. There was movement beyond that widening, bright circle. Slow, oily pulsations. Dimmer patches which undulated against the brightness.

No time to find the airfield. They had to put down now!

Leigh's plane was little more than a pale blotch in the gloom. Hoping she could see him clearly enough, he drew a thumb across his throat in a vastly exaggerated movement. He followed it up with violent groundward gestures: hurling pantomime thunderbolts. With a prayer that she'd understood, he pushed his stick forward, dropping the P-12 into a punishing dive.

Not taking his eyes from the altimeter, he kept the stick forward until he was less than fifty feet off the ground. Yanking the controls back, it felt like he was raising the whole airplane by his fingertips. It howled at the brutal abuse. He was in luck: the ground was open and looked pretty even. There was a stand of trees far enough away that he could ignore them.

Cutting the engine, he dropped the flaps and allowed the plane to glide down. Even so, he came in too fast. He felt the wheels hit dirt. The landing gear shrieked, and then the P-12 lurched back into the air. It bounced, bounced once more; then it was down.

He was out of the cockpit before the plane had come to a halt, watching for Leigh. Maybe she hadn't guessed just how urgent his descent had been: she was lazily circling him. He waved as the Hawk roared overhead. It pulled a horizontal turn that had Paladin's heart in his mouth. A wingtip clipped treetops; then Leigh straightened, cut the engine, and came down in a textbook three-point landing. Paladin figured it was time to start breathing again.

He glanced up at the sky. There wasn't a cloud to be seen.

VI

Leigh took another sip of coffee. Letting it go cold hadn't improved it one bit. She set the almost full cup down next to the remains of dinner and silently watched Damy. He'd barely said two words since they'd found the diner—empty except for an ancient waitress and an old guy sat at the counter—not even to order. The waitress had shoved plates of jonnie cakes and a local version of chowder on their table anyhow. Leigh figured it was the only thing on the menu. Along with coffee, which tasted like it'd been brewing since the Revolution. Damy didn't touch his food, just gulped down endless cups of joe.

Eventually, Leigh took a pack of Lucky Strikes from her purse. As she put a cigarette between her lips, Damy looked up from whatever he'd been seeing in his coffee.

"Can I have one of those, princess?"

Leigh offered the pack and he took a smoke. "I've never seen you smoke a ciggie before." She pushed matches across the sticky table.

He struck a match, lighting first her Lucky, then his own. He took a deep pull, exhaling smoke slowly. As the blue cloud dissipated, he seemed to find it fascinating.

The broody silence grated on Leigh's already itchy nerves. "Well?"

Damy's dark eyes twitched away from the last wisps of smoke.

"Well what?"

"You're giving me the jitters, Damy! What's the big deal? Give already!"

He slipped a hand into a coat pocket; it came out holding a box so dark it was almost black. He placed it carefully on the table. Leigh stared at it a moment: it was just a simple wooden box, except for carvings running all around its sides. The design was abstract as far as she could tell; at least, she couldn't make anything of the wriggling, swirling shapes. But it made her nervous for some reason: there was something nasty about it, but she couldn't say what. Maybe it was the way the shapes seemed to move when she wasn't looking at them dead on.

"A cigarette box?"

He shook his head. "There's a powder inside … or something like powder…"

"Powder?" Leigh felt herself growing mad. She hated when Damy tried to be all mysterious.

He sat back, his coat creaking against the shabby leather seat. "You ever wonder why New England's got so many legends about witches and magic, princess?"

Leigh shrugged, puffing on her own cigarette. It wasn't something she'd thought about. "The European settlers brought their own superstitions, I guess."

"Maybe. But this part of the world has a—" He gazed out of the diner's streaked window, taking a last pull on the cigarette before mashing it out. "Let's call it a weakness… a place where the walls of reality are thin. There are several across the world, some worse than others. Here—" he gestured up at the evening sky "—is particularly bad. Things can bleed through. Both ways…"

"Wow." Leigh sat back herself. "You mean those planes fell through a kind of hole in the sky?"

"No." He looked back at her; the haunted look in his eyes scared her silly. "They were pulled."

"That storm having anything to do with it?"

"That was no storm." He started tapping the dark box with a forefinger. "Least, not the kind you're thinking of." The tapping became fiddling as he slowly rotated the box on the tabletop. "Storms are created by colliding weather fronts; I guess you could say this one's made by colliding worlds…"

Leigh ground her burned-out Lucky into the ashtray. "This has happened before…?"

"Back before the Great War, there were several cases in Europe: England, France, Bavaria… Planes went missing; sometimes just the pilots. A couple of machines came down, and the pilot's injuries couldn't just be explained by the crash. One was missing his head."

"And you were there?" Leigh had long accepted that Damy, throughout his crazily long life, had a talent for being where the trouble was. He nodded. "Since I've never heard of anything like that happening in Europe, so I guess you fixed it?"

He smiled: kind of sad and strained, but it was an improvement. "No, princess—but thanks for the compliment. I just helped. The guy who did all of the work, he—" Paladin took his fingers off the box "—He gave me this…"

"The box." Leigh glanced at it again. Dammit! The shapes *were* moving! "That's it? We fly up, and when the storm-thing reappears we throw a box at it? What is it? Some kind of magic itching powder?"

Damy kind of laughed. "Not a bad description. It sure irritates the hell out of what we're after. Sends it back to wherever it came from."

"Really does take a powder, huh?"

Damy slipped the box back in his pocket. "I won't lie to you, princess: it's going to be dangerous."

"Isn't it always?"

"This time, more than ever."

"Hell, you kicked its butt last time. You and your pal."

"Yeah…" He stood, tossing a handful of dollar bills on the table. "But last time—"

Leigh waited for him to finish. When it grew obvious he wasn't going to, she did it for him. "He got killed. Am I right?"

"Not—" He paused before nodding. "Yeah… He was killed."

Damy called to the waitress, asking if there was a phone. As Leigh came to her feet, it occurred to her that maybe Garrard Graves wasn't the only one looking for revenge.

VII

The next day started misty. A heavy dew carpeted the grass. Wisps of low-lying vapor drifted around the airfield, softening the two airplanes' silhouettes and muffling the sound of their engines. Above, the sky was already a luminous blue. It had all the makings of a good day.

Paladin watched Leigh as she cheerfully directed the fitting of under-wing tanks to his biplane. With her charm turned up to full, blue eyes wide and fluttery, it had taken her around five minutes to turn a bunch of surly locals into eager riggers. She hadn't even needed to toss her platinum curls at them.

Last night they'd actually landed less than a mile from the airfield. Even though it was dark once they had the planes turning over, they'd hedge-hopped the distance. The fires he'd called ahead and ordered lit guided them down fine.

But he'd spent a lousy night, barely sleeping. The few minutes he did grab were choked with dreams of screaming clouds and what they hid. He was up before sunrise, looking for coffee, checking over the tanks which had been delivered from New York the day before, and preparing the small amount of powder in his dark box. His head felt thick, his eyes gritty.

He also felt bad about lying to Leigh. Maybe he hadn't actually lied, but he hadn't been completely honest, either. The last time he'd been up against something like this, no one had died. It had been worse. Just the two of them, in a balloon, against God knew what. Paladin was going by the name of Dexter Phillips at the time, and his old friend was calling himself James Morton Stanley. Professor James Morton Stanley: he'd talked himself into a visiting professorship at the University of Ingolstadt. They'd known each other for more years than either remembered; expecting to be around for many more. Jim had taught Paladin a lot in that time: life, and death, and the alternatives.

Armed with just Jim's boxes of powder and a few other trinkets, at an altitude so high the cold and thin air would have finished normal men, they'd taken on things not born in a sane universe. And beaten them. Or at least driven them back.

They actually saw the gap in the worlds shrink—*heal* was how Paladin thought of it—dragging the thing, or things, back. Dexter Phillips and Jim Stanley leaped about in the balloon's frail basket, punching each other's shoulders and shaking hands. Once it was all over they could admit neither of them had expected it to work. But it had. They'd won.

At which moment a pallid, gelatinous limb had uncoiled out of the thinning cloud. Jim was engulfed in a second: dragged from the basket and hoisted toward the shrinking rift. Between heartbeats, Paladin's old friend was gone. Sucked into a black, oily, vanishing whirlpool. The sky above him was clear and blue.

He hadn't died. Not then. James Stanley Morton was special: one of a few men who measured their lives in centuries. An immortal, almost: indestructible, as far as either of them knew. Like Paladin, he couldn't die; at least, not like an ordinary man.

In all the years since, Paladin had hoped the laws of whatever hell Jim had been drawn into were different. Different enough that he could find death, sooner rather than later. The alternative was too terrible.

Paladin pulled himself together. Unbuttoning one of the larger belt pouches, he drew out a palmful of small objects. Crudely shaped chips of stone: like tiny, star-shaped arrowheads. The centuries had lent them a mirror polish. He turned them over with a thumb before dropping them back in the pouch. From another he removed something like a flower bud. Small, dirty-white in color, hanging off a length of pale, shriveled stem. For all its resemblance to a plant, it was cold, damp; unpleasantly soft. Quickly he put it away, wiping his hands on his pants. He checked on Leigh. "We ready to roll?"

She looked up from her supervising and snapped to attention with an exaggerated salute. "Aye, aye. Tanks filled and the cannons loaded, cap'n."

One of the locals glanced Paladin's way. "Strange time o'year for crop dustin'." His accent was a pure, undiluted New England drawl.

"Ain't it, though." Paladin took a deep breath and swung himself up into the P-12's cockpit. "Time's a-wastin'."

Once in the air they climbed to four thousand feet, Paladin's full attention on the clear skies above them. For an hour they circled, the airfield at the center. The blue sky remained cloud-free. The sun rose higher, though the chilly air didn't warm noticeably.

Paladin knew he was going to have to force the issue. He couldn't guess what had summoned the cloud in the past, supposing yesterday had been a fluke. They couldn't waste gas chasing their tails in the hope something might happen.

He took a few of the tiny, star-shaped stones out of the belt-pouch, muttering bizarre words to himself. One by one, repeating the same phrase every time, he threw the stones overboard. Each flared with a dazzling, violet light as, rather than fall, they hurtled upwards like tiny, brilliant missiles. Glancing across to Leigh's plane, he could see her head poking out of the cockpit, watching him with curiosity.

He waited several minutes before repeating the process. After fifteen minutes, there was still nothing: the sky was as clear and cloudlessly blue as ever.

He drew out another handful of stones. "Well, they do say third time's the charm." He began the invocation again, reciting every phrase carefully; none of the alien words sat easy on his tongue.

As the last bright stone shot heavenward, small clouds began to form to the north. Starting as wispy tendrils which writhed slowly across the sky, they thickened with unnatural speed. In minutes vast thunderheads were bearing down on the two biplanes: high and purple and black, edged with a sour yellow light.

Paladin bit his lip. Pulling back on the stick he aimed his P-12 toward the clouds, easing the throttle forward, coaxing as much speed from the engine as it would give. Glancing back, he noted

Leigh's Curtiss was holding position, as agreed. If anything went sour, the Hawk's speed might be the only thing that could save her.

A gap opened in the cloud. As he flew closer, Paladin thought it looked more like the cloud was rolling back; peeling apart. More pallid yellow light glowed inside the opening, and there was movement: slow, oily waves; huge and opaque, uncoiling. He cocked both of the plane's .30-caliber cannons: they wouldn't kill what was up there in the clouds, but they'd slow it down; confuse it. Just a little time was all he asked.

Tendrils the length of a freight train unfurled from the gap; they glowed with the same acid light. Paladin was reminded of a jellyfish's stinging tentacles. They probed the air with a misleading slow grace Paladin recognized too well.

One swept toward his plane. The moment it was in range, he fired a short burst. Incendiary shells raked the viscous mass, flames erupting in several spots. The limb flinched—a vast, opaque slug sprinkled with salt—and retracted into the gap. It was instinct; Paladin knew it wouldn't stay up there long.

He banked the P-12, heading for the mass of waving tendrils. Opening up the cannons in short, careful bursts, he raked the undulating limbs with fire. They all withdrew, like an alarmed sea anemone.

"Now for the clever part."

Pulling back hard on the stick, he drew the P-12 into a steep climb: right toward the center of the writhing, glowing gap. If he could, he'd have flown above the cloud mass, but the Boeing's ceiling was just above 26,000 feet; the towering thunderheads soared far higher than that. For his plan to work, his only choice was to fly into the cloud. Right up to what was hiding behind the yellow light.

By his estimation, he was less than a hundred feet below cloud base when the dark flecks appeared against the glow. Hundreds of shapes dropped out of the gap: things that looked like wriggling sacks of black guts hanging from leathery wings. From somewhere, an edgy screaming began, rising and falling. A dull pain grew in Paladin's stomach, his bones began to ache.

He pushed the throttle to maximum, and climbed to meet them.

VIII

Leigh saw Damy opening up on the glowing tentacles. She saw the brief blossom of fire, and for a moment allowed herself to hope it was over. They'd done it. Then the shrieking began—a giant trying to shout above deafening radio static—and the hideous black things appeared.

She lost sight of the P-12 as swarms of the horrors mobbed her own plane. Masses of black worms hanging off wings; each wriggling and stabbing. Some seemed to have eyes on the tips; others had mouths or some kind of claws. It was hard to tell, everything was moving so fast.

She dived her plane to the left, cocking the guns, then yanked up the Hawk's nose and raked the things with a burst of incendiary shells. They writhed and shriveled under the flames, but didn't die. She wondered how many shots it would take to destroy just one. Blown apart, probably; each fragment burned to ash.

She dived again, evading bat-wings and snapping limbs. At least she could out-fly them: they didn't seem to have the speed to match the Hawk. One drifted across her sights, and she fired by instinct. Flames licked across its glistening body, cooking one skeletal wing. It dropped, thrashing vainly with the remaining wing. Leigh watched it spinning toward the distant countryside. "That'll be a talking point tomorrow."

Her plane shuddered. One of the things was attached to the

upper wing, writhing toward her like an ink-stained octopus. She reached inside the cockpit, fingers closing around the hilt of a Very pistol. Pressing the wide muzzle right against the thing's wriggling center, she fired. The distress flare blew it clear, coated in white-hot phosphorus. Burning, it struggled to stay aloft, and failed. Leigh hummed the opening bars of *Bye-Bye Blackbird* to herself.

She banked left, firing in short, calm bursts at anything crossing her sights. She wanted to glance up, see how Damy was managing above her, but she couldn't afford the distraction. She'd learned that lesson.

Instead she kept firing, and prayed.

IX

Paladin felt like he was surrounded by movement. The air glowed; hidden inside sour light a vast shape pulsed. Clear as a jellyfish, mantle hundreds of feet across, it filled the hollow cloud. Countless filaments drifted on a breeze the aviator couldn't feel, each thicker than his plane's wingspan. It took all of his skill to avoid being crushed, or swatted from the sky.

The noise was beyond deafening. A deep, anguished howl echoing off invisible walls. It surged in crescendo after crescendo, dropping to an almost bearable volume before building to another agonizing peak. All the while, at a pitch that flooded Paladin's throat with bile, the black-winged things shrieked mindlessly: swooping at the biplane in a nightmarish dogfight. He fired the cannons economically, just enough to clear a space in front, trusting in the P-12's maneuverability to keep him out of trouble.

He was still climbing. For his plan to have any chance of working he needed to be above the pulsating titan. A glance at the altimeter confirmed he was already at 25,000 feet. In theory he had another thousand feet but the engine wasn't in the best shape. It was already beginning to labor, the throttle wide open. He was risking a stall.

"Come on, baby. Just for me."

The whole plane shuddered; the engine howled, faltered for a second, spat out a thick plume of oily smoke, then smoothed out.

Things weren't going so well.

One of the black things crashed into the starboard wing struts, its thrashing limbs anchoring it in place. The Boeing dipped to the right with the extra weight. Paladin clung onto the stick with his left hand, desperately keeping the plane level, unholstering one of his automatics with his right: a heavy Mauser 9 mm, already set to rapid-fire. At a squeeze of the trigger, the entire clip emptied in a second. The black thing was cut in two. The halves slid off the wing, leaving a few shreds hanging off the struts. The stringy black remains fluttered in the slipstream like a flight commander's ribbons.

With an uneasy feeling, Paladin also noticed they were leaving a trail of blood, or something like it. Glancing back, he could see a glittering wake as the stuff crystallized in the cold, thin air. Like airborne sharks, more of the black fliers were homing in on the trail.

X

Leigh risked a quick glance at the roiling sky above her. The gaping, lurid hole was still there, but the flying black squid things weren't falling out of it any more. Just that god-awful noise. It was starting to blur her vision; not something she needed when her sky was still full of bug-uglies.

And they were tough little sons of bitches. Even after getting toasted with incendiaries, they'd tumble a while, then come screaming back, half-crippled. She'd swear they healed after a while, too: grow back shriveled limbs and shredded wings. Maybe it was just her messed-up vision.

Another one tried to crash land across her top wing. She side-slipped crazily, almost losing the Curtiss, but the thing clung on. Tentacles snapped like whips: claws, eyes—parts she didn't even have a name for—straining for her face. She flinched, momentarily losing control. The P-6E plunged into a spin; Leigh forgot all about the thing above her as she fought to control her plane. The spin slowed, she pulled back into a shallow climb. A quick glance at the top wing revealed ugly was gone: lost somewhere in the dive, leaving several smoking rents in the surface.

She figured it wasn't such a good idea to get splashed by whatever came out of the ugly bastards.

XI

Paladin's Boeing lurched as another of the black things lashed itself onto the port wing struts. That made five in all, clinging to the biplane in various spots. Their combined weight was slowing the plane; it was losing height. A sixth swung by. It spewed out a bunch of tentacles, found purchase around the root of the lower starboard wing, and reeled its winged body closer.

He no longer had a choice. Nowhere near the top of the cloudy cavern, it was clear he could never make it. He'd have to release the contents of his tanks now.

As he reached for the jury-rigged release wires, the P-12 shuddered violently. He was thrown back in his seat, the release snatched from his fingers.

Something huge and glowing slid across the top wing's surface. As thick as the P-12's fuselage, the massive tendril crawled along the wing: an endless, colorless slug. Reaching the trailing edge, it dipped, slid underneath. Paladin figured it intended to wrap around the whole wing, bring his plane to a halt, hanging like a bug from flypaper.

He reached forward again, gripped one of the wires, and pulled. A fine spray trailed back from the port wing tank, fanned by the propeller's wash. Glistening in the sick light, a mist of Morton's powder suspended in brine spread out behind the Boeing. Buoyed and spread by air currents, part frozen, the mist became a cloud within a cloud. Black things hanging off the P-12 were the first to be touched. The effect was instantaneous.

Where the mist reached, black flesh erupted into boils and running sores. Pale violet pus oozed through crackling skin. Smoke black as the creatures boiled into the slipstream. As tentacles disintegrated, the collapsing things fell away, leaving gaping holes in the plane's structure.

The P-12 reacted immediately. The weight gone, it leapt forward, soaring high. The huge tendril, now engulfing half of the upper wing, tore apart like Jell-O. Paladin gagged at the stench that washed over him, but at least it took his mind off the gut-pounding noise.

He opened up both cannons, careless if there was anything in range. As the plane climbed, he pulled on the second wire; the starboard tank spewed its contents.

The crushing noise grew even louder. He hadn't thought it possible. Squinting against the tears flooding his eyes, he brought his plane round in a complete circle. Even hidden in the sour light, he could see the titanic, opaque creature was squirming. Tendrils the size of office blocks writhed in ponderous agony, shredding the cloud. Beyond, vast peristaltic waves slowly distorted the main body. Rents bigger than the Empire State Building split its surface; blackness poured out.

Paladin began to laugh. It wasn't a pleasant sound; not the kind of laugh a regular guy made. He was glad Leigh wasn't around to hear him.

He reached inside a belt pouch and drew out the pallid bud, blinking back tears to see it better. In the sour, deep-sea light the strange bud was opening. The flower it revealed was like no earthly blossom: perfectly round, wet and glistening; more like some kind of eye. For a moment Paladin and the flower stared at each other, before he flicked it carelessly toward the agonized colossus above him. His question was answered.

He dropped the P-12's nose, diving away from the noise and madness. Around him, the briny suspension still swirled. Decaying winged things tumbled away, disintegrating as they fell. He began to chant: screaming incomprehensible words at the boiling inferno overhead. They tore at his throat; he tasted the blood. But that was good: some things required blood. Better a little of his than anyone else's.

His plane vibrated as he dived. A quick check showed the wings' surfaces peeling off, struts splintering. Those flying black bastards had really done a number on his kite. If she didn't hold together, he'd be reaching the ground a little faster than was healthy.

He glanced back over his shoulder. The clouds were thinning, shrinking; for all the world like they were being sucked away. The nauseating light was fading. A clean New England sky showed beyond it. Paladin nodded in triumph. Notch one up for the good guys.

There was one final blaze of sour yellow, and the last wisps evaporated. For an instant, the vast entity hidden deep in the cloud was revealed. Even looking directly at the thing, Paladin couldn't begin to describe it. Then it was gone, and he could no longer remember it.

He also realized that it was blissfully silent.

A moment later, with a lethal crack, both sets of wing struts parted.

XII

Leigh watched the boiling thunderheads collapse in on themselves and vanish. With a final glaring flash, the sky was clear.

And she could hear, again.

The black flyers disappeared, too, if not so quickly. She wished she could say they collapsed into dust, but it wasn't so clean. Melting was the best she could describe it: melting and slowly boiling away in the clean sunlight. If it wasn't for all the smoking holes in her plane, she could believe they'd never existed.

But where was Damy? Panic grabbed at her throat as she remembered what had happened to his old pal. She scanned the sky, looking for his plane. For too long she didn't see anything: then she spotted the silhouette of a biplane, falling a mile or so to the south of her position. She pulled the reluctant Hawk around, opening the throttle, aiming the nose toward the tumbling airplane.

She caught Damy up around a hundred feet above the ground. It wasn't a good place to try a landing under any circumstances: too many trees and ditches. She could see how beat up the Boeing was. The top wing flapped like a bird's and the tail section was Swiss cheese. She couldn't see if the landing gear was okay.

The Boeing slipped between two trees—missing them by inches—dropping toward a half-ploughed field. Leigh brought her plane lower, hoping for the best, convinced she was about to witness a fatal plane crash. She kept a parallel course, watching

Damy fearfully. He was focused on the ground; Leigh wasn't sure he even knew she was there. His plane was a few feet above the field when the engine cut. A moment later, the top wing folded.

Instantly the nose dropped. The P-12 ploughed engine-first into the rough ground, flipped over, and came to a shattered halt, upside down.

Careless of the ground, Leigh dropped her plane. It lurched and bounced, the landing gear creaking and snapping, but she kept it upright. She cut the engine, leaping out of the cockpit as the plane staggered to a halt, running toward the wrecked Boeing. There was no movement she could see.

She fell to her knees, scrabbling under the grounded fuselage. "Damy! Damy goddammit! Talk to me!"

From the half-buried cockpit came the muted snaps of a released harness, followed by an equally muffled voice. "Keep it down, will you princess…? I got a lousy headache—!"

His head appeared in the gap between ground and the hump formed by the headrest. He was pale, streaked in mud, blood and Christ knew what else, but there was a battered smile on his face. "Any landing you can walk away from…"

"You're going to have to crawl away from this one, wise guy." She dragged him out from under. Shakily, he got to his feet.

"What was that slogan again? We investigate and eliminate?" He pulled off his helmet and goggles, movements stiff. "Remind me to be a bit more particular about who gets eliminated—"

Leigh threw her arms around him, ignoring his complaints. "Jesus, you scared me!"

"I scared *you*?" He turned to look at the wrecked P-12. "Guess we won't need that new engine after all…"

Leigh rested his arm across her shoulders. "C'mon, hero—it's a long walk to a phone."

XIII

Leigh stared at him levelly, one eyebrow cocked. "So what you going to tell Graves? Not the truth?"

They were back in the deserted diner, less than five minutes from where Paladin crashed. The same old guy was still nursing his coffee at the counter; the same waitress bringing them more chowder and jonnie cakes than they could eat. Paladin wondered if it was the kind of place that just popped into existence right when you needed it.

"Who'd believe it?" He wiped his bowl clean with a piece of jonnie cake. Unlike the last time, he felt real hungry. There was nothing like crashing from thousands of feet to give a man an appetite. "Maybe you were right about them ditching in the Narragansett, after all…"

"I'm always right, Damy. One day you'll realize that."

"In that case I'll leave you to figure out what to tell Graves."

"Thanks a million." Leigh lit up a Lucky. "Did you get rid of it? For good, I mean…"

He took a sip of coffee, instantly regretting it. "I sealed the breach. Whether it'll stay sealed—" He left the rest unsaid.

"So maybe it wouldn't be such a bad thing if Graves lost his license… At least, if there are no planes flying by… and if it opens up again—"

"Did I ever tell you you're a hard woman?"

"Only as nails." She stood. "C'mon boss—somehow we have to get two of us back to New York in a single-seat plane…"

"Cozy."

As Leigh wandered over to the counter to pay the check, Paladin allowed his mind to replay the last moments before the breach had closed. How the pale flower had bloomed: a flower that blossomed only under the diseased light of a certain world. The breach to which he'd last helped seal back in 1908.

He closed his eyes and addressed the darkness. "Found you, Jim." After almost thirty years, he knew where to look. And he'd be back.

PART TWO:
ALL THROUGH THE NIGHT

I

The corner of East 10th Street and 2nd Avenue felt cold and hostile. Only the church was welcoming, even if it looked out of place. So much older than any of the faded buildings around it, yet still immaculate. In a place where despair was the major currency, the church's promise of peace and hope obviously kept it safe from the petty larcenies common elsewhere.

In all New York, someone wanting ghosts couldn't find a better place.

He scanned the neighborhood, gently shutting the door of his Chrysler Airflow. All he got back from the squalid tenements and flop-houses was echoes. Everywhere was uneasily quiet. Behind every dark window he figured there'd be eyes: wary, suspicious; some even angry. Only two kinds of men drove an automobile into The Bowery this time of night: cops and hoodlums. Neither would be welcome. Paladin might not fit into either category but when the chips were down, there'd be no time for debate.

The only life in the street was two kids, standing on crumbling steps near the 10th Street intersection, back to back. Their heads turned as they watched him, eyes insolent. He gave them back their stares with interest.

"Either of you mooks want to earn a couple of bucks?"

They shared a conspiratorial glance before swaggering across in the best Jimmy Cagney fashion. Thirteen going on thirty, they were dressed in the street uniform of scuffed baggy pants, tight faded sweaters and caps that were several sizes too big. They stopped an arm's length away, looking Paladin up and down as disrespectfully as they could.

One spat in the gutter. "You a G-man?"

The second sniggered. "Don't be a chump!" He nodded at Paladin's battered, sleeveless flying coat, roll-neck sweater, riding pants and boots. "It's Doc Savage!"

"Maybe I'm a big game hunter." Paladin deliberately hiked at his heavy belt and rested hands on the two holsters.

The first kid laughed bitterly. "If yous sees an elephant, give me a call. I ain't eaten in weeks!"

"We can fix that." Paladin dug out two five dollar bills. The punks stared at the green like they were hypnotized. Likely it was more money than they saw in a year. "I got business in the church. I'd appreciate it if you'd keep an eye on my automobile while I'm gone."

The bills were snatched from his fingers, vanishing instantly. "You got a deal, mister!"

"Sure thing. How long yous gonna be gone?"

Paladin shrugged amiably. "Hard to tell. Elephants are tricky animals, you know."

Both kids laughed like he was their new best friend. He started to walk away, but the second kid called after him.

"So what do we call ya, mister?"

Paladin wondered about it. Handing out names was risky: names were power, even in The Bowery. "You go first."

The first kid hooked a thumb at his pal. "That's Nussy. I'm Jayo."

"Damian Paladin." Neither of the kids so much as blinked; so much for fame. He continued toward the old church. There was only one path, and it stopped a couple of yards short of the long porch. He craned his head back to take another look at the place.

The church's architecture wasn't planned, just grown over the centuries. Originally built by the Dutch when everywhere was still farmland, the English settlers had added to and refined it. The final addition had been the bell tower, built to celebrate the Revolution. After that it had fossilized: a hold-over from another age, somehow surviving the city that grew around it.

He gave himself another moment before starting to walk around the small chapel. He did it deliberately, thoughtfully; placing each booted foot just so. Three times he circled the church, the air growing colder with each pass. Darkness began to fall.

The third and final lap completed, Paladin sat on a worn bench inside the porch. He unholstered his Browning and Mauser automatics, placing them on the bench within easy reach. Not for the good folk of The Bowery: you never knew what else might be passing. He dug a pint of good Scotch out of his belt, too. It was likely to be a cold night.

He checked his wristwatch: it was coming up to nine. A couple hours to go yet; still, he was always early. The courtesy of kings. Somebody told him that once; could even have been a king. Paladin smiled to himself, rested his head back against the porch, and settled in for the night.

II

Leigh was growing increasingly exasperated. It was bad enough that she had to run a business in someone else's name—none of *The Palace* restaurant's success ever got credited to her—but when the joint's supposed owner did a disappearing act, on a night when the joint really was jumping, she figured she had every right to feel sore.

She batted aside the doors into the kitchen. The chef was stirring something in a deep pan. "Franco, have you seen Mr. Paladin?"

He turned his head, checked to see who was disturbing him, and gave it a staccato shake. "No Miss Oswin. Haven't seen the boss all day."

He returned his attention to whatever he was preparing. It must have been fascinating, or so difficult it required all his consideration. It just looked like soup to Leigh. She didn't miss the *boss* reference, though it didn't rattle her unduly: Franco had always referred to Damy as the boss. Never mind that everyone at *The Palace* formally worked for her—even Damian Paladin—they still treated Damy like a lord, or something. On the rare occasions he actually showed his face.

"He's not back at the apartment." Leigh felt like she was talking to herself.

"Can't help you, Miss Oswin." Franco's face edged nearer to

the pots and pans. Leigh figured he was deliberately avoiding eye-contact.

"Then he must be out at the airfield." It was the most likely place for him to be hiding, playing with his collection of ratty old planes, although Leigh didn't want to drive all the way out to Chaykin Field if she could avoid it.

Franco spooned up a sample of whatever he was cooking, sniffing it. "Why's it so important?"

"Because he's the main reason we get any customers in this place—!" She caught the hurt look on Franco's face. "Sure, sure. They stay for the food; but they come to see the crazy guy who chases ghosts. We got a full house tonight; would it be too much to ask he got out there and glad-handed a couple of diners? Especially when those diners include a bunch of city aldermen…"

Her rant finished, Leigh glared at Franco to see how much of an impression she'd left. None, as far as she could tell. She narrowed her eyes, trying to nail the chef through the back of the head with a look. It didn't work, so she glanced around for an ice pick. "What aren't you telling me, Franco?"

"Nothing." He tasted the soup, seemed satisfied.

She couldn't spot an ice pick, but a huge ladle hanging on one of the kitchen's walls looked handy. "Tell me, Franco…"

"Lady, I'm just the cook round here. Least I would be, if someone let me…"

"Franco!"

He sighed theatrically, putting down the tasting spoon. Finally, he met her gaze; she was disappointed when he didn't flinch. "It's April twenty-fourth, Miss Oswin." He sounded as though he was explaining something real obvious.

"So?" She tried to sound offhand, rather than confused as all hell.

"He always disappears the night of April twenty-fourth."

"Why?"

"Beats me." He picked up a ladle and started to give the soup hell. "Like I said, I'm just the cook…!"

"You can always be an ex-cook…"

Franco paused, giving the soup a break. "Look, the night of every April twenty-fourth, the boss goes off somewhere. Has done as long as I've known him." Leigh picked up on the unspoken

Which is longer than you have, lady, but let it pass. "Once I tried to ask him where he went, but he just made a gag out of it…"

"What did he say?"

"That he went to church." Franco laughed at the absurdity of the idea. "Church! The boss don't even go to church on Christmas!"

Leigh found herself smiling too. It was true: she'd never known him show much interest in that ol' time religion. "He say which church?"

Franco shrugged. "New York's got a lot of churches, Miss Oswin."

"Sure. And I don't see Damy in any one of them."

"Maybe he's Jewish." Franco glanced at her briefly, his black eyes flickering with mischief. "You ever see any… indication of that…?"

For a moment, Leigh felt herself coloring-up; she got the better of it, putting all the heat back into the glare she gave Franco. He broke eye contact first; the pan of soup became fascinating again. Leigh allowed herself a brief smile of triumph.

"He once said you'd see the funny side of it."

Leigh frowned. "What'd he mean by that?"

"Beats me."

Leigh stared at the back of Franco's head for several more seconds, but it was clear he'd said all he was going to. She sighed. "Okay, Franco. Guess I'll have to wait for him to get back." Wherever he's gotten to, she added silently, leaving the kitchen

As she made her way back to the restaurant's main entrance, and the alley beyond, Leigh couldn't shake the notion of Damian Paladin vanishing every April twenty-fourth. Not only something he never let on about, but something to do with a church, yet. She was used to his secrecy: she knew there was plenty he never told her, and that suited her fine. Everyone had secrets. There was plenty she wasn't letting on about, too. But what in hell did he do on this night, every year? Visit a sick relative? An ex-wife? Or maybe, and she went a little cold at the thought, not so ex, after all?

III

Paladin had raised and cocked the Mauser a fraction before he actually heard the footstep. Call it luck, call it intuition. He was just made that way. "Step up to where I can see you."

A tall guy walked into the thin light cast by the porch's single bulb. His gray three-piece suit was expensively tailored. Paladin didn't need to know every button was gold to recognize it had cost the wearer more than *The Palace's* annual takings. There was something about the cut that said it had been tailored far from America; nothing Paladin could put his finger on. His gleaming shoes were part-masked in equally immaculate spats. The newcomer was good-looking too: Cary Grant and Clark Gable would have hated him on principle. He was sporting a mustache this year, a thin, well-clipped pencil, and his hair was slicked back. Maybe he was going for the English look: Ronald Coleman, someone like that. Paladin hated to admit it suited him.

He placed the Mauser back on the bench. "You're late."

The newcomer pulled a gold pocket watch out of his suit vest—big, heavy, and so fat it was almost a sphere—and peered at it. "Actually, I believe I'm exactly on time." There was an accent, but faint and unrecognizable. Just as wrong as his suit; and just as hard to figure out. The watch dropped back into the vest pocket.

Paladin tried not to sigh. The arrogant son of a bitch always got to him; there were some things you just couldn't help. "So. What d'you say, Saint-Germain?"

There was another bench on the porch, facing Paladin. The self-styled Count Saint-Germain sat, carefully arranging the knife-sharp creases in his pants. His cold, steely blue eyes flickered up and down once as he took in Paladin's outfit. He smirked, lips as thin as his fancy mustache, and took a gold cigarette case out of his coat. "My, don't you look nice."

"Funny, I was about to say the same about you."

Saint-Germain fitted a cigarette into a long ivory holder, clenching the mouthpiece between impeccable teeth. At the last moment, he thought of offering Paladin one. Instead, the ghost hunter pulled out a briar pipe.

"Still trying to master those things?" The count lit his cigarette, puffing a ghostly cloud of smoke into the cold night. Paladin drew on the pipe, sucking a match-flame into a bowl of tobacco he knew would be out in less than a minute.

"A touch of failure now and again… keeps a man humble." Paladin threw the dead match away. The other grinned around his cigarette holder: he looked like a shark sucking on a harpoon.

"We are many things, my friend; men isn't one of them."

"I was being allegorical."

The count huffed. "You're just trying to annoy me."

"Is it working?" Returning a grin of his own, Paladin raised the whisky bottle. "Fancy a slug? Keep out the cold." He knew Saint-Germain never touched Scotch any more than the ghost hunter smoked cigarettes. Not expensive enough.

The count ignored the bottle, staring into the darkness instead. Paladin wondered if he thought the good people of The Bowery were about to come screaming at them with pitchforks and flaming torches.

"I understand you may have located James Stanley…" The question was phrased laconically: a simple ice-breaker. The off-hand manner didn't fool Paladin.

"Where'd you hear that?"

"I think I read it in the funny papers." A curlicue of smoke spiraled around Saint-Germain's head. "Will you be attempting a rescue?"

"What do you think?"

The cold eyes appraised him once more. "I think you are very much your father's son so, yes, you will go racing blindly where angels fear to tread." He grinned the shark grin again. "And speaking of fatherly angels, I understand there's a family reunion in the wind."

Paladin took a slug of whisky, determined to not let the smug bastard get a rise out of him. "Meaning…?"

"Don't be obtuse. Raven is in town; has he not contacted you?"

"What makes you think he'd—?" He broke off as Saint-Germain tensed; cool, alert gaze fixed on the darkness. The ghost hunter could have sworn he saw his ears twitch.

"It's starting."

Paladin rammed his already dead pipe back into a belt-pouch. "How can you tell?"

"Experience."

Paladin tried not to laugh. Saint-Germain always had to act the big shot. After all these centuries, he hadn't caught on that he was fooling no one.

The count pointed his cigarette holder at the porch light, flourishing it like some two-bit magician. Within seconds the porch seemed dark as the churchyard, in spite of the bulb still glowing away like a tiny, distant sun. Paladin saw lightning bugs flashing on and off like defective neons.

"There." The man in gray took the spent cigarette from its holder and crushed it underfoot. "Better—"

Paladin hushed him. He thought he heard something: a faint, high buzz; crickets who'd been sucking on helium. There was no direction to it, coming from everywhere at once but so faint it was easy to believe it was imagination.

Saint-Germain sat back lazily, but Paladin wasn't fooled. The man was excited; it flashed in his eyes like cold blue electricity. Paladin's own nerves buzzed along with the sub-aural noise. He dug out a steno pad and pencil.

The buzz didn't get any louder, but it grew more intense. Even though he could still barely hear it, it was drilling straight through Paladin's ears. A city's worth of invisible dentists having a real good time.

"Here they come." For once, Saint-Germain's voice wasn't at all steady.

Out in the churchyard the lightning bugs had competition. Faint lights pulsed brighter and bigger than the insects' display. They drifted closer, growing larger, moving with a purpose: cloudy, human-sized clots of gray light. And the nearer they came, the more detail Paladin could make out: faces, clothing, expressions; even hair and eye color. An army of spectral individuals advancing through the churchyard. Somewhere in the night, a clock struck twelve.

The future dead: wraiths of everyone who would die over the next year. The gift of the night of April twenty-fourth: St Mark's Eve.

IV

Leigh closed the door to their ritzy Teton Building apartment. She tossed purse and hat onto a table, poured herself a tall drink and flopped into a chair. Thoughts in a jumble, she stared out of the window at Central Park; all the streetlamps were flickering on as night fell. It was a swell view, all right, and she could only afford it because of Damy. And not just the restaurant. It was the spook hunting: his crazy reputation was money in the bank. It didn't matter if anyone believed or not, the Depression was easing, and New Yorkers were greedy for kicks. She'd seen some pretty crazy stuff herself over the past couple of years, and still couldn't be sure it wasn't all some kind of stunt. The occasional fat check from grateful clients didn't hurt any, though.

But none of that answered her one question: where in Hell was Damy?

And what did it mean: her seeing the funny side? Sounded like the kind of dumb thing Damy would say: all smart and mysterious, probably nonsense. Her eyes flickered to the phone book. She picked it up and skimmed through it, finger tracing down the page. She didn't know what she was looking for, or even if she'd recognize it if she spotted it. There was a small cluster of churches under *S*; all named after saints of one kind or another. *St Anthony's, St John the Baptist's, St Mark's, St—*

Leigh's finger jerked to a halt. It couldn't be. St Oswin's. In

The Bowery. No wonder Damy had thought she'd see the funny side. The last time she'd seen the name *St Oswin's* had been in 1934, on the side of a women's mission close by the docks. It had inspired half of the phony name she'd given a down-at-heel fly-boy calling himself Damian Paladin. She snapped the phone book shut. It was so apt. It *had* to be the place.

But The Bowery… at this time of night?

She grabbed a raincoat that was more practical than glamorous, slipping a small .38 revolver into one of the pockets. She'd have to drive there: no cabby was going to take her across to The Bowery in the dark. Too much sense. Unlike Damy, obviously.

Or her, come to think of it.

V

One by one, the shades drifted by the porch and back into darkness. They were silent, except for that faint, high, annoying buzz. All of their faces were etched with a stark emotion: fear, anger, disgust; some even looked happy. Paladin had never been certain what those looks meant: was it a mirror of their final thoughts, a hint of what would kill them? He'd given up trying to figure it out long ago.

Some faces Paladin recognized: city officials, radio and movie stars, Broadway producers and other big shots; but most he'd never seen before. With luck, he'd never see them again. He wrote down anyone he knew on the pad, in the order they came. It wasn't exact, but the earliest shades tended to be the first to die. Those bringing up the rear would see out most of the year. He'd always found it useful to know who was going to take the big sleep sometime in the next twelve months: it limited the surprises. Paladin had no idea why Saint-Germain wanted to know; last he'd heard the stiff wasn't any kind of sleuth, just a very rich bum.

The parade started to thin out; there was only a handful of glowing wraiths out in the churchyard. Paladin took the opportunity to take a mouthful of Scotch. Saint-Germain yawned and stretched. "No real revelations; although I was slightly surprised by that senator."

Paladin sniggered. "You wouldn't if you knew what they keep

out of the papers."

"And how would you know?"

"Mind your own beeswax…"

"You're just saying that to annoy me."

"Is it work—?"

The words jammed in Paladin's mouth. Likely because it was suddenly so dry his tongue got stuck. He took another heavy slug of the whisky. It didn't help.

Saint-Germain glanced over. "Is there a problem?" His smug, over-concerned tone told the ghost hunter he knew damned well what was wrong. But sure, he was just ace; he was real crackerjack.

The final shade was drifting past the porch, the last one to die in the next twelve months. The look on the face was so unhappy, so desperately sad, it tore Paladin up. He suddenly wanted to know exactly what those final expressions meant. More than anything.

The last shade was Leigh Oswin.

VI

Leigh made her way down to the parking garage under the Teton Building. Stowed way back against a wall was an old Cunningham Phaeton: a brute of an automobile that looked like it should be crammed with bootleggers. It had, of course; right up until the previous owner met with an accident involving a handful of lead slugs. Now she just kept it around to remind her of the good old days she didn't miss one bit.

Firing the Cunningham up, Leigh swung out of the garage and turned south east. As she approached The Bowery, traffic quickly thinned to nothing. Cruising along East 10th Street, Leigh felt like a rabbit walking into a canyon full of coyotes. There were no lit streetlights, and less than half of the windows had lights on. No prehistoric, wolf-filled forest had ever gotten darker than this.

She spotted Damy's car easily enough: his Chrysler Airflow. Only Damy would think nothing of parking a brand new coupe in the middle of The Bowery; at night, yet. She pulled in behind the Chrysler. Immediately, two ragged kids appeared out of the darkness, flanking her Phaeton: one on the sidewalk, the other in the empty street. She reached inside her raincoat, taking comfort in the weight of the .38.

Cracking her door window, she gave the nearest kid her best smile. "Have you seen the owner of that coupe?"

He hunched his shoulders and tried to look a foot taller. "Who wants to know, sister?"

"I do, obviously. You can't miss him: he dresses like something out of the comics section."

The second kid sniggered. "I think she means Mister Damian Paladin, Jayo."

"The big game hunter!" Jayo leaned closer. His sour breath crawled through the window gap. Leigh blinked it away. "That your guy, sister? He on the square?"

The second kid scuffed the sidewalk with the toe of a worn boot. "We think he lied to us, lady."

"What about?" She squeezed the revolver's grip tighter, drawing it part way out of her pocket.

"What's your name, doll face?" Jayo was almost pressing his face up against her window now.

"What's it to you?" She pulled the small .38 free and rested it on the wheel. Jayo didn't react, or was careful not to.

"Aw, c'mon sweetheart, don't get fresh. We'd just like to know your name, is all." The second kid was leaning on her limo now, his arms stretched across the canvas roof. Leigh couldn't help being reminded of bookends: life-sized, street punk bookends.

"I'll make you a deal." Leigh never took her eyes of Jayo. She'd had years learning to read two-bit yaps like these; she'd lay money he was the dominant one. "You little punks scram back into the shadows and I won't make your lousy excuses for a life any worse. Keep up the tough guy impressions and—Well, let's just say I know how the real wise guys operate. I'd be happy to give your boyfriend back there a demonstration." She flicked her head toward the second kid.

Jayo just grinned wider. "I don't think she likes you, Nussy-boy."

"Nah. She just needs to get to know me better."

"Now." Jayo pressed his face against the window; Leigh had the peculiar impression the glass was bending. "We do the threats. Your name, lady—"

"And you'd better be on the square." Nussy's voice was intimate, cajoling. It raised the hairs on Leigh's neck, scraped at her nerves. She opened her mouth, about to tell them how everyone knew her, following it up with a few ripe suggestions on where they could stick the information, but her jaw froze.

Something just wasn't right. Even for Bowery punks these kids were wrong. There was no bravado, no empty posturing. The best threats were always hard promises, and these two were as sure of themselves as the meanest hood.

She raised her revolver and pointed it vaguely in Jayo's direction, keeping her voice quiet and level. "Romanova. My name is Ludmilla Tatiana Romanova."

Jayo pulled back from the window, leaving a moon-shaped smear. His smile had softened; his whole demeanor loosened. "There. That wasn't so hard…"

Nussy sounded petulant. "She forgot the Duchess. Don't forget the Duchess, sweet cheeks…"

Jayo glanced across the roof of her car. "Aw, I reckon we can let that go, don't you? Duchess ain't a name, it's more of a… title. 'Sides this is America; they don't got no titles…"

"I dunno—"

Jayo looked back down at Leigh. "Don't pay Nussy no attention, lady. He's too stiff. Ain't too… what's the word…?"

"Flexible…?"

He beamed. "Flexible! That's the word! Far as he's concerned, what says goes; but me, I'm flexible as the day's long." As he spoke he grew harder to see: like he was backing up into the dark street, even though he wasn't moving a step. His voice was gradually fading, too.

"Well, so long, duchess. Catch you later…"

"It's been swell, doll face…"

Both voices faded to nothing, the street was empty; or as empty as Leigh could tell in the poor light. Dawn was a couple of hours away; already the streets were turning a dirty gray.

She stepped out of her car, listening to the echoes her footsteps stirred. They were alone. She slipped the .38 back in her pocket, hand trembling.

VII

Paladin sat in the porch, staring across the grounds, mechanically sipping at his Scotch. He couldn't shake that last image: the shade of Leigh, so desperately sad. By the end of the year, she'd be dead.

"Penny for them." Saint-Germain was loading another cigarette into his ivory holder. He lit up.

Paladin just glared at him.

"All this time, and it still affects you." The count sat facing him again. "She'll die eventually. It's the mortal condition." He exhaled a thick blue cloud and pointed at the bottle with his cigarette holder. "All the cheap hooch in the world can't change that."

"That's what makes us different." Paladin got to his feet and pushed the almost drained bottle into his coat. "You lost the ability to care long ago; I'll never get used to it."

"Doesn't make you a better person…"

"Says you." Paladin pulled up his collar; the approaching morning had somehow made the air colder. "I'm going home."

Saint-Germain laughed. "Home? Is that what you call it—?"

Paladin spun around, drawing his Mauser. "One more word, Leo—just one! Let's see if you can dodge a slug!"

The other stood languidly, hands raised like a two-bit hood in a gangster movie. His smug grin never wavered. Paladin waited several seconds before holstering the automatic. He turned away—

and saw Leigh standing halfway down the path, watching him curiously. With an effort he choked back his feelings and stretched a smile across his face.

"Princess! What brings you out on a cold night like this?"

She stared, her eyes frosty. "Oh, I don't know… Maybe because we have a busy restaurant and I find you out here playing at stick up with—" Her glance flickered toward Saint-Germain. "Who is he, anyhow?"

"Him? Likes to call himself the Count Saint-Germain. You wouldn't like to hear what I call him."

The count cleared his throat. "Don't stop there, David, please introduce me to this vision of loveliness."

Paladin resisted the urge to gaze up into the paling sky: there was no help there. "Saint-Germain, this is Leigh Oswin. She runs *The Palace* restaurant."

The other man stepped past Paladin, took Leigh's hand, and bowed over it. "Charmed, my dear. His tastes are obviously improving."

Leigh peered at Paladin above the count's bowed figure, her expression a picture. "Kind of fruity, isn't he?"

The investigator felt a genuine smile flowing into the phony one. "She's got your number, Saint-Germain."

The count turned his still ducked head in Paladin's direction. "You can be such a pill."

"Well, good to have met you, count." Leigh took her hand back. "C'mon, Damy, shake it. This isn't my kind of neighborhood." She glanced toward the street in a way that Paladin might have described as nervy.

"Suits me, princess." Both their parked automobiles stood out clearly in the growing light. He took her arm as they walked toward them.

"Hold it!" Saint-Germain called. "There's something out there. Something rather unpleasant. I'd rather we waited for full light…"

Leigh's hand slipped into a coat pocket. "What's he mean?"

Paladin shook his head. "Smoke and mirror, princess. Cheap stunts. It's how he pays for the chintzy suits."

The count was insistent. "I'm perfectly serious!"

Leigh paused. She gave Paladin a twitchy look; she really was on edge. "I think he's got a point, Damy."

He looked hard at her pale face; glanced back at Saint-Germain. The count was staring into the fading gloom, cigarette holder held like a weapon. Leigh was right: the count wasn't fooling. Not this time.

"What is it?"

Saint-Germain shook his head; he'd gone as pasty as Leigh. "I don't know…"

Paladin released Leigh's arm and drew both of his automatics. If Saint-Germain was clueless as the rest of them, then things were real bad. "I must be losing my touch."

All three made it slowly down the path. Just off 10th Street the two street punks, Nussy and Jayo, were waiting: each propped against opposite sides of the lych-gate. They were relaxed, arms folded, faces serene.

Leigh jerked to a halt. "Those are the punks who tried hustling me."

Paladin grew even more uneasy. "I paid them to watch my car."

Saint-Germain gave a brief, unamused laugh. "They charged me entrance money," He shrugged at Paladin's expression. "They looked like they needed a couple of dollars."

Nussy was the first to speak. "The count, the investigator and the duchess." He made it sound insulting.

Jayo's face warped into a sneer that was far too knowing. "Nice t'see yous all again."

Saint-Germain spoke, just loud enough for Paladin and Leigh to hear. "Tell me, did they ask your names?"

Both replied in unison. "Yes."

"And did you give them?"

It took Paladin a moment; then it hit like a sandbag. "Holy shit!" Too much was getting past him tonight. He stared at the punks, trying to see through their exteriors, but they were too good. A beam from the rising sun made it through the tenements and fell across Nussy and Jayo. They glowed with soft, deep orange radiance.

Paladin nudged Leigh, offering his Browning 9 mm. She shook her head, taking a snub-nosed revolver out of a coat pocket. That's my girl, he thought, always prepared. He offered the gun to Saint-Germain instead. The count shook his head.

"I doubt they'll be of much use."

"Then I hope you've got something better in that stogie stick." Paladin gave Nussy and Jayo his full attention, snicking the safeties off both Browning and Mauser. "So what do you say, boys?"

Jayo jerked upright from the support, facing them. "You lied. So did he."

"But not the duchess." Nussy mirrored Jayo's actions: they were bookends.

Paladin addressed the count, never taking his eyes off the punks. "I guess you told them you were the Count Saint-Germain?"

"And I imagine you said you were Damian Paladin..."

"Guess neither of us were paying too much attention."

Leigh butted in, her tone impatient. "Hate to interrupt the debate, boys, but I don't suppose either of you would like to tell me what's going on?"

Paladin was rueful. "Our friends here aren't the local punks they seem."

"That much I worked out already."

The count was fiddling absently with his cigarette holder. "David and I may well have talked ourselves into a little trouble. We think it—they—might be a *genius termini*."

Paladin smiled to himself. "*We* think?"

"I'm sorry, am I going too fast for you...?"

Leigh was frowning in thought. "I'm guessing you don't mean like in bus stations?"

Paladin tried to explain. "Think of them as kind of like doormen. They guard borders, boundaries, stuff like that." He was mentally kicking himself for strolling wide-eyed into this jam; he should have sensed it. That Saint-Germain also got rooked didn't make it any better. But a *genius termini* had no need for oracles and mediums, it could pierce the veil masking the future. It knew just where its victims were together, at their most vulnerable and distracted. It was an apex predator, with all the tricks and dodges it had learned over an endless existence.

"More like vagrant doormen." The count sounded distracted, as though he wasn't concentrating on his words. "Wandering all the tiers; picking spots to hijack."

Nussy was grinning at him, enjoying the show. "Picked good this time, didn't we?" His lips spread far too wide, showing too many teeth.

"So what's so special about them?" Despite Leigh's casual tone, Paladin couldn't help noticing her revolver was pointed levelly at Jayo's gut.

"Before they let anyone pass they ask their names. Their real names…"

Nussy grinned. "And you lied… *Damian Paladin*."

"You too… *Count Saint-Germain*." From out of the stunted, malnourished kid, Jayo was growing into something bigger, brighter. It pushed and heaved below his skin.

"Sounds like they get pretty sore when you try and fake it." As she spoke, Leigh removed a pack of Luckies from a pocket with her free hand, tapped one out and slipped it between her lips. Each movement was slow, controlled.

"Terminally." Jayo laughed. It was a piercing, window-shattering keen that should have echoed up and down The Bowery tenements. All it did was set Paladin's teeth on edge.

"So how do we get past them?" Leigh struck a match and lit her cigarette.

Nussy looked at her, his ghastly smile softening. "You can go, duchess. We got no beef with you."

"Your chums, though—" Jayo flicked a thumb across his throat. "They don't go nowhere."

"Am I the only one growing tired of your sub-Hollywood dialects?" The count pointed his ivory cigarette holder at Nussy and Jayo. "It occurs to me you're pretty fake yourselves."

Paladin had to agree. "Phony accents; phony characterization. You couldn't get a bit part in a Cagney movie."

Nussy shrugged. "Fooled you though, didn't we?" Shark-grin growing wider, his shape began to smear and stretch. Across the path, Jayo was an indistinct blur of slowly writhing, pallid color.

Saint-Germain shouted something Paladin couldn't make out, flourishing his ivory holder in an elaborate gesture. The investigator couldn't be sure if a blaze of light spat from where a cigarette should be, but the air pulsed and rippled, converging on the two transforming shapes. For a moment they paused, frozen into grotesque statues, then an answering throb ricocheted back at the count. Saint-Germain was thrown to the path, hitting the ground in a tangle of well-tailored limbs. Even though Paladin wasn't the target, the backwash sent him staggering.

Dropping to one knee he fired both automatics. All twenty shells from the Mauser sprayed around Nussy and Jayo in less than two seconds, splintering the wooden lych-gate beside them. He was more clinical with the Browning, picking his shots thoughtfully. None made a difference. It was like trying to plug water: each slug passed through the undulating shapes without trace.

Leigh was firing with detached fury, and no more success.

Both automatics empty, Paladin got to his feet. There was going to be one hell of a repair bill for the gate: it looked like a pin board.

The things that had been Nussy and Jayo were growing taller and thinner, their nebulous forms more brilliant with every moment, stretching up toward the lightening sky. Each reached for the other with dazzling, tenuous arcs that might once have been arms.

Saint-Germain raised his head. "Don't let them touch!"

"I know, I know!" Paladin holstered his Mauser, hastily switching magazines in the Browning.

Leigh's lowered her automatic. "What happens if they touch?"

Paladin glanced at her. There was no time to explain a Tangential Gate. "Do you really want to know?"

She pursed her lips. "Guess not."

Paladin's free hand fumbled at his belt pouches. He dug out two dull spheres like small, smooth grenades. Thumbing a switch on each, he tossed them at the *genius termini*: now a growing, incomplete arch filling the width of the lych-gate, towering above it. Between them, East 10th Street was getting harder to see as a luminescent mist gradually filled the space. So far, the reaching limbs hadn't touched. Not quite.

The spheres exploded with a faint thump; blood-red smoke billowed out, masking the blazing outline. From somewhere behind the thick fog bellowed a harsh din that could have been either a scream or a laugh. Paladin pulled out two more grenades, waiting.

"I doubt that will stop it." The count was at his side again:

bruised, blood speckling his left cheek, suit ripped.

"We don't need to stop it, just slow it down." Paladin juggled the grenades like worry beads. "Give Leigh a chance to get out. Us too."

"You heard it: she gave them her real name. She should be quite safe." Saint-Germain fitted a cigarette in his holder with a hand that wasn't quite steady. "Besides, you saw the prophesy…"

Paladin fought back an urge to slap the stupid holder out of the other's hand. "Go to Hell!"

The smoke was clearing, two pillars of light cutting through the bloody clouds. As Paladin readied the next two grenades a faint breeze struck up from nowhere, rippling the smoke like a curtain. A moment later the *genius termini* was exposed, the bright arch inching closer to completion. As Paladin primed and pitched the grenades, the two branches connected. The arch blazed with a harsh, actinic light that seared Paladin's eyes.

Even as the grenades exploded, the breeze erupted into a gale. A moment later it was a hurricane. A tornado whose eye was at the very center of the *genius termini*: the Tangential Gate was completed.

VIII

Leigh fired her bean shooter until it was dead and empty. It did no more damage than Damy's cannons, but it made her feel better. Even if those little creeps were rapidly changing into something else, she'd let off steam. Too bad she hadn't had the chance while they were human enough to bleed.

She glanced toward Damy and the count: they looked pretty sore. A trap of some kind, and they'd both fallen for it. That she hadn't was sheer dumb luck; Leigh didn't see any reason for either of them to get all bent about it.

Nussy and Jayo had stopped changing, far as she could tell. The mouthy street punks were gone, replaced by figures that reminded her of the Greek and Roman statues she'd seen in the Metropolitan Museum. Pure white, perfectly proportioned, draped with simple robes, some kind of woven crown sitting on wavy hair. The things' eyes were colorless and lacking in detail; even so, Leigh couldn't shake the feeling they were looking at her. Their full, almost feminine lips were poised on the edge of a conspiratorial smile. Each was reaching an arm out to the other, their second arms hanging carelessly at their sides. Through the arch they formed, East 10th Street was gray and quiet.

They didn't look one bit threatening; Leigh wasn't fooled for a minute.

Red smoke erupted in front on them, blocking Leigh's view.

Just before the clouds had billowed in front of the faces, Leigh could have sworn both heads looked at Damy, laughing in delight.

The fog cleared. As far as Leigh could see, nothing had changed. No: the figures were almost touching now, fingertips a fraction away from brushing. And that would be bad; Damy had said so.

More smoke exploded across the scene. This time it dispersed in a moment, like an invisible airplane engine was blowing it to shreds. Another quick glance at Damy and the count added strength to that crazy notion: both were crouching, fighting against a hurricane she could neither feel nor hear.

The figures stood quietly, hands interlaced like they were about to play some kids' game. They were definitely smiling at Leigh, now: open, friendly grins that were meant to reassure her.

Like hell.

She snatched a final look at Damy and his chum: they were still miming their battle against a wind that was blowing them toward the archway. Damy wasn't even getting the chance to level his Browning.

She took a step toward the archway. Was it her imagination, or did the figures' smiles falter, just a little? She stepped forward again; their serene expressions hardened. They didn't like it at all. That was aces with Leigh: anything which rattled those smug faces was all right in her book.

She pocketed her .38 and walked steadily toward the street framed by the archway. "Here comes a chopper to chop off your head."

She was regretting the words even before they'd cleared her lips.

IX

Paladin saw Leigh starting to move. She was walking straight for the ugly purple vortex boiling in the center of the arch. Couldn't she see it?

"Leigh!" The howling wind ripped the words from his mouth. She'd never hear them. He inched toward her, going with the hurricane rather than fighting it. He felt his arm pulled, his body tugged back. It was Saint-Germain, hanging onto him.

He screamed into the count's pinched face. "I have to stop her!"

"No! No, you don't!" Paladin just made out the words above the storm.

"It'll kill her!"

"It's not her time! You saw—!"

Paladin shrugged off the hands, stumbling as the winds dragged at his flapping coat. He crashed to the ground. Saint-Germain leapt on him, trying to pin him down. The wind tore at the count's ripped clothes, half-lifting him. Paladin swung a fist, connecting with Saint-Germain's movie star jaw, and the count rolled away.

Paladin staggered to his feet, leaning away from the sucking storm. Leigh was only a few feet away from the bruised maelstrom: if she reached out she could have touched the blazing sides, the agonizing brilliance of the *genius termini*.

"*Leigh!*"

She couldn't hear him; it was impossible. He took a step toward her, the hungry storm instantly sucking him six feet closer to its heart. He dropped to his knees, raising his Browning 9 mm, for an insane moment trying to aim at Leigh.

Something cracked down on his wrist. He dropped the gun, cursing at the sudden, sharp agony. It was an ivory cigarette holder. Saint-Germain loomed over him, wielding the holder like a whip. Paladin snatched for it; the count lashed him across the face. Paladin's vision blurred.

"You can't help her!"

Paladin grabbed at Saint-Germain's foot, misjudging it. The count stamped down on his hand, pinning it to the ground, even though Saint-Germain could barely stay upright himself.

Paladin looked on helplessly as Leigh stepped into the maelstrom; through it. He yelled her name one last time—

—And all was silence, save for his voice echoing off tenement walls. The *genius termini* had vanished, the lych-gate empty of everything except Leigh: standing under its roof, staring back at them, her face confused.

Saint-Germain removed his foot, stooping to help Paladin up. The investigator stared at him, angrily rubbing at his wrist. The count was talking softly, just loud enough for Paladin to hear.

"She gave it her real name. It had no hold over her. It was there for us, the ones who lied to it. By stepping through she broke the seal: a willing sacrifice."

"You didn't know it would work!" Paladin rammed his clenched hands into coat pockets.

"Such sacrifices have always propitiated the gods. Like I said, it wasn't her time… I was confident—"

Paladin's right fist, looped by brass knuckles, smashed into the count's jaw a second time. He dropped like he'd been sandbagged.

"And in my experience, you're a self-serving, careless son of a bitch!" Paladin slipped the knuckles back in his pocket. "You were lucky this time; you guessed right. Just don't go thinking either of us owes you so much as a plugged nickel!"

He stepped over Saint-Germain's body, waving at Leigh, somehow finding a cocky smile that hurt more than his stamped-on wrist.

She raised an eyebrow. “You boys finished playing?”

“For now.”

“Good, because I’m in the mood for breakfast.” She looped an arm through his, guiding him toward the parked cars. “And an explanation.”

“Sure, soon as I’ve worked it out myself.” He glanced back at Saint-Germain: the count was sitting on the path, nonchalantly lighting a cigarette. He waved the holder, smiling crookedly, ignoring the blood dripping from his square chin. He mouthed words Paladin chose not to understand.

The investigator shivered, telling himself it was the early morning cold.

PART THREE: ZOMBIE DANCE

I

Stamping along the empty sidewalk, Leigh was feeling pretty evil. Damn Enid Walden! Leigh had been looking forward to watching Clark Gable and Franchot Tone all day. But what movie did they catch instead? *Bride of Frankenstein.* Because Enid got the wrong day. And it *would* be a double feature with a three year old Bela Lugosi movie: *White Zombie*. Even if Colin Clive was kind of cute, he was no Clark Gable.

On top of that, she was managing to spook herself. It had to be that second hot dog. No movie could get her imagining zombies lurching about the streets of Manhattan. She'd seen *real* monsters; experienced weirdness beyond what some Hollywood hack banged out. It *was* that second hot dog. The black guy who'd been following her for the last three blocks didn't really look like a reanimated corpse…

With some relief she realized she'd reached the alley which housed *The Palace*'s front door. She glanced at her wristwatch: it was just five after ten. The place would still be jumping, the staff around. Damy might even be there.

"And why's that such a big deal?" She was sore with herself for just thinking it. "I'm in no trouble. I don't need Damy to bail me out—" She glanced down the sidewalk one last time. The black guy was still there, lurching in her direction, most likely completely ossified. Why did tonight have to be so quiet? Leigh wondered angrily. Where were all the damned crowds?

She slid her purse strap back up her shoulder and headed into the alley. *The Palace* was a few yards away: an ex-Juice Joint she owned and mostly managed. The safety she so obviously didn't need.

It was only when she was halfway to the restaurant door that it occurred to her: if she was really being followed, would a dark back alley be the best place?

II

Paladin looked suspiciously at the dish he was holding. From under a crust of cheese and tomato sauce, the glazed white eyes of several small fish stared back at him. Beside him, Franco was enthusing wildly.

"The customers will love it. No place else in New York will be serving it." *The Palace's* chef positively quivered with eagerness.

"You amaze me." Paladin tilted his head to one side. He silently dared any of the fish to blink. "And what do you call it?"

"*Occhi dei morti.* Literally 'eyes of the dead'. The name will go great with your reputation, boss."

Paladin dipped a finger into the cooling cheese sauce. He tasted it and winced, hoping Franco didn't notice. Far too salty. "What? Being the city's best supplier of ptomaine poisoning?"

Franco laughed politely. "No—New York's resident occult detective!" He paused dramatically, like the idea had only just struck him. "We could rename the menu! Give all the food connected names—!"

Paladin stared levelly at Franco. "You mean like fur of bat and eye of newt?"

Franco's face lit up. "Now you're on the trolley, boss!"

"You've been hanging around Leigh too much."

As though summoned by name, Leigh burst into the kitchen, looking hot and flustered. She pulled off her hat and began to fan herself. Paladin was glad of the interruption.

"If Clark Gable has that effect, princess, maybe I should grow a mustache."

Leigh shot him a look. "We never got to see *Mutiny on the Bounty*! Enid and her lousy taste in movies!" She dug a pack of cigarettes out of her purse, lit up and blew a plume of smoke in his direction. "And on top of all that I thought I was being followed." She took another twitchy pull on her ciggy.

Ah, thought Paladin. That's why she's so balled up. "Were you?"

"No! Just my imagi—!"

The shrieks and yells from the restaurant stamped a period to her words. Paladin, Leigh and Franco all pushed their way through the swinging kitchen door. Beyond, it was chaos.

Customers leapt to their feet in fear or outrage; the band was scrabbling off stage, instruments clutched tightly; waitresses and cigarette girls headed for the exit. It was, Paladin thought, just how the joint must have looked during a raid back in the good old Prohibition days. Although back then a bunch of flat-feet would be causing the ruckus, not a scrawny black guy hurling tables and people about with equal ease.

Paladin kept his tone casual. "That wouldn't be the ape you thought was tailing you?" Leigh was concentrating on the chaos in the middle of the restaurant, likely adding up the cost of each systematically shattered chair and table. She jerked out a nod.

"I blamed the lousy movies, or the lousier food." She ducked as a plate bounced off the wall to her left. "I got it in my head he was… you know… a zombie…"

Paladin watched as the black figure ploughed effortlessly through the warzone he was creating. Some brave souls were trying to tackle him, and getting plenty of lumps for their efforts. His skin had an unhealthy gray pallor; his staring eyes unfocused. His movements were rigid and poorly coordinated.

"You know, princess, you may just be right…" Paladin tapped his lips in thought. "So how do we stop a zombie…?" He was talking to himself, trying to dredge up scraps of forgotten lore. It had been a while.

He remembered that he was still holding Franco's over-salted *occhi dei morti*. Paladin smiled: it was so apt. Raising the dish level with his chest he stepped forward, straight toward the lurching figure. The floor was thinning out: everyone had either beaten it or out cold. Most of the tables were only good for matches. The thing in the center was stumbling forward; Paladin couldn't be sure if it was heading toward him, Leigh, or just looking for another mug to sock. He didn't want to disappoint.

"Hey—ugly!"

The creature paused, tilting its head in Paladin's direction. He marched right up it, halting just outside what he hoped was its reach, raising the dish of cheese and fish. "You're just in time to sample my chef's latest creation."

He pitched the *occhi dei morti* straight into the black guy's face. The dish bounced away, leaving congealing strings of cheese, slices of tomato, diced mushrooms and flaking bits of fish dripping off the dark gray features. The scrawny figure reached up an uncertain hand to touch the goo. It licked at Franco's specialty.

The creature twitched violently. Its left knee buckled, collapsing to the floor in a thrashing mess of limbs. Paladin stepped closer, watching thoughtfully. After a handful of seconds, the spasms eased, and the thing sagged like an unstringed puppet. Paladin nudged a shoulder with his toe; it was already growing rigid.

"Knew it. Far too much salt..."

III

Paladin found a relatively unscarred table and chair, a bottle of house Scotch, and sat himself down. Pouring a generous slug, he relaxed and watched a baffled posse of New York's Finest sifting through the ruins. The body had been removed for examination, and a couple of the flat-feet had been detailed to get witness statements. But any diners still conscious had taken a powder. Those staff whose brains weren't rattled halfway back to kindergarten hadn't seen much; or so they said. Paladin wondered just what the cops expected to learn. It was a regular three-ring circus.

Over by the wrecked stage, Leigh was frantically scribbling on a cocktail napkin, chewing on her lip, a cigarette, and anyone dumb enough to interrupt her. A dazed-looking Franco retrieved his dish. It was one of the few things still in one piece.

Paladin took a sip of hooch, trying not to wince. Once he got back to his apartment he'd rinse his mouth with some good stuff. "I guess we can say goodbye to tomorrow night's bookings. Even if we could get the place fixed up in time."

Franco laughed. "You kidding, boss? After tonight you'll be beatin' 'em off with sticks."

"You figure?"

"Sure!" Franco righted another chair and sat down. "Who needs a torch singer with a floor show like that? Word will already be going round."

Paladin finished off his Scotch and stared at the chef. "Let me get this straight: you think people will come here just to be knocked silly…?"

"Not exactly." Franco's hand twitched toward the cheap whisky. For a moment, Paladin considered telling him off, but then he saw the pale face and too-bright eyes behind the chef's swagger, and nudged the bottle toward him. It was easy to forget this was the first time Franco had seen the kind of thing Paladin regularly went up against. The chef gulped a couple of noisy mouthfuls.

"You just want to scare 'em, but in a safe way. Like that giant monkey movie a few years back. Folks went to get scared even though they knew it was camera tricks."

"You want me to take on King Kong in the middle of *The Palace*?" Paladin had an idea Franco was trying to sell him another circus.

"Nah. Just a guy in a rubber suit that you beat the bejesus out of every night. Safe scares. Everybody gets to scream and laugh. It'll bring 'em in from outta state."

"And just who's going to pay for tonight?" Leigh's voice suddenly rose above the general background nose. "Anybody want to tell me that?"

Paladin just favored her with a sour look. He knew about her little box, not so secretly buried out by Chaykin Field. She'd used a part of its contents to bankroll the restaurant; contents any court would happily waste years figuring if she was entitled to. Contents that were a long way from exhausted. They'd survive.

He was more interested in zombies strolling the sidewalks of New York; especially one that was stopped in its tracks by just a little salt.

"I got just one question, boss." Franco slid the bottle toward himself.

"Just one?"

"How come that thing dropped dead after tasting my food? I mean, everyone's entitled to their opinion, but—" He sucked on the bottle. "That was my mother's recipe… God rest her soul…"

"Salt, Franco. Salt revives a zombie, brings back its memory."

"Didn't look to me like it had time to remember much before—" He slapped his left arm flat onto the table, raising the bottle with his free hand. This time, Paladin reached over and took it off him.

"Exactly: salt doesn't destroy a zombie. Or it shouldn't. Which leaves *me* with just one question…"

"What's that, boss?"

"You paying for that booze…?"

Franco's exit was the smoothest and quietest Paladin had ever seen.

IV

Morning found Paladin on the streets of Harlem. If zombies were about to start parading down Fifth Avenue, he wanted to know. Hidden away in these crumbling brownstones was someone who could tell him.

It was a fine day: not too warm, the sun hanging unchallenged in a blue sky. All the more remarkable that the sidewalks were empty. No women gossiping from windows, no men hanging around on corners, no kids playing. Everywhere was an eerie hush; not so much as a radio playing. The only soul around was waiting at Paladin's destination.

At the foot of worn steps leading inside a tired brownstone sat an ancient black man. His hair and whiskers were pale gray, eyes a watery brown. He looked old enough to have seen Atlanta burn, and mean enough to have supplied the matches. Paladin stopped and removed his hat.

"What d'you say, Lakwa? Long time no see." He nodded toward the open door. "She in?"

The old man scanned rheumy eyes down Paladin's suit. His expression was both defensive and pugnacious. "Nice threads."

"Didn't you hear? I got a job."

"What you got ain't no job for a decent man…"

"Who said I was decent?" Paladin glanced toward the door again. "Well?"

"She in." The old man returned to gazing down the silent street. "An' she expectin' you…"

"Of course she is." Paladin trod lightly up the steps. "I've enjoyed our chat, Lakwa, we must do it again sometime. Say in another hundred years."

The old man snorted what may have been a laugh and spat.

Paladin stepped into a dim, stale lobby. The mailboxes to his right had all been jimmied open; a wall phone was on the floor in pieces. Had there been an elevator, he guessed that wouldn't have worked, either. Paladin made his way up creaking stairs, careful not to touch banister or walls: he didn't much like the color of either.

Her apartment was on the third floor. As he made his way toward it, the darkness took on substance. Serrated shadows nodded in a breeze Paladin didn't feel. The stagnant air grew fetid: a rankness belonging to distant jungles, not New York. The roaches in the walls were doing a crackerjack impersonation of monkeys.

By the time he reached the apartment door, Paladin's smart suit was wrinkled by out of place humidity; thick rivulets of sweat rolled down his face. Before he could knock, her voice came from the other side, oddly muffled. "Come in *cher*. It not locked…"

He pushed the door open and stepped inside.

If he thought it had been warm in the hallway, the apartment was a furnace. The air was thick and wet enough to drown in. Incense, spice, the fierce scent of tropical flowers: all fought for dominance. Behind him the apartment door, now a heavy bead curtain, rattled together. He tried not to think of it as a net closing.

"Do you really need it so hot?"

He was answered by a loud, bass laugh. "Appearances, *cher*! You know how important they are. Clients have… expectations…" Another bead curtain on the far side of the room parted and a large black woman sailed through. She was swathed in garish robes, mostly in red and gold; an equally bright turban covered her head. Her wide face was as radiant with humor as the old man outside had been sour. The heat and humidity didn't seem to be bothering her one bit. "Besides, it remind me of home."

"I don't remember New Orleans ever being this hot." He looked around for somewhere to drop his hat before it was reduced to a mangled ruin in his hand. He dropped it onto a small table to his right before loosening his coat, tie and collar.

"Not N'Orleans, sugar." She flopped into a broad armchair that Paladin could swear hadn't been there before. "I mean *home…*"

Paladin managed a drained smile. He wished there was a chair he could fall onto. "Lakwa's his usual cheerful self."

She giggled. "Don't you pay him no mind, *cher*. You know how he get roun'… people like you and me."

Paladin couldn't miss the pause before *people*. As if any of the trio, himself, Marie *or* Lakwa, could claim to be ordinary Joes. "How you been, Marie?"

"You know me, *cher*: I'm indestructible. How 'bout you?"

"The same."

She pouted. The childish expression looked out of place on her large face. "'Cept you meanin' it, honey." She picked up a glass dripping with condensation, something else Paladin thought she just conjured out of not so thin air. She took a sip. "What this I hear 'bout your father bein' in town?"

Paladin felt an irritable stab. "You know how it is: he never calls, never writes…" He tugged at his necktie. "Zombies, Marie…"

"Yeah. I hear 'bout that, too." A little of the sparkle left her eyes.

"Just hear? I guess you wouldn't know anything else about them?"

She stared at him; for a moment her expression was as hard and unforgiving as Lakwa's. "They nothin' to do wi' me, *cher*. They not true zombie is what I hear."

"You got that right. I fed one salt last night. Stopped it dead—" Bad choice of words. "If not you—?"

Marie's harsh expression stayed a moment longer, then it was brushed aside by a vast grin. "Okay, I tell you what I *know*. And that ain't much, sugar…" She leaned forward and the robes rolled away from her body, her head perched on top of a gold and red tent. "There another *bokor* in town. A *bokor* who ain't *bokor*. And people bin disappearin'; I mean *my* people. You seen how quiet the streets is? They scared, *cher*. They scared to go out—!" The grin faltered for a moment. "And I don' know why!"

She leaned back, taking another drink from the cold glass.

Paladin knew how much that last admission hurt. Marie had spent her long life trading on what she knew, which was plenty. If there was something she didn't know, that something was a very big deal.

"That it?"

She stared back. "Ain't it enough?"

"Thanks, Marie." He picked up his crumpled hat. "I owe you."

"Sure do, honey. And I'll collect." Her grin grew even wider. "One last thing, *cher*. For what it worth…"

Paladin paused in the act of pushing the bead curtain aside.

"Try the warehouse district on the East River."

"Any reason?"

She shrugged, her robes swelling like a colorful sea. "A feelin'. Nothin' more."

Paladin shoved his half-ruined hat on his head and returned her grin. "One of your hunches is worth a dozen cast-iron leads, Marie. Thanks."

"*Au revoir, cher* Baron. You be careful among *Les Americains*—"

He was out in the hallway, back in Harlem. A door that was once again solid wood shut behind him, cutting her words off. "Thanks again, Marie."

Outside, the step was deserted, Lakwa nowhere to be seen. The place was a ghost town. Paladin hoped that wouldn't prove to be more than just a metaphor.

V

Leigh climbed out of Paladin's Chrysler, frowning at the faceless ranks of warehouses marching in all directions. He couldn't take his eyes off her; or rather, her new get-up. She spotted the wide masher's grin and her frown rapidly soured into a scowl. "Put your eyes back, mister. They're leaving big sticky marks all over my duds."

"What there is of them."

Her scowl became a sly grin. She did a little twirl. "Don't you like it?"

"I'm all for it, princess. Just not sure how the League of Decency is likely to react…"

He joined her on the sidewalk. Back in the apartment, he'd changed into what Leigh had long ago dubbed his hero suit. He never imagined Leigh might want her own version. Before they'd quit the Teton Building, she mentioned changing into something more comfortable. Ten minutes later, she'd joined him in the Airflow, done up in the threads presently getting him all steamy. Maybe it wasn't so different from his own: short brown leather jacket, pants and boots; with a belt and large holster hanging off her waist. Though he had to admit it fitted her a damned sight better. Kind of snug in all the right places.

Leigh's impatient voice brought him up to date. "Well? We off to do some kind of investigating, or you just going to stand there and drool?"

Paladin grinned back. "If I gave you the honest answer you'd like as not plug me, princess. So I suggest we get on with the sleuthing."

"Fine." She looked around at the quiet buildings. "So what are we looking for? Keeping in mind it's Sunday and smart people are at home."

"You'll—"

"If you say I'll know it when I see it, I will most definitely drill you."

He shrugged. "Like you said: it's Sunday. Apart from the occasional security guard, I don't expect the place to be jumping. But—"

"If we find someone with a warehouse containing half of Harlem, he's our guy?"

"Something like that."

"I love it when you plan ahead." She faced him again. "Where to?"

"Beats me. There's a lot of ground, and only two of us. I don't want us to split up, but I can't see any other way."

Leigh's face was solemn for a moment, then she cracked a grin. "Okay. You take the west side and I'll take the east." She patted the holster on her hip. "And if you hear Old Faithful here, come a-runnin'!" With a defiant toss of her blonde curls she set off.

"If only to protect you from yourself…" He watched her striding away for a few moments; she looked so small against the deserted building. "Take care, princess!"

"You know it!"

He shook his head. My, but that coat and pants were tight…

***

As he'd predicted, Paladin's search was fruitless. Aside from a couple of aging guards who were under the impression that the half acre of empty real estate they were protecting was the Federal Reserve Bank, he'd come up empty. No matter how big or small, full or obviously deserted since the Depression hit, he hadn't found anything that gave him a clue. If only Marie had been more specific.

He returned to his coupe after three hours. Leigh wasn't back yet; he hoped she was having better luck. He dropped into the driver's seat, wondering if there was some kind of wireless phone system he could get fitted: something they could use to keep in touch. If Leigh wanted to dress up like Wilma Deering, maybe it was the kind of doodad she'd go for.

What felt like an eternity passed. Paladin glanced at his watch: four hours since they'd started the search. Where was Leigh? He stepped out of the car, looked up and down the empty avenues like he could summon her up by staring hard enough. He realized he was drumming his fingers on the car roof.

"I knew we shouldn't have split up!" He slammed his palm on the roof, scaring up echoes. It hurt but didn't make him feel any better.

He unholstered both automatics. Kicking the car door shut, he set off, following Leigh's path as well as he remembered it.

Within minutes he was experiencing déjà-vu: this part of town looked no different from the section he'd prowled. Just as quiet; all the buildings, from squat lean-tos to three-floor monsters the size of airplane hangars, just as empty. Except for a few birds making staccato chirps from where they perched on the power-lines, there wasn't a sound. Most doors were locked, and those that weren't led nowhere. Peering through grimy windows just revealed crates and boxes, bits of machinery, sometimes nothing at all. He was never going to make any progress like this: his approach was too random. If he'd been anybody else, he'd accuse them of panicking. He needed a plan.

He stopped and took a deep breath. C'mon, hotshot! You can track down ghosts and monsters; how hard can it be to find a living, breathing human? If she still—

He wasn't even going to entertain *that* thought!

Above him power lines dissected the sky, leading off a few at a time to various buildings, feeding whatever utilities the warehouses needed.

A few at a time?

Half a block away, an innocuous, single floor building had more lines leading to it than every other warehouse combined. Looked like half the city's power was being fed into that one small depot. Each line entered at ground level, which must have violated half a dozen zoning statutes. What in the name of God would need that much power?

He just had to find out.

VI

It was too much like the Karloff movie. The same crazy equipment, the same noisy sparks and lightning zapping between polished domes. The metallic, almost sweet smell reminded Leigh of Coney Island for some reason. At least the place was too well-lit for a castle cellar, and there was no creature on a nearby slab waiting to be resurrected. The guy in the white coat was no Colin Clive, either: too short and fat; too bald. She wasn't happy about being tied to a trolley like Dumb Dora, though. If only she could get a hold of her gun…

She still wasn't too sure what had happened. One moment she'd been checking every door and window, then the universe had exploded and she'd woken up lashed to a gurney. Her head was pounding like a troupe of Russian dancers were kicking away inside, the back of her neck felt sticky. If she'd gotten blood on her new leather coat, boy, was someone going to pay!

Movement snagged the corner of her eye, she turned her head as far as it would go. The two-bit Frankenstein was coming in her direction, rubbing his rubber-gloved hands together in a way Leigh found disturbing. He reached the gurney, pulling a bizarre kind of apparatus over his eyes, like a welders' face-mask with a set of field glasses stuck to it. He stared down at Leigh silently. She appreciated how a bug on a microscope slide must feel.

She tugged at her bonds; it felt like the one around her left foot gave a little. "They better not be some kind of X-ray specs, mister!"

Frankenstein flinched, pushing the weird goggles up off his face as he moved. His round face was slick with sweat, two bright red patches burned high on his cheeks. Give him a bushy white beard and a red cap, Leigh thought, and he'd be the perfect Santa. Except for his habit of tying people up. "Madam, I can assure you—!"

Leigh realized his flushed face had nothing to do with heat. She almost laughed. "While I'm here strapped to this table, you couldn't assure me diddly, fatso! How about setting a girl free before I introduce you to my side-kick, here!" She tried pointing to the holstered automatic, but it was an empty gesture, hog-tied as she was.

"Indeed, madam." He shuffled, licking his lips and glancing around the warehouse. "I'd be delighted to remove your bonds… but—"

"But you get a kick out of tying women up?"

"No—no!" He grew even redder. "It's just that… the nature of my work… I have to take precautions…"

"Listen, mac, if I get outta here precautions won't save your sorry ass—!" She strained against her restraints again. Yes, they were loosening. Fun-sized Frankie had obviously never been in the Cub Scouts.

He edged away, her threats or actions rattling him. "No, madam: I assure you—!"

"Like hell!" Her right hand was almost free.

"The precautions are not for myself—"

"Too bad! You're going to need them!" With a snap, her right arm broke free. As the little man backed further off, she fished out a pocket knife. Cutting her left arm free, she sat up, making fast work of the remaining bonds. Her captor seemed to be in no hurry to stop her: he just backed off, wringing his rubber gloves and looking furtive.

Leigh swung herself off the gurney, looking around. She was in a warehouse, crammed with more of the fizzing machines, spider webs of hoists and pulleys, more gurneys—

And a workforce of gray-faced zombies. All looking at her.

“I was trying to protect you from them…” His apologetic voice tailed off as the silent creatures stepped closer.

VII

Paladin sized up the situation in a moment. Even through the grimy, ground level window he made out the huge basement and its bizarre set up. He saw Leigh cutting herself free from the trolley; the small, white-coated man backing away from her; and the parcel of lurching zombies.

He switched his Mauser to rapid-fire and squeezed the trigger. In a second most of the window frame was kindling. Holstering the empty automatic he kicked away the last splinters of frame, launching himself carelessly through the gap.

Before he'd dropped a dozen feet, his hands clamped around a length of chain. He dangled high above the floor, looking down at a dozen or so faces gazing up in shock, disguised relief, or simple incomprehension.

Leigh folded her arms. "High time!"

There's gratitude, he thought. Taking all his weight on one arm, Paladin drew his Browning, and took careful aim at a braking mechanism. The chain slackened, and he made what he hoped was a controlled, heroic descent. Once both feet were planted on concrete he grinned at Leigh. "Did I miss the main feature?"

"Only the cartoons."

"No, no!" The small guy was shuffling uncertainly, wringing gloved hands like there was someone's throat between them. "You'll ruin everything! This is too soon! Too soon!"

Paladin winked at Leigh. "Friend of yours?"

"We never got round to introductions..."

Paladin aimed his automatic at a point just above the small guy's nose. He went boss-eyed staring at the muzzle, but at least he stopped squirming.

"Thanks, professor." With his free hand Paladin dug a ten dollar bill out of his pants. He waved the sawbuck in front of the small guy's face before tucking it into his flying coat. "Made a bet with myself I wouldn't meet a mad scientist before the year was out."

The small guy's fat face crumpled, for a moment Paladin thought he was going to cry. "Please, sir, if we must have this conversation, could we have it away from—?" He jerked his head in the direction of the silent black figures who were all watching like the trio were the most fascinating people on the planet. Other than that, they didn't move a muscle.

Paladin frowned. "Don't look dangerous..."

"No, no... I don't believe they are. But they are easily distracted."

"Especially by blondes, huh?"

Leigh wrinkled her lips in mild disgust.

"Please." The small guy shuffled backwards, motioning the others to follow. He led them behind a packing crate, out of sight of the motionless creatures. Paladin never once lowered his automatic. Out of eyeshot, the guy seemed to relax, but Leigh was not about to allow him that luxury for long.

"Okay, Frankenstein. Let's have it."

"My name is Doctor Brook." He peeled off his rubber gloves and unbuttoned his coat. "Not that of some fictional character." He glanced at Paladin in what may have been injured pride. "Nor am I a deranged scientist from the worst excesses of a Hollywood screenplay!"

"We'll be the judge of that." Paladin made great play of looking around the warehouse and its weird machinery. "So what have you done with those people."

"The Negroes?" Brook fiddled with his tie like a half-sized Oliver Hardy. "Lab rats. The results of continually failing experiments. Luckily they still have a use around my laboratory: carrying, cleaning... nothing too demanding."

"What experiments?"

Doctor Brook sniggered. "The spark of life—the soul, if you will! I've been trying to isolate it—to detect and remove it whole!"

Leigh muttered in disgust. "Hell, no. You're not mad…!"

"And all you got were zombies." Paladin risked a glance around the packing case: the shuffling creatures were aimlessly shoving small boxes around, or polishing brass domes. They moved with less grace than automatons. "Give that man a cigar."

Brook was warming to his theme. "I took my clue from those African and Haitian witchdoctors. I reasoned that something they used in their so-called voodoo, some compound or drug, was capable of isolating the element which I sought." His round face grew sly. "After all, do they not claim that it is the soul, imprisoned by the primitive magician, which keeps the zombie in thrall…?"

Paladin nodded. "Until fed salt. That cancels the spell, reuniting body and spirit. Except it doesn't work on the things you've made…"

Brook sneered. "You talk as though you believe that mumbo-jumbo! Mine is scientific research, not primitive superstition!"

"But you've used that superstition as the basis of your experiments."

"Indeed. The witchdoctors use all sorts of potions, and I was able to collect samples of most." A little of Brook's self-assurance dropped away; he grew shifty. "I distilled a drug from those potions. A drug which, combined with my apparatus, can simulate death—"

"And extract the soul."

"Indeed. Gonbatine, the name I have given my drug, is very effective." His confidence wavered again. "I had planned to detect and isolate that vital force, much as the witchdoctors claim to do, but in a specially-designed piece of apparatus…"

"Except you haven't; or can't. The soul escapes, leaving you with things even less than zombies, since they've no hope of regaining their souls, and peace."

Brook's shoulders slumped. "Indeed. I'm only thankful that I used Negroes in my work. Imagine what a catastrophe it would be to do the same to a white man…!"

Leigh bared her teeth; she looked ready to blow. "Imagine—"

Paladin gestured with his gun. "I think you've got an appointment with the cops, doctor."

Brook didn't move. "And they will charge me with what? Stealing souls? That would look fascinating on the station blotter…"

Paladin smiled, though he wasn't feeling very happy. "How about operating a death chamber without a license?"

Leigh's own smile was deadly. "Or he could be a foreign agent. I'm pretty sure we could find a transmitter around here someplace…"

Paladin pushed the Browning's muzzle into Brook's face. "Move it, short round. I'm all out of patience!"

Brook raised his arms like a prisoner in a Western movie. Leigh and Paladin stepped aside to let the doctor pass; closing up behind him. As they emerged from the back of the packing case, the zombies froze again. Just their heads moved: tracking the three. The only sounds came from Brook's arcing, humming apparatus. Paladin didn't know which was the spookiest: the creatures' silence, or the way they simply watched, motionless.

Leigh voiced Paladin's thoughts. "Those things give me the creeps! What's so fascinating about us?"

Not us, princess, Paladin thought, remembering the night before. It's you: something about you draws them like moths.

Brook shrugged without lowering his hands. "I've never been able to ascertain their motives. But they can be unpredictable."

They were halfway across the floor, detouring around a piece of apparatus covered in growling neon lights. Five zombies stood idly by, glazed eyes locked on Leigh. They showed no more sign of animation than the others. When the attack came, it was with no warning.

VIII

The creatures went from immobility to frenzy in an instant. One tried to scramble across a steel table; two more lurched into a parody of a run; the last two wrenched at pieces of the apparatus, tearing it apart for weapons.

Brook shrieked, colliding with Paladin and knocking the Browning from his hand. Paladin snatched the doctor's left arm, twisting it. Brook shrieked again, trying to pull loose. Paladin hissed into his ear, "Keep still or I'll tear it off and use it on them!" The doctor subsided.

Around them it was like a switch had been thrown: all of the zombies had a new, deadly life. They marched erratically toward the living, batting each other aside, stumbling against the apparatus. One fell into a collection of gleaming rods and was consumed in a dazzling, acrid bolt of electricity.

Leigh glared at the doctor. "What's he doing?"

Paladin weighed up giving a full answer, settling on a half-truth. "It isn't Brook. It's our life force. Our souls. Whatever you want to call it."

He backed toward the distant warehouse doors, dragging Brook along. The doctor was whimpering faintly, in fear or pain. Paladin paused for a moment, reaching into the deep pockets of his flying coat. "Here." He threw a small sack toward Leigh.

She glanced at it curiously. "What's this?"

"Two pounds of salt. I brought it along, just in case."

"Salt?"

"Remember what happened to that thing in *The Palace*?"

Her face lit up with understanding. "Attaboy!"

As she untied her sack, Paladin grabbed another for himself. He tore it open with his teeth, wincing as the contents trickled into his mouth. Paladin loosened his grip on Brook for a moment, and the doctor tore away. Paladin considered going after him, but changed his mind. The madman could take his chances among his creations; it would save the city the cost of a trial.

He dipped his hand into the sack. One of the creatures lashed out an unsteady hand. Paladin ducked the blow and threw a handful of salt into the blank face. The zombie reared up, ripping at its face, before collapsing with an awful keening sound. After a moment it lay still and silent.

To his left, four of the things were already at Leigh's feet, truly dead, or dying. She marched resolutely forward, tossing handfuls of salt at anything that came within range. He lost sight of her as soulless creatures came at him from all sides; within seconds he was as much an automaton as they: throwing salt into the nearest face, dipping his hand in the sack, throwing again…

Until it was all over. He grabbed a handful from a near-empty sack, but there was nowhere to throw it. Corpses littered the concrete floor; he and Leigh were the only things moving. "Just getting into my stride."

Leigh up-ended her sack; only a few grains fell out. "Not me, coach. I'm out."

A disgusting smell hung on the air: burnt meat and hair, smoldering rubber. Machines and several of the corpses were on fire. Some of the flames were crawling a little too close to the crates. Paladin tossed his almost empty salt bag to the floor. "Time we weren't here, princess."

As he turned, Doctor Brook stepped from behind one smoking machine, holding Paladin's Browning in a shaky hand. His voice was high, quivering as much as the automatic's barrel. "I don't know who you are, sir! But you have ruined me! Set back the cause of science decades!"

"You did that yourself." Paladin sounded calmer than he felt: people with twitchy fingers should never play with guns. "Trying to control things you barely understand."

"What do you know about it—?"

"You'd be surprised."

Brook raised the shaking gun higher. "Well, they'll find your body here, mister busybody! Just one more burnt corpse amongst so many—!"

Purple flames erupted beside him. The doctor leapt to one side. Paladin winced; somehow the Browning didn't go off.

"Give it up, Brook! It's over—"

"For you, certainly! This is no grave for a white man, I'll grant you, but you leave me no choice…" He took the gun in both hands, trying to quell the shakes. Paladin could see his joints whiten. A shot resounded like a cannon against the warehouse walls.

Brook howled, dropping the Browning as he grabbed his left arm. The white sleeve rapidly turned dark red. With a sob he half fell, half ran, disappearing among the smoke and flames.

Leigh stepped out from behind the now blazing apparatus, a still-smoking gun dwarfing her hand. Paladin gazed at the black automatic in mild disbelief. "A Luger?"

"Why? Is it only men who get to play with big toys?" She holstered the 9 mm, all the while gazing around. "Think I need more practice, though. Missed the little rat bastard—"

A loud explosion cut her off. Wordlessly, Paladin jerked a thumb toward the line of windows above them. Leigh nodded.

They found the bodies of Lakwa and Marie lashed to gurneys of their own. Marie's cheerful face was pale and cold; Lakwa's more shriveled than ever. "Sorry, Marie."

Leigh touched his arm. "You knew them?"

"Yeah. I do."

"Then we've got to get them out—!"

He took her hand. "It's out of our hands, princess. Death, it's—it's kind of their territory."

"That doesn't make sense—"

"Come on, before we choke on the fumes."

They climbed up to the broken window on the chain hoist, crawling through to the sidewalk. Oily smoke followed. As the flames grew hotter, Paladin heard more windows shatter, dull pops as the apparatus exploded or collapsed. They headed back toward his Chrysler, hoping to be gone before the fire department arrived.

IX

Brook staggered through his burning dreams, right hand pressed against his left arm. It was so hard for him to think: the agony of the gunshot, the stupidity of those fools and their guns…

He collapsed against a crate, thoughts swimming as his legs grew numb. Nearby something shattered, covering him in shards of hot glass. The pain was insignificant.

Time passed: a moment; a lifetime. He grew aware of two silhouettes: shadows cast by flames growing in heat and intensity. The meddlers…? All of the Negroes were dead—

The silhouettes came closer, or did they become bigger…? One was stick thin, the other round and flowing. They bent toward him… or reared over him… or…

Their faces were ancient and dead and alive. They looked at him with contempt and compassion and hate…

The larger silhouette engulfed him. He realized the pain had gone. Everything had gone…

The voice was intimate; kindly. "C'mon, *cher*. It time to go…"

X

Leigh glanced back at the blaze as Damy opened the coupe's passenger door. The fire had spread from the basement; soon the whole place would be an inferno. Just for a moment, she imagined three figures walking away from the flames. One thin, another billowing, the third small, stooped. "Hey!" She pointed toward the shimmering figures just as they evaporated. "You know, I thought I just saw—!"

Paladin glanced the way she was pointing, wiping at his face. "Brook didn't care whose souls he took for his experiments. Thing is, some aren't up for grabs. And I told you death was their territory."

***

Back at their apartment, Damy called the bathroom before he'd even unlocked the door. Steam curled lazily under the door as Leigh heard him murdering something from a Broadway show, voice punctuated by splashing bathwater. She was distracted from the performance by a hesitant knock on the apartment door. Leigh opened up: out in the hallway stood a black man and woman. Her large frame was draped in the most exotic, billowing get-up Leigh had ever seen; the thin guy leaned against the wall, chewing moodily on a matchstick. Hot, scented air rolled into the apartment. The hallway had too many shadows, dipping in a ghostly breeze.

The woman smiled: the grin huge and friendly. Leigh relaxed. "Why, *cherie*, ain't you the picture." Her eyes took in Leigh, missing nothing. "And you is…?"

"Leigh Oswin—"

The woman's smile grew even wider. "Now, sugar, we both know that ain't the whole truth." She waved a hand at Leigh's unborn protest. "It don't matter. He in?"

Leigh nodded in the direction of the bathroom. "Back there, failing his Radio City audition."

"Always did have a unique voice." She held up what Leigh thought was a kid's toy: vaguely pistol-shaped, like something out of the Buck Rogers newspaper strip. It was twice the length of her Luger; when the woman placed it in Leigh's smoke-grimed hands, the weight surprised her. Leigh raised it to eye level. It had to be some gizmo from Brook's madhouse; it sure looked crazy enough. "When he's finished stranglin' the cats, give him this. He goin' need it."

Leigh was about to ask what for, but the sudden look on the other woman's face stopped her. It wasn't fear, not quite; but it came a close second. "You okay?"

The woman shook her wide head a moment, the big smile was back. "You's special, *cherie*, real special. More so than the baron in there knows." She took Leigh's hand in her own, engulfing it. "But you's goin' be just fine, sugar…"

Behind her, the old guy's sour face twisted. He looked like he wanted to spit.

Leigh was feeling lost. "Swell… I guess." She raised the pistol-gizmo and aimed it along the shadow-infested hallway. "So what's this do?"

"Do I look like somebody who'd know that?" The woman leaned in closer; her breath smelled of fresh rain and oranges. "Jus' don' be shootin' it till I'm long gone, hear…?" She laughed and backed away. Her miserable companion took the toothpick out of his mouth and stabbed it into the wooden doorframe. In the moment Leigh's eyes were distracted, both figures vanished. Seconds later, the toothpick joined them. The hallway lost its shadows.

Closing the door behind her, Leigh took the dingus into the apartment. She couldn't take her eyes off it, or forget what the large black lady had said. *Special*? How was *she* special…?

Damy must have heard: his voice echoed from the bathroom. "That the door?"

"Yeah." She was only half-listening, lost in her thoughts. "Uh, special delivery… I guess."

Real special.

PART FOUR:
DOIN' THE UPTOWN LOWDOWN

I

The only door in the unlit warehouse opened and shut. Andy Raven squeezed himself further into the darkness, half-drawing a Colt automatic. In his black suit he was all but invisible. A harsh voice croaked in the darkness.

"Hey, boss! You in there?"

Raven swore silently, letting his gun slide back into a pocket. South Side Eddie came cheap, and most of the time was on the square. Too bad his brain was always three steps behind him.

"Quiet!" He flicked on a single light: a low-wattage lamp standing on an upturned packing case. The cone of light only made the shadows beyond denser. "I'm over here!"

South Side Eddie's rail-thin figure materialized out of the darkness. His battered hat was too big for his narrow, horsey skull, and he looked swamped in a brown suit. He smiled; teeth big as grave-markers glittered in the poor light. "Relax, Mr. Raven. Everything's copacetic."

Raven bit back his irritation. "If it was, would I be here?" His ears strained against the silence: had there been a footfall, masked by his voice? "Did you hear that?"

South Side's oversized head swung back and forth, looking like a Budweiser dray horse shaking his reins. "I don't hear nuthin'."

Raven wasn't convinced. A whole precinct of New York's Finest could be marching in step behind South Side and he wouldn't notice. "Did you get it?"

"Sure, Mr. Raven. But it wasn't easy." His right hand slid into his coat pocket, Raven found himself tensing again. Maybe South Side was playing it straight, but it wouldn't take much cabbage to make him stray.

The hand came free of his pocket, holding a slip of paper. Raven relaxed a little and reached to take it. He froze as South Side grunted, a perplexed look washing over his equine features. Eddie's shoulders sagged and his head began to droop, like an ugly, wilting flower. He was staring intently at his body. "Mr. Raven—"

He never finished. About a foot of ugly blackened metal jutted from his chest. South Side's knees buckled. Before Eddie could fall, Raven lunged, grabbing for his right wrist. His fingers closed around the paper as Eddie collapsed. Most came free of the dying man's hand, but Raven felt it tear: pinched between the other's bony fingers.

South Side was an indistinct shape on the floor; Raven couldn't see how much blood there was. He pocketed the torn slip, digging into his coat for the Colt. Its weight wasn't as reassuring as it might have been.

"The interfering Raven." The voice from the shadows beyond the lamp was calm and urbane, faintly amused. Very English. "You do realize I must ask for that note."

"Then you're going to have to take it," Raven hoped he sounded a hell of a lot more confident than he felt. The gun wasn't going to be much use; and he needed to see whoever was talking before he tried anything else.

"I shall. If necessary. But I much prefer you hand it over. I have no wish to harm you."

"Unlike Eddie, huh?"

"We both know I can't kill you, Raven; not in this world. But I can certainly hurt you."

The speaker was good; Raven gave him that much. He felt it rolling across him in oily waves. There were maybe a dozen who might have recognized it, even fewer who could resist. Anyone else would have just slipped under the voice's spell. If only the speaker would step into the light. The single lamp cast too many convenient shadows.

"If you don't mind, Raven: the piece of paper." The voice sounded bored.

"Like I said: come ahead and take it."

The invisible talker sighed. "You're being unreasonable, Raven. Perhaps I ought not be surprised."

Raven caught a sound to his left and spun his automatic toward it. Too late. Something hard and colder than an Arctic winter slid through his chest. It didn't hurt at first. He didn't need to look down to know the same dark blade which had slain South Side Eddie was now jutting from his own body.

Numbness spread rapidly. He was on the floor, looking up at the lamp, but his vision was clouding, dimming. He felt the blade withdrawing: a blast of cold fire. As blackness closed in, he figured the paper was gone, along with his assailant.

But it was growing hard to care—

II

Damian Paladin bit his lip as cold water lapped over his boot-tops. He didn't want to think what might be floating in the sewers under Lexington Avenue: he'd already lost his flashlight after slipping on… something. His left hand keeping contact with the arched roof, moving slowly to reduce waves, he kept doggedly on. In his right he cradled his trusty Mauser automatic.

Leigh's voice echoed so loudly in his head it could have been bouncing off the encrusted walls. *"I can see the headlines: 'Damian Paladin, Ghost Hunter—Rids City of Deadly Menace!' You can't buy that kind of publicity!"* She'd said nothing about tiptoeing through pitch black sewers, he was pretty sure of that.

"She'll have me tap-dancing at Radio City next—"

His left toe caught on something; he staggered, almost falling. This time his pants received a generous splash of icy water. Paladin hissed in anger, not opening his mouth any wider than necessary. He dug into one of his belt pouches, pulling out a stubby candle. Lighting up and placing the candle in a wall-niche, Paladin glanced down into the murky water. Five bloated human fingers jutted out of the sluggish flow.

Paladin holstered his automatic and reached both hands under the water. They closed round a large and heavy bulk. He gave a heave. The oozing head and torso of a man emerged. Even in the thin candlelight, it was obvious the guy hadn't just crawled down here for the atmosphere before dying. There were three regularly spaced holes in his forehead, marking out an isosceles triangle. Puncture marks.

Something giggled. Paladin let the corpse drop back into the sewer run-off, drawing his Mauser again. He thought the sound came from not too far ahead. "Step out where I can see you."

He got the impression that a chunk of darkness broke off and drifted closer. He heard splashing. Two brilliant red sparks ignited in the shadows. Paladin cocked the Mauser's hammer. He was betting whatever lurked just beyond the candle's light couldn't shrug of a fusillade of 9 mm slugs.

"What's the matter? Afraid of the light?"

The sparks grew larger, nearer. A short, hideous creature stepped into the dancing candlelight: a balding ape crossed with some kind of warped goat. Its forearms were long and gnarled. Three twisted horns sprouted from its skull. From its stooped back two spiny fans radiated out, like ribbed wings that had long ago lost their feathers. But for all that, it still had a rubbery, boneless look about it. Like it wasn't as solid as it should be. There was an unhealthy sheen to its skin. In all, it was the ugliest son of a bitch Paladin had seen in a long time. "No wonder you stick to the sewers."

"We all wear masks..." The creature spoke slowly, taking great care over each syllable. As it pealed back thin lips, Paladin could see three sharp, forward thrusting tusks: two in the upper jaw, the third nestling between in the lower. Unlike its horns, there was nothing ungainly or second thought about them.

"Philosophy, yet. I bet you're a wow at staff parties."

"Your humor is tedious, Paladin."

"Laugh this off, pal."

The thing moved the moment he fired. Somehow it dodged the stream of bullets. They ricocheted off arched walls, exploding into a deafening stream of echoes. And the magazine clip was empty.

Jaws opening impossibly wide, the tusks came at Paladin like a living trident. Throwing himself out of its path, no longer giving a damn about the filthy water, Paladin pushed his free hand inside another pouch. As the thing passed by, he lashed out a boot. With a degree of satisfaction, he felt something give under his heel. The thing yowled, leaping clumsily back into the darkness.

Paladin came to his feet, back against the arched brick. He pulled a spare clip of twenty shells from his belt. As his eyes flickered around the sewer, waiting for the thing to strike again, his fingers worked independently: ejecting the empty clip, loading the fresh one, cocking the pistol. Paladin didn't have another reload; he couldn't miss a second time.

The candle winked out, dropping the sewer into total blackness. Paladin readied himself.

Twin red pinpricks lit up. Without thought, he aimed and fired at the gap between them. The slugs were nothing more than plain lead, even so, something exploded with an intense light. For over a minute, he was blind and deaf; his eyes filled with throbbing purple stars, his ears belling.

***

Dawn was paling the sky over the East River as Paladin hauled himself up through a manhole cover on Lexington and 48th. It wasn't quite a ticker-tape parade. Just the Chief of Police and a tweedy nobody from the Mayor's Office standing alongside a visibly relieved Leigh. As he stood, before he could warn her, Leigh lunged forward and gave him a spine-cracking hug.

"Damy! You've been gone—" She snatched her head back, blonde bob snapping in indignation. "What is that *smell…*?"

"I'll leave that to your imagination, princess!" He turned to the nobody and Police Chief. "All clear, gentlemen. New Yorkers may take a bath in comfort once more."

The nobody was clearly debating the wisdom of shaking Paladin's hand. Instead, he fiddled with a pair of wire-framed eyeglasses. "What was it?"

Paladin winked at Leigh. "Rats. Big ones."

The Chief repeated the word in disbelief. "Rats." It was written all over his ugly face what he thought of that idea. "I never seen rat bites like that before…"

"Probably came over from Hoboken." Paladin was already walking away. He went to put an arm round Leigh, but her expression made him think twice. "Somewhere out of state, anyhow."

III

Back at their apartment, Paladin quickly showered and changed. He sat down to breakfast as Leigh strolled in, dolled up in her ritziest suit, fixing a new hat over her blonde curls.

Paladin gave her the once-over. "I don't remember getting an invite." He lifted a forkful of scrambled eggs to his mouth.

"You wouldn't." Leigh fished inside her purse and dug out a cigarette case. Removing a long cigarette she lit up, holding it an elegant hand, angling it just *so*. "Got a call from the Mayor's Office. LaGuardia wants to see me." Breathing out a huge cloud of smoke she beamed at him,

"So what do they want to see you for?" He took a sip of coffee, wincing: his arm was stiff from cold sewer water.

Leigh grinned mischievously. "Maybe you're not the mayor's type."

"And maybe the city's welching on the deal."

Leigh pulled a childish face. For a moment she looked all of her twenty-one years. "The Mayor can't pretend the past six months never happened!"

"Can't he? None of the victims survived. That leaves half a dozen who know what happened. Is the Chief of Police going to shoot off his mouth? You think Mayor LaGuardia will admit some guy who chases spooks in his spare time did what every Precinct in the city couldn't?"

Some of Leigh's elation had vanished from her face, making Paladin feel bad. He stood and walked around the breakfast table to give her a hug. This time she didn't back away. "Maybe I'm wrong. Maybe the city has a heart, huh?"

She looked at him, eyes suspicious. "You think so?"

He dropped his arm. "Nah. But make sure our silence is expensive."

She slugged him playfully with her purse. "You're playing my kind of tune, Mr. Paladin! I must be rubbing off on you."

"Like cheap paint. Amscray! Go get your pat on the fanny and a barrel-load of excuses."

"Smooth talker." Leigh kissed him lightly on the cheek. "Catch you later."

She swayed out of the apartment; Paladin returned to breakfast. There was a timid knock on the door: it was Jimmy, youngest of the Teton Building's roster of concierges. He cast his eyes theatrically around the apartment.

"She gone?" On the day they moved in, Jimmy took one look at Leigh and fallen for her hard. He hadn't come within twenty yards of her since. Paladin couldn't figure if it was because Jimmy was embarrassed, didn't trust himself, or what he imagined a jealous Paladin might do. As if he ever got jealous.

"If by that you mean Miss Oswin, Jimmy, she's the one whose swelled head is jammed in that doorway. What's the shtick?"

"Sorry, boss. But I had to make sure you was alone. The guy said to."

"What guy?" He scooped up the last of the eggs. "Want some coffee?" He poured two cups.

Jimmy held out a visitor's card. "There was this guy. Said to give it to you. But to make sure you was alone."

Paladin took the card. It was unmarked, one side pure white, the other totally black. In an instant, he felt like his gut had stepped out into an empty elevator shaft. One that dropped a few thousand years. His eggs were on their way back up, too. "This guy. What'd he look like?"

Jimmy shrugged. "I dunno. Regular guy. Normal height… thin, kinda ugly… suit, hat… smelled of cheap cologne…" He picked up a cup and sipped noisily.

"What color suit?"

"Gray, I think. Or maybe brown. It important?"

Paladin allowed himself to breathe again. "When did you see him? This morning?"

Jimmy shook his head; he looked unhappy. "Nah. Three days ago—"

Paladin just stopped himself from leaping up, grabbing Jimmy by the throat and slapping him around. "Three days! What kept you—?"

"He said to!" Jimmy was getting jitterier by the moment; he almost dropped the coffee cup. Paladin expected him to burst into tears any second. "He said if I didn't see him again in three days I should give you the card! Otherwise, forget I ever saw him!"

"Okay…" Paladin noticed he was crushing the pasteboard in his fist. He forced himself to relax and pocketed the card. "He say anything else?"

"Only that you'd know where. At nine tonight."

"Nine o'clock." Paladin repeated the time in a whisper. He realized Jimmy was staring wide-eyed at him: half fearful, half expectant. "Thanks, Jimmy. I'll take it from here." He passed the young concierge a battered five dollar bill.

The five-spot cheered the kid up immediately. Jimmy smiled, flipped a shaky salute and dashed out of the apartment.

"Nine o'clock." Paladin sipped at coffee that tasted of cold blood.

IV

Leigh was ushered into the Mayor's office by a secretary who looked like she'd been weaned on a pickle and eaten nothing but starch since. Mayor LaGuardia was already inside, talking to a handsome guy with slicked-down hair and a Ronald Coleman mustache. Even seated it was obvious he'd tower over the stocky Mayor. Both rose to their feet as she entered: the Mayor smiling efficiently, the other guy suddenly displaying a perfect set of teeth. He has to be a movie star, she thought, though she didn't remember ever seeing his face on a poster. And he had a mug you couldn't easily forget.

LaGuardia indicated a seat. "Miss Oswin. I hope you don't mind if Mr. Lancaster stays?"

"Oh?" Leigh sat and favored Lancaster with a smile of her own. "And why is that?" She opened her purse to take out a cigarette; Lancaster offered one of his own from a plain silver case. The cigarettes inside were long, probably European. Leigh took one, he lit it for her.

LaGuardia introduced them. "Miss Leigh Oswin from *The Palace* restaurant; Mr. Edmund Lancaster from England."

The Englishman smiled again. "Charmed, Miss Oswin. Fiorello has told me some of what your associate, Mr. Damian Paladin, did this morning. Intriguing."

Hell, he even talks like Ronald Coleman, Leigh thought. "He

also tell you what he promised if Damy did with the Pied Piper act?"

LaGuardia had the grace to look uncomfortable. Leigh wondered how much practice it took. "We've been discussing that, Miss Oswin. Edmund has suggested that it might not be in the city's interests to say too much about the events of the past days."

"He did, huh?" Leigh took another, colder, look at the Englishman. Movie star looks apart, she wondered if he wasn't a bigger rat than the ones in the sewers.

Lancaster's smile was as smooth as his voice. "I understand your position, Miss Oswin. You wish to advertise your partner's—" He waved a hand in the air for a moment. "—Shall we say, exotic hobby. No doubt you see it as a strong lure for future patrons."

Leigh drew on her cigarette: it was cool and fragrant; she could get used to it. "Uh-huh."

The Mayor stepped back into the conversation. "It's not that we won't pay you—" Leigh began to wonder if they'd scripted the whole scene. She stubbed out her cigarette.

"Double."

"Pardon me?" A little of LaGuardia's amiable, guy-next-door mask slipped.

"You don't want to talk about it, swell. But I figure the publicity neither the city nor *The Palace* is going to get is worth double what you were going to pay." Strangely, she didn't feel all that mad. Damy had been right: they were trying to chisel her. So why wasn't she screaming in their faces and demanding blood?

Was this what maturity and acting responsibly felt like? It wasn't half so much fun.

"Pay it." Lancaster's brilliant white smile was an orthodontist's dream. "The city can afford it."

LaGuardia looked at the Englishman sourly. "Double? You want to make up the difference? Maybe you haven't heard in England, but there's a Depression!"

"Use the Federal subsidies. I thought you vowed to 'clean house, and clean it thoroughly'." Leigh was sure Lancaster was laughing at the Mayor, in that strange way Limeys have. She didn't understand why LaGuardia wasn't kicking him out on his urbane keister. It wouldn't be unheard of. "It sounds as though this was one hell of a house-cleaning."

"Okay, already!" LaGuardia threw up his hands and stalked toward the office door. He started to twist he handle before looking back at Leigh. "You get your money, lady. But understand this: it buys a lot of silence. I see one word in the papers, or hear anything on the radio, you and that crazy partner of yours will be kicked out of New York so hard they'll hear it in Amarillo!" He slammed the door behind him.

Leigh chuckled. "Kind of thorny for a Little Flower."

Lancaster removed a cigarette from his case and lit it. He held it between the tips of thumb and forefinger. "Oh, Fiorello's a decent enough chap. But he tries too hard to be the bluff, honest politician."

"Sure. And what's your angle?"

"I'm here in an entirely unofficial capacity, Miss Oswin." He drew on his cigarette. "As you may know, the situation in Europe is growing… how can I put it? Tense? Herr Hitler is set on a course of aggression, but our governments have shown little will to tackle him. As the representative of certain interested parties, I have come to the United States to see if I can't enlist America's support, as it were."

She snorted. "Good luck. With all the Neutrality Acts the government is forcing through, you'll be lucky to get Joe Public to care if Plague breaks out. Americans aren't interested in getting a bloody nose in another foreign war."

"I am fully aware of popular feeling, Miss Oswin." Lancaster's eyes were glowing with what she guessed was missionary fervor. "But for evil to win, it simply requires that good men—"

"Do nothing. Yeah, I read that in a fortune cookie. And you think that gives you the right to interfere in a private deal?"

He looked hurt. "Miss Oswin, I apologize if you think I have been in any way too forward. I am by nature and profession a diplomat; allowing the news to break would have been to no one's advantage. For your colleague, perhaps, and briefly. But if the people were to lose confidence in their new Mayor, who can say how things might change at the next election."

Leigh fought the urge to laugh. "I'll say this for you, Mr. Lancaster: you sure talk like a politician."

"Call me Edmund, please."

"Then you'd better call me Leigh."

"With pleasure." He smiled again. "Leigh, it occurs to me that I might owe you more than an apology. Would you allow me to take you to dinner tonight? To make full amends…"

Like you hadn't planned that from the start, Leigh thought. Why not? Where was the harm? Besides, it would give her chance to look over another joint: steal a few ideas. Something she'd been aiming to do for months.

"Okay, Edmund," she said. "You've got a date. Pick me up at nine-thirty."

V

The rain started around seven, and was showing no signs of letting up. By the time Paladin had reached his rendezvous point, the city was slick. Streetlamps highlighted it, turning the rain into a glistening coat.

For almost half an hour he sat behind the wheel of his precious Chrysler coupe. He'd left *The Palace* early, unable to take anymore of Leigh's endless costume changes. Maybe he *was* jealous, just a little. Eventually, he stepped out into the weather's fury. In moments rain ran off the brim of his hat like a small Niagara. It wouldn't be too long before it soaked through his overcoat. Beyond the open wharves, the East River was just a black absence. The lights of Brooklyn and the bridge were lost in the rain.

The pier was deserted, but the rain hadn't washed the reek of old fish from the air.

He made his way toward the rendezvous, hanging onto his hat, rain blowing in his face. It was a relief to kick the heavy warehouse door shut behind him, although inside smelled worse than the fishy exterior. It gave him unwelcome memories of the city sewers.

The unlit warehouse was as black as it was fetid. Paladin stepped cautiously, listening to the echo of his footsteps. He unbuttoned his overcoat and flicked rainwater from his hat. He bit back the urge to call out: the sounds of the door and his footsteps would be announcement enough.

A faint light snapped on to his left: a single, low power bulb. It looked like a table-lamp. Paladin reached into his overcoat and pulled free his Browning automatic. He moved toward the light.

A tired, pinched voice came out of the shadows, close by the lamp. "Enough with the melodramatics, Junior…"

"You're one to talk, Raven. What kind of a jam you in this time?"

"Get over here and sit down."

Paladin reached the table-lamp. It was standing on a single packing case, throwing enough light for him to see the man half-lying against another crate. His hat, shirt and suit were all black, his necktie white. Under the hat-brim the face was long and delicate, almost feminine, much too pale. It was a face Paladin had hoped never to see again.

He slipped the automatic back into a pocket. "So the rumors are true. How come I only get to hear from everyone else? Not so much as a postcard…"

Raven's fine features twisted. "I didn't know you cared."

"I don't." Paladin looked around for a crate to sit on, there was nothing. He'd have to remain standing. "So, what d'you say, Raven? Want to tell me why I had to come out on such a lousy night?"

Raven started to shift position, but flopped back with a hiss. For a moment, his white face twisted in pain. Paladin dropped to one knee and gently pulled back Raven's coat. Both shirt and tie were soaked in a clear ichor.

Paladin released the coat. "What the hell happened?" He realized his hands were shaking.

"I cut myself shaving. What do you think?"

"You stuck your neck out once too often is what I think. How long ago did this happen?"

Raven groaned. "Two days, near as I can tell. It's this lousy New York weather. Gets into the bones…"

"Bullshit." Two days! In that time, Raven could have grown himself two more arms, never mind heal a stab wound. "Who did it?"

"If you'll shut your mouth for a minute—" Raven took a deep

breath, trying not to show how much it hurt and failing. "You know the *Thule Bund*?"

"Sure. Just after the war the German *Thule Gesellschaft* group turned into an extremist, anti-Semitic bunch of power-crazy occultists. A self-styled Baron Rudolf von Sebottendorf was the charmer behind it all."

Raven nodded slowly, like his head might fall off. "Several months ago, they held one of their dumb Aryan rituals … they wanted to raise Thor… Loki. They got something else… something worse…"

"How much worse?"

"Hitler's always wanted the Grail—" Raven took a shallow, quavering breath. "I think what they actually called up is a… a seeker of some kind…"

Paladin waited to let that news sink in, torn between adding a couple of slugs to Raven's wound, or thanking him for the warning. "And you didn't think to tell me earlier? Maybe like three days ago?"

"I had somebody checking it out for me… Someone who knew the city…" Raven's voice was growing hoarser with every breath. If Paladin didn't know better, he'd swear the guy was growing worse. "If the thing hadn't been in New York, I could've moved on…"

"I'm guessing your shamus is dead?" The sewer smell blew up strong for a moment. Paladin wrinkled his nose.

"He drew more attention… than a fifty-foot neon sign—" Raven drew in a fitful breath. "Really loused this one up—"

Paladin stood. "Get a look at who stuck you?"

"Too dark…"

"Next time get a stronger light bulb—" The stench hit him like a freight train. His hand dove for the Browning. He pivoted and fired point-blank into a three-fanged muzzle. The thing's head flew apart like mud; the rest hit the ground with a dull slap. Another leapt out of the dark. He fired again, taking its bent legs out from underneath. One by one they came on: jumping into the light. Paladin's automatic blazed fast as a machine gun.

Fast as it began, the onslaught ceased, the warehouse echoing with the sound of gunfire. Acrid smoke just about masked the cloying stench of the creatures. The floor around the packing cases was thick with oozing corpses.

Paladin unclipped the magazine from his Browning. There was one slug left. "A couple more and we might have been in trouble."

Raven croaked a feeble laugh. "Hooray for us."

Paladin stood over one of the bodies, prodding the muddy remains with the tip of his shoe. "Exactly the same as the thing in the sewers."

"They are… all the same—" Raven heaved each word out, staring at a liquefying corpse. "They're ectypes… replicas of each other… or of something else—"

"Like your demon?"

"Demons…? You gone… native, junior…? You'll be talking about… angels next—" He rasped a short laugh that ended in a cry of pain. Paladin looked at him again: the man in black's graceful features were getting too corpse-like.

"You going to be okay?"

Raven attempted a smile; it looked more like a skeleton's grin. "I'm not going to die… if that's what's bothering you… At least… not for a… considerable time… But the waiting will… be a bitch—"

"Say we pretend I care for a minute: anything I can do?"

Raven stared at him for the longest time. "Find this… *demon…* get whatever he stuck me with—"

"Sure. And in the afternoon I'll cure world hunger…"

"You'll find it, Junior… it wants to be found… It's playing a game… Leaving clues… Leading us on. I've had two days to think about it… it's pretty obvious—" He nodded weakly at the nearest body—it was little more than a foul-smelling puddle. "You think they stopped by… because they like the décor—?"

Paladin dropped his near empty Browning back into a pocket. "So?"

"So—" Raven felt inside his coat like it was the hardest thing he's ever done. He held out a shred of paper, hand shaking. "This was conveniently left behind—"

After he'd let Raven sweat for a couple of seconds, Paladin bent to take it. Their fingers touched—

—Across an endless plane radiant creatures both more and less than human lived and died...

—They soared through a sky that was much too blue; flying on

blazing coronas of energy resembling skeletal wings...

—They enjoyed the company of beautiful human women whose beauty was coarsened in comparison with that of their ravishers...

—The women bore sons—

Paladin wrenched free. He staggered back, weak and sweating, and the visions faded. "You lousy, stinking son of a bitch!" He took a deep, ragged breath, any sympathy he'd started to feel for Raven gone. Those visions had shown him more than he'd ever wanted to know.

Raven sighed. His voice was stronger; his delicate features had lost some of their pallor. "I'm sorry, but I can't leave these bodies lying around. I didn't have the strength before."

"You could have asked!" Paladin wiped a shaky hand across a cold and slick forehead.

Raven wasn't listening. He'd closed his eyes and begun to mumble to himself. There was a soundless concussion that Paladin felt deep in his guts, and the putrid remains of the creatures weren't there anymore. Raven sank back like a punctured balloon, his face ghastly once more. "You going to stand... around all night—?"

"I don't owe you any favors, Raven—"

"I'll owe you... Think about it—"

Paladin stared down at the pale, ichor-soaked figure, absent-mindedly putting the scrap of paper in his overcoat pocket. "Let's not make a habit of it."

"Deal..." Raven's voice trailed off into harsh, rattling breaths. "Thanks, Junior—" The words were barely audible.

Paladin left the warehouse, plunging himself into the rain. He couldn't shake those strange visions; he was pretty sure he never would. Maybe that was what Raven wanted all along. Either way, they'd stirred up old questions; including one he thought he'd buried long ago. One he didn't think he'd ever have the guts to ask.

VI

Lancaster turned up dead on nine-thirty in a chauffeured Rolls Royce. He was togged to the bricks in white tie, black tails and a thick ebony cane. The only thing missing was a top hat. Leigh was kind of glad: she didn't think she could have kept back the giggles all night.

He greeted her with a smile, taking her hand and bowing quickly and stiffly; a gesture she found a little odd. She'd expected a brief kiss on the hand, not clicking heels. Worse, Jimmy insisted on hanging around, watching everything, his goofy smile plastered all over his kisser. He even had the nerve to crack wise with the chauffeur; but she didn't catch whatever smart-aleck remark he made.

The chauffeur held an umbrella over them as Lancaster guided her into the limo. A moment later, they were pulling away from the sidewalk; Jimmy, standing in the alley, waving a cloth in exaggerated farewell.

Except they didn't keep to Manhattan, and all the glitzy joints Leigh was expecting to visit. The Rolls swung north on Third Avenue. Funny way of showing a girl a good time, she thought. "I didn't think we'd be eating uptown."

Lancaster turned his smile on her again, but it had lost some of its glow. In fact, Leigh was starting to find it, and its owner, kind of creepy. "A little excursion before dinner, I thought."

Leigh's suspicious nature asserted itself. "How little?" She couldn't believe the urbane Edmund Lancaster was going to turn out to be a regular, foursquare masher after all.

"A trip to the zoo, perhaps?"

Leigh tried to laugh, but all she could manage was a slack-jawed gasp. "At this time of night? Mister, you're nuts!"

"There will be no problem entering, if that concerns you. I have influence."

Leigh thought back to how he'd played Mayor LaGuardia. "You ain't kidding,"

"Have you never done anything spontaneous, Miss Oswin… Leigh?"

"Plenty. But it didn't usually involve closed zoos, at night, in the pouring rain."

Lancaster laughed. It was such a natural, pleasant sound that Leigh almost relaxed. Carefully, she patted her purse, relieved to feel the weight of a snub-nosed Colt .38; glad she'd never gotten out of the habit of packing heat.

"You won't be needing that."

Leigh snapped her head in Lancaster's direction. Despite his calm, reasonable tone, she felt like he'd slapped her. He was half-looking her way, his eyes dreamy. Although he wasn't smiling at the moment, she could see it wasn't too far away: like his skin was partly transparent.

"I really think I should take it, don't you? Just hand me the gun, Leigh…"

For a moment, Leigh was about to snap something short and pithy, then it seemed so unnecessary. Why not hand him the gun? She didn't need it. Lancaster was with her, and even though he didn't look like he could handle too much rough work, the chauffeur was a big guy.

She opened her purse and lifted out the .38. For a moment her finger tensed on the trigger before handing it over, basking in Lancaster's smile as he took the gun.

"Thank you, Leigh." He slid the bean shooter inside his coat. "Why don't you have a cigarette?"

Absently, she reached back inside her purse and took out two Luckies. Putting both between her lips, she lit them, passing one to Lancaster. He accepted with a nod.

"Ah." He exhaled a thick pall of cigarette smoke. "We've arrived."

Leigh glanced through the rain-streaked window, wondering how in hell Lancaster could tell where they were. Outside was a tar pit as far as she was concerned.

The Rolls lurched gently as they drove over some unseen bump. Leigh felt herself leaned to one side as the limo took a sharp right, and a few moments later turned left. They drew to a halt, and Lancaster opened his door. The chauffeur was already waiting, umbrella in hand, as the Englishman stepped out. Lancaster turned and, bending slightly, helped Leigh from the car.

As far as she could tell they'd pulled up close to the Bronx Zoo's main offices on Astor Court, right by the sea lions. But she could hear nothing from their tank. Did sea lions sleep? Or was it another part of the night's general craziness.

Lancaster gently took her elbow and walked her toward the administration offices, pointing the way with his black cane. The chauffeur kept in perfect step, umbrella held steady; never allowing a single drip to fall on either of them. Lancaster swept the office door open with a flourish. He even flicked the lights on. Didn't he care if anybody saw them? Leigh wondered. The zoo must have security: nosy keepers, cops swinging by on Southern Boulevard! Anybody!

Lancaster released her arm and turned to the chauffeur. "Thank you. You may leave now."

The baby grand bowed silently to them and backed out of the building. He left the wet umbrella behind.

"Talkative little stiff." Leigh looked around the deserted offices. "You must be paying him a bundle."

"No more than he would expect for a night's work." Lancaster waved toward a chair ranged up against a far wall. "Please sit."

Leigh did so, crossing her legs slowly as she thought. There was something about Lancaster's remark. Did he mean anything by it? Although she couldn't figure out why, she was feeling jittery. "So what do you want from me?"

"From you, Leigh: nothing. You've done your part—and done it beautifully, may I say. The stage is set for tonight's drama. Two of the principal players are ready, we merely await the last actor."

Leigh just shook her head. Frankly, she couldn't figure out

what Lancaster was gabbing about. “Mister, you sure can talk.”

His smile grew wider; he looked like a sleek, mustached shark. “Oh, I can do much more than talk, Leigh. Believe me. For example: I have all but forcibly abducted you, taken your gun, and now hold you captive. Would you care to explain to me why you’re not doing your best to escape?”

Leigh simply stared back at him, confused. What was all this bullshit about abduction? “Sorry… I’m listening in English… what language are you balling me up in?”

He laughed, and Leigh knew everything was okay again. “You see! Even when I explain your predicament it fails to move you. I could tell you exactly what I am, even show you, yet it would mean nothing.”

Leigh shuffled in the chair. “Edmund, you’re making me nervous. Are you tight…?”

He laughed again. “Drunk? How delightful!” He turned away from her, leaning both hands on the cane, peering out of the window.

Abruptly, he turned back to face her. The Ronald Coleman looks were gone. Now his face looked sick: green and glassy. The three tusks growing forward from his jaws distorted his mouth: two in the top, one centered in the bottom. The pencil-thin mustache was a red slit drooling thin, yellow pus. “There! Are you revolted? Do you want to run? Are you finally afraid of me?”

Leigh stared back impassively. Somewhere, a part of her brain was screaming at her to get up; to run like hell. But it seemed so unimportant. So remote. Whatever game Edmund was playing, she was perfectly safe. She knew it.

Something in the night caught his attention. “Ah.” He raised his heavy cane and twirled it. “That will be Paladin.”

VII

Paladin paced his apartment floor. At some point, he'd changed into his flying coat, riding pants and boots; he couldn't remember when. Showed just how antsy he'd gotten since leaving Raven.

The scrap of paper hadn't given much away. All there was, written in pencil in a childish hand was a single word: *Astor*. Just what in hell did it mean? Even Raven was in the dark! That irritating son of a bitch was another Saint-Germain, with poorer dress sense.

And that reminded him of the day's big shaker: Raven was hurt. Hurt bad. And not getting better. Beings like Raven rarely got injured, and if they did, they healed fast. They called themselves Eternals; it wasn't an empty title.

A knock on the door startled him out of his funk. He swung the door open, hoping it might be Leigh, but out in the hallway was Jimmy. Whatever the boy was about to say dried up when he saw Paladin's expression

"What do you want, Jimmy?" Paladin wasn't in the mood for Jimmy's special brand of humor.

"Just brought up the mail, boss." Jimmy sounded like a guy with an itchy nose tiptoeing through a crocodile swamp. He handed over a wad of envelopes. "Miss Oswin back from the zoo yet?"

"Zoo? What d'you mean: zoo?"

"Her date. The driver guy, he told me. Said something about the crazy Limey wanting to drive to the zoo. We had a good chuckle about that—"

Paladin almost grabbed Jimmy by the lapels. "Which zoo?"

Jimmy shrank back, his eyes large and nervous. "Why, the Bronx—"

"Astor! That's it: Astor Court! The Bronx Zoo!" Paladin raced out of the apartment, leaving the door wide open. "Jimmy, I love you!"

Jimmy was left shaken and confused. He closed the door, checking the hallway sheepishly. "Jeez," he muttered. "I hope no one heard that…"

Paladin raced down the stairs to the parking garage, too impatient to wait for the elevator. His Chrysler was in its designated lot. He leapt inside, gunned the engine, and peeled rubber up to street level. Once he was heading north he floored the gas, the coupe's engine relishing a chance to cut loose.

Paladin silently raged at himself. Raven had been right: he was being led. But who by? And why? This Lancaster bromide was an obvious candidate, but what was his angle? He bit back on the fury, and the endless questions stoking it. He'd need a cool head when he arrived.

He somehow made it to the Bronx Zoo without attracting the attention of any passing traffic cop. Swerving through the Southern Boulevard Gate without slowing, Paladin didn't ease off on the gas until he slammed his coupe into a skidding halt in the center of Astor Court. He was out of the car, Mauser already in his hand, before the wet gravel had settled. Before him, offices were lit up like a beacon. He couldn't have been given a bigger clue.

He stalked toward the building, drawing up sharply when he saw a figure coming confidently toward him. White tie and tails, cane, movie star looks.

"You must be Lancaster."

"Until recently. The body you see did belong to one Edmund Lancaster, a minor functionary in the British Foreign Office. But last month—" He smiled broadly. "Why, he became a whole new man." He took a step closer. Paladin raised his Mauser an inch. The figure halted.

"Where's Leigh?" Paladin didn't know what kind of dumb

game the thing in front of him was playing, and could care less. He had his own priorities.

Lancaster spread his arms wide, dangling the walking stick from his right hand. "Inside. She's perfectly safe. Not all Eternals share this perverse desire to copulate with mortals."

"Who are you? I mean really?"

Lancaster twirled his ebony stick, twitching his head to one side in a curiously birdlike gesture. "We are legion, Paladin, and names are power. You know that. Why else have you spent the centuries constantly changing your own? And that preening Raven: as many pseudonyms as worlds."

Paladin tried to figure how easy it would be to sprint past Lancaster. He slid a foot slowly across the gravel, trying to make it look like he wasn't moving at all. "Just another Nazi stooge, huh?"

Lancaster's mouth twitched with contempt. "Publicly, the *Ahnenerbe* Institute scours the world for the most potent occult relics. A front of course. There have already been significant finds; all of them mine." Abruptly, he raised his cane and threw aside the ebony cover. Inside was something that glowed like a neon tube, throbbing with its own crude life. Paladin watched as it twisted and writhed; broadening, flattening out, losing its harsh radiance. Moments later, it was a crude type of sword, with a short, age-blackened blade.

"The *Thule Gesellschaft* still calling the tune? Herr Hitler know how much his chain's being yanked?"

"The Führer is an ardent disciple of von Sebottendorf and Drexler." Lancaster flourished the blade. "And I would appreciate it if you didn't insult us both with such a childish attempt to pass me."

Paladin closed his feet together. He'd moved less than a yard. "Got it!" He used the barrel of his gun as a pointer. "Myphas the Searcher. Am I right?"

Lancaster's movie-star smile vanished. "One name, Paladin, and much good will it do you." He came *en garde.*

The investigator aimed his pistol at a point just above Lancaster's eyes. Water ran off the barrel in heavy drops. "Can you fence past a slug?" He fired once. Lancaster slammed back and crashed to the ground, pale ichor tracing an arc as he fell.

Paladin began walking toward the lit offices. A sword blade

flashed. He recoiled, right hand dripping blood from a deep cut. He'd heal soon enough, a family trait he shared with Raven, but that slash hurt. Far too much. And he'd dropped his gun.

Lancaster was coming slowly to his feet. The oozing hole in his forehead wasn't the only thing spoiling his matinee idol looks. His face was twisted: bestial and triple-fanged. A thin stream of pus from the slit above his mouth mingled with the rain. The horns on his skull grew straight and proud like a crown; the ribs jutting from his back crackled with a fierce blue radiance. His voice was thick, distorted by the fangs. "I'm disappointed, Paladin. You have obviously been living among *untermenschen* and criminal classes for too long."

The investigator had a brief rush of déjà vu. "You don't have any relatives running round the sewers, do you?"

"Tiny sendings; barely noticeable expenditures of energy. Bait."

Paladin considered drawing his Browning as Lancaster weaved his sword with hypnotic grace. He should have recognized it at first glance. "The Spear of Destiny. Last I heard, the Hapsburgs had that carefully hidden away."

"Let's say they made a perhaps not so willing contribution to the Reich." Lancaster slashed at the air twice. "Delightfully symbolic, don't you think?"

"The thing might work on Eternals, but far as I'm concerned, it's just an old spear-head." Paladin circled, mind racing. Despite his bravado, the cut in his hand sure burned more than it should.

"Even so, let me assure you it's keen enough." Lancaster lunged suddenly. Paladin leapt back to avoid the point.

"Oh, I'm perfectly assured." Paladin dodged the blade, slipping on the wet gravel. He hit the ground painfully, at the same moment spotting the discarded black cane scabbard. Lancaster reared above him, poised to thrust down.

The investigator rolled, snatching up the cane. Lancaster impaled a few stones on the ground. On his feet, Paladin felt less like the sacrificial lamb. When Lancaster thrust, he parried with the cane. Clumsy—it had been a long time since he'd wielded a sword, and his hand throbbed like hell—but effective.

Lancaster withdrew. "Not exactly Heidelberg."

"You got enough dueling scars." Paladin charged, using the

cane like a club; it was no time for finesse. He slugged Lancaster hard across the face. The creature faltered for an instant, just long enough for Paladin to make a run for the office building. He burst through the door, yelling Leigh's name. She was slowly getting to her feet.

"Princess! You okay?"

She looked confused. "Damy? What's going on? Where's Edmund—?"

Both spun around as a window exploded. Rain and glass followed Lancaster as he leapt through.

"Vermin! Drinking your soul will cleanse the world of another scrap of impurity!" He lashed out. Paladin blocked a succession of rapid cuts; each time splinters of ebony skimmed off the scabbard, inches from his face.

He risked a glance in Leigh's direction. Her expression was unreadable; baffled.

Lancaster's advance was relentless. He, or whatever inhabited the body, was a superb fencer. Out of practice and flailing with a less than perfect weapon, Paladin was at a disadvantage. He gave ground constantly, watched by Leigh. Her expression suggested there was another kind of duel going on in her mind.

Paladin stumbled over a high-backed chair. He scooped it up and hurled it at Lancaster, who tried to ward it with his arm. He staggered, dropping the sword. Paladin dived for the weapon; Lancaster beat him to it.

Paladin stared at the blade hovering about an inch from his eyes, inhumanly steady. Carefully, both men straightened, Paladin unable to take his gaze off the ancient spearhead.

Lancaster smiled, fangs bared. "It's no use, I don't think I could get used to fighting with furniture."

Paladin's mind was racing; even the hypnotically weaving sword point couldn't distract him. "If you won't answer to Myphas, how about the clouder of minds, Elaurin?"

Lancaster flinched. The sword drew back, just a little. "Reaching, Paladin!"

"Edmund?" It was Leigh: she sounded confused; just a little frightened. She's coming round, thought Paladin. Whatever whammy he put on her is wearing off.

Lancaster's warped head twitched toward her, just briefly. It was enough. Paladin twisted away from the spear point, dropping to the floor and lashing out with both feet. He connected with Lancaster's knees, knocking the other's legs out from under him. Lancaster came down like a felled tree, landing heavily on Paladin. The three tusks snapped together inches from the investigator's face.

Paladin grabbed at Lancaster's throat with his undamaged hand. The thing strained closer, fangs gnawing on air. Paladin's free hand scrabbled for the sword, but he had no idea where Lancaster had dropped it. Assuming it was dropped.

"That's it! I've had just about enough!"

It was Leigh's voice: baffled and angry, coming from somewhere above Lancaster's distorted, champing features. His head recoiled. Lancaster grunted and half-rolled off Paladin. The investigator blinked at the sight of Leigh standing over them, swinging her purse like a mace.

"That son of a bitch hypnotized me!" The look of righteous anger on her face was so vivid Paladin almost laughed.

He rolled into a tense crouch. The Spear of Destiny was lying not six feet away. Lancaster had seen it too. Paladin dived for the sword. Both hands closed around the hilt. Something smashed across his neck. He half-somersaulted onto his back, dazed. Lancaster lunged forward—

—Onto the upraised blade.

Impaled where the heart should be, the thing calling itself Lancaster thrashed and swore as Paladin pushed and twisted the blade deeper into the wound. Lancaster tore at the naked blade with both hands, pushing, trying to lever himself off. Flesh smoked, foul pus dribbled from the torn chest. The room filled with a nauseating stench. Whatever was impaled on the sword burned and charred, and still tried to free itself.

Paladin got to his feet, hauling the thing upright with the embedded weapon. His face was so close to Lancaster that filthy smoke filled his nostrils. "If you won't answer to Myphas the Searcher, nor Elaurin, that just leaves me one last guess…" He heaved at the sword, twisting the blade again. The thing that somehow still lived, howled.

"How about the Grail's one-time guardian. The one who lost it centuries ago and who's been trying to find it ever since—"

"Go to hell, Paladin!"

"You first, Abbron—!" He snatched the sword free, swinging at the thing's exposed neck. With a blow that almost shattered the blade, the smoking head spun free. The body collapsed to the floor, disintegrating into charred bone and viscous flesh. Paladin watched as it turned into black wax, dribbling slowly off its bones. Eventually, there was nothing left but a few unpleasant stains, and the smell.

Leigh was staring at the floor in revulsion, her purse hanging forgotten. Paladin put an arm around her; she didn't flinch.

"Enchanted blade." He held up the spear point: it was curiously clean of the dissolved thing's remains. "Lucky for us it works both ways."

Leigh's voice was small and girlish. "Can we go now, Damy? I… this place… I don't know. I feel dirty, somehow—"

Paladin couldn't wait to get out into the rain himself, get the spearhead back to Raven, and wish him out of his life. Again. "Some people have that effect."

VIII

"So… Abbron the Maimed all along…?" Andy Raven held the Spear of Destiny like it weighed a hundred pounds. Up close, in the poor light from the table lamp, the weapon didn't look so special: an ancient spearhead, fitted to a worn wooden hilt. No ornamentation, no frills. It could easily have passed for an oversized letter opener. "I wonder if I'm supposed to appreciate the irony." Raven's hands were shaking; his expression unreadable. He handed the sword to Paladin, hilt first. "I'm going to need your help."

The investigator was already starting to regret coming back at all. "Exactly how much help?"

"Nothing you can't handle. You just need to stab me in the back."

"Sure, I can do that. Mind telling me why?"

"Reversal. You need to repeat the original action: penetrate the wound… then remove the blade…" Slowly, every movement speaking of the agony he was suffering, Raven turned until his back was to Paladin. The investigator could see the tear in Raven's coat, the clear ichor glistening in the lamplight.

Paladin aimed the spearhead, bringing it to within a finger's width of the torn coat. "You'd better hope my hands are steadier than yours." He licked arid lips. "This is going to hurt you—"

"Just do it…"

Paladin closed his eyes and took a deep breath. He didn't need to be an expert to know that if he was out, even by just a half inch, whatever Raven planned wouldn't work. He opened his eyes again, but couldn't release the breath. Steady as he could he slid the blade through the torn coat, and into Raven's body.

Raven tensed. Paladin could tell he wanted to pull away, to scream, but somehow was keeping rigidly still. The Spear of Destiny slid deeper, filling the wound; blocking it. Paladin imagined it would never stop: the tear in Raven's flesh was too wide, the blade would never fill it again. Then he felt the slightest of resistance: the spearhead was in as deep as the original thrust.

Raven groaned. The sound seemed to fill the entire warehouse, echoing off its invisible walls. "Now... Pull it out... Slowly—!"

As carefully as he'd slid the blade in, Paladin extracted it. This time there was resistance, like Raven's body was trying to keep the ancient weapon embedded. Paladin could smell roasting flesh,. Raven's voice was a mindless rasp.

The Spear of Destiny reluctantly slid free. Through the tear in Raven's coat, Paladin clearly saw the Eternal's inhuman flesh flowing together behind it. The wound closed, leaving no mark; only a wisp of opalescent smoke.

Raven slumped, his breathing shallow but regular. Paladin smiled, amused at how closely the being before him aped mortal behavior. Even down to breathing air he didn't need. Placing the Spear on the ground, the investigator stood up.

"Okay. Our business is over. And remember: you owe me one."

Raven also got to his feet, slowly facing Paladin. He propped himself against a packing case. "I don't need... reminding—" Although his face was deeply etched with suffering, he was plainly growing stronger. Paladin might have said color was returning to his strange, fine features, if such a thing was possible. "There's something you need to know—"

Paladin felt his hackles rise again. Raven held up a placating hand. "Not what you think... It's just another reason why I was here." He took a deep breath, standing up straighter. "The mounds the Caddo Indians built... in Texas..."

Foreboding took hold of Paladin. "I know them..."

"Guessed you would." A thin smile stretched Raven's pale lips for a moment. "There's an archaeological dig at one. I think you might want to be around… when they… find whatever there might be to find."

Paladin snatched up his hat and made for the door. Raven called after him, "I'll catch up to you, Junior. Soon as I'm fit enough to travel—"

Paladin slammed the door shut, drowning out his father's voice.

PART FIVE:
AU REVOIR, CHER BARON

I

Professor Safka stepped out of his tent into another perfect East Texas morning. He breathed in deeply, smile growing across his face. My, he could actually smell success this morning.

He took another deep breath, let it out, and began to make his way toward the dig. Some of the men were already at work, even Doctor Theobald was on site, supervising them. Safka's elation dissipated, smile growing frosty. He hoped that oily jerk wasn't going to try and grab some of the glory. The Elmcut site was *his* discovery; no amount of money from the Columbus Foundation was going to change that.

Theobald was standing on top of the oblong High Temple Mound, staring intently into the dig. In his pristine khaki and pith helmet, he would have looked more at home in the Egyptian desert. He didn't hear Safka's approach until the professor was no more than a yard away. A broad smile, almost as big as the professor's had been, stretched his handsome features. "Morning, professor." His smooth voice gave Safka the creeps. "Thought we'd get started early. Might grow kind of sticky later."

Safka struggled to the peak. Although it hadn't rained in weeks, the dirt was damp and clogged. "Are they close?" Piqued as he was, he still couldn't keep the excitement from his voice.

Theobald waved toward three of the hired locals who were brushing carefully at what appeared to be a stone floor. "I'd say that's the most likely spot, given its location."

Safka barely stopped himself rubbing his hands in satisfaction. "I hope you appreciate the gravity of this find, doctor. The Caddoan Mound Builders are supposed to have quit East Texas by 1300, yet everything about this site indicates this village was still here as late as 1500!"

Below them, one of the workmen got to his feet, dusting off his pants. "Doctor Theobald! I think we got somethin'."

Both Theobald and the professor scrambled into the hollowed mound, careless of how much dirt cascaded alongside them. All three workmen were on their feet now, batting at their clothes. Even above his excitement, Safka couldn't help thinking they were looking kind of shifty: giving each other edgy glances. He overlooked it quickly. All three were at least part Comanche or Apache; he wasn't about to start paying attention to whatever superstitions they'd brought along with them.

"What is it?" Safka scanned the brushed surface for a clue. The workman who'd originally spoken pointed at the ground.

"It's some kinda face, professor."

"Where?" Safka dropped on all fours, oblivious of his professorial dignity. The spokesman shuffled closer, pushing at the dirt with his boot-cap. Impatient, hardly wondering why the man didn't just point, Safka waved a hand for a brush. He finished cleaning the carved stone himself.

"Theobald! Give me a hand here!" He'd found deep lines carved between stones. There was no doubt they formed a pattern: a broad oval that could well be a face. Theobald joined him in clearing out the lines. In less than five minutes, the image was exposed.

Safka got to his feet. It was a face, sure enough. But what a face. Long and angular, with a large nose, a shock of long hair. And a beard. If Safka didn't know better, he'd have said it was the face of a white man. A European. "What do you make of that?" His grin was back, and so wide he felt his cheeks ache.

Theobald never got a chance to reply. Abruptly the stone floor quivered, vibrating like a drum. The few traces of dirt left over the inlaid face danced across the surface. Somewhere deep below, Safka heard the roar of an enraged giant; a moment later he was smothered in a heavy, airless blackness.

II

Leigh steered the aging Cunningham off the road. For a while she just sat behind the wheel, enjoying the sense of familiarity. The peeling truck company sign was still there, just more illegible. Now all that was left was the cryptic message: *F G KIN O. M R ERS.* If it lost many more letters, she reflected with a salacious grin, someone from the city would have to take it down.

Eventually, she opened the limo's door and swung out. The air had a kind of smoky chill to it: Fall wasn't so far away. A skein of geese picked that moment to arrow overhead, honking mournfully, already heading south. Leigh hugged her coat to her neck.

Across the road, Damy's Chrysler was parked right next to the new fencing which ran the length of Chaykin Field. Hard to believe it was only two years since she'd found herself here, one freezing July night. Back then it was just another nameless, deserted airfield, a dumping ground for tired and rotting airplanes. A lot had happened in that time.

She crossed the deserted road, passing through a simple gate. The new fence wasn't the only change: the battered hulks she'd seen that first night had been replaced by a squadron of immaculate, brightly-painted biplanes, all lovingly restored to their former glory. Mostly war-vintage, but several were more recent. In fact, two large two-seaters were parked up on the field's far side, still in US Marines markings. If he kept on adding machines at this rate, Damy would have a private air force bigger than the one Howard Hughes had boasted about owning.

As she'd guessed, Damy was fussing over one his babies. It was the Curtiss P-6 Hawk, patched up and repainted in red and gold after getting beat up over Rhode Island earlier that year.

"So there was this guy, kind of worked for me; but I hardly see him anymore. Haven't seen him hanging around, have you?"

Paladin raised his head out of the open cockpit. "Huh?"

"The Algonquin Set is in no danger here." She reached his side and, hoisting herself up on tiptoe, tried looking inside the cockpit. "What ya doin'?"

Whatever it was, she could tell it was something he shouldn't have been. For a guy who'd been around the block so many times, he couldn't mask his feelings worth a damn. Guilt was stamped all over him. "Just a bit of maintenance."

"Uh-huh." Carelessly, Leigh looked around the airplane. There were emptied gas cans lying on the grass, boxes she recognized as ammunition crates, and Damy's sleeveless flying coat was hanging off a propeller blade. "No party favors?"

"Leigh, I—"

"Save it." She thought about getting mad, then reconsidered. It wouldn't get her anywhere. Ever since the Edmund Lancaster business last month, Damy had been more close-mouthed than usual; to the point of shutting her out. "Not thinking about heading south too, I hope? We got a business to run."

Paladin opened his mouth to speak, shut it again, frowned, and took a deep breath. Jesus, this is serious, Leigh thought, her stomach doing a sudden backflip.

Eventually, he spoke. "This is something that can't wait, princess. I have to go." The way his shoulders drooped, Leigh thought he looked like someone heading to the electric chair.

She could hardly bring herself to say it. "You're coming back?"

He grinned, and the tense lines around his eyes melted. "Sure. There's stuff in New York I never want to give up."

Leigh stepped a little closer. "Really?"

"Yeah." He waved at the airfield. "Think how much this lot cost me."

"Rat!" Leigh punched his arm. For an answer, Paladin pulled

her tight and kissed her. It seemed to go on forever and still wasn't long enough.

When he finally let go, Leigh's head was swimming: like having the flu, but a whole lot better. "Wow… Maybe you ought to skip town more often…"

Paladin grabbed his coat off the propeller. "Stay away from Jimmy while I'm gone, princess."

In a daze, Leigh watched him start the P-6 up and, with a cheery wave back at her, taxi away across the dusty grass. The last time she'd watched him fly away from this airfield, he'd come back. Now she found herself wondering if he always would.

She headed back to her limo. A tall guy, ritzed up in black suit, shirt and hat, was leaning idly on the hood. Leigh reached for the snub-nose revolver that was a permanent fixture in her purse. When he spotted her, the bird straightened up, adjusting his white tie and removing the hat.

"He flown?"

"I know you?"

He smiled, showing white, even teeth. Leigh noticed for the first time how thin his face was; how pale. Delicate, even. He held out a hand. "Andy Raven. Guess you could say I'm a friend of the family."

She ignored the outstretched hand. "Uh-huh…"

"I helped Junior out with that Lancaster job. He failed to mention you…"

"Junior—?"

"Paladin." He pulled the offered hand back and reached into his coat. Leigh cocked her .38. He paused a second, finally producing a cigarette case and flipping it open. "Gasper?"

Leigh took one: they were long, the tobacco dark, almost black. Handmade, she figured. Raven lit it for her; the first lungful hit even harder than Damy's kiss. She tried not to cough. "This hop?"

Raven smiled again. "Not exactly." He took an appreciative draw on his own cigarette, glancing at the gun she was still aiming in his direction. "You won't need that."

Leigh shuddered, and her fingers twitched. "I still get nightmares about the last guy who said that to me…"

"You remember?"

She took a steadying drag on the exotic cigarette. "Just in my dreams. Most of it fades when I wake; but I think I'm recalling more each time."

The man in black nodded, his fine features solemn. "I'm sorry. Maybe I can help?"

Leigh shrugged and slipped the .38 back in her purse. "I doubt it. But you're not here to discuss the weather, are you? What's your angle?"

"He needs our help, though he'll never admit it."

Leigh bit back a mischievous grin. "Junior?"

"Paladin. As usual he's flying straight into a fix, with no idea how to dig himself out."

"Where's he heading?"

"East Texas. Elmcut County…"

"So he is heading south…?"

Raven glanced at her quizzically; Leigh took a last pull on her cigarette before crushing it out. "You want me to fly us down there?" Without awaiting the answer, she glanced back at the airfield, checking on each of the parked up machines. Most were single-seaters; but a beat-up Curtiss JN4 Jenny stood alone in a corner. Even the sparkling red and gold paint job couldn't disguise the years of abuse it had spent as part of a barnstorming outfit.

She looked again at Raven. "You a good flyer?"

His smile was broad. "No idea. Never tried."

"It'll take an hour or so to get the plane prepped; two tops. You need to fetch anything, now's the time." She was all business: doubts and fears forgotten.

Raven slipped his broad hat back on. "Then I'll meet you back here in an hour."

"Sure. You can take—" Leigh tailed off as she realized she was taking to nobody. The guy had simply vanished. The thing was: she no longer found anything screwy in that at all.

III

Paladin carefully banked the Hawk over the dig, turning back for another look. It looked like Raven had been right; partly, anyhow. Work had already started, but at the moment, there didn't seem to be too much activity. The whole site looked deserted.

From the plane, everything was easy to make out. He could see the Burial and both Temple Mounds—one of which was a complete mess—along with the outlines of the long-gone village. There was a plane on the ground: pulled up to the far side of the High Temple Mound, hidden from the road and row of tents. He couldn't make out what model it was, not from this height, but was clearly another biplane: all over white, with large crosses on the top wing. Anyone who'd been in the Great War might have thought they recognized the markings; but they weren't the black, Maltese crosses of the old German Imperial Army Air Service. They were eight-pointed and blood red. Paladin was irresistibly reminded of a medieval sailing ship, red cross prominent on its sails.

He'd been hoping to get there first; he should have known better.

Paladin allowed the Curtiss's nose to drop, and he came in for a landing alongside the other machine. It was a rough ride; the ground was no one's idea of an airfield. He winced at every creak of his kite's landing gear. He cut the engine, drifting to a stop only a few yards away from the white airplane. He sprang from his cockpit, peeling off his helmet and tossing it onto the seat. There was definitely no one around: just him, two planes and the sagebrush. Paladin's unease twitched up a notch.

It didn't get any better as he walked toward the other kite. It was much older than his own, a leftover from the war. A Fokker D VII, the most advanced scout the German war machine produced before the Armistice. In its day, the cat's pajamas; now, just about good enough for roles in war movies.

He leaned inside the D VII's cockpit: it was empty. He noted both Spandau machine guns were still fitted. They looked well cared for. He heard footsteps and turned quickly, drawing his Mauser. A tall figure halted immediately, some two yards away, raising his arms and smiling faintly.

The newcomer's face was full without being fat. His hair was unfashionably long, and almost pure white. A thick, grizzled mustache drooped over his mouth. Like Paladin he was wearing riding pants and brown boots, but his white leather coat was ankle length, and bore a thick fur collar. A red, eight-pointed cross was stitched to the breast. Underneath he wore a pale cotton jacket and turtleneck shirt. If he was armed, there was no sign of it.

"I wondered if you would be here." His voice was rich, still colored by a French accent. He bowed formally. "I salute you in the name of the Order, de Payens."

The old man was still observing the niceties, which meant he hadn't gotten a proper look inside the mound yet. Even so, Paladin was damned if he'd bow back. He holstered his gun. "Hugues de Payens died eight hundred years ago, de Molay."

"And yet you look so well for it."

Paladin couldn't help laughing. "Well, so do you, de Molay."

The other shook his head. "I do not have your advantages, *mon ami*. I will be sixty-two next month. That is no age to be flying around the world on foolish quests."

Paladin glanced at the D VII again. "You're not telling me you came all the way from France in that?"

De Molay snorted. "You must keep up with events. I divide my time between Cuba and San Salvador. The climate is so much better for my old bones."

Paladin grunted noncommittally. "Have you looked at the

mounds yet?"

"I had just begun when I heard your approach. It is not an edifying sight."

They walked toward the High Temple Mound: the wrecked one Paladin had spotted from the sky. "Anyone about?"

De Molay shrugged. "I've seen no one thus far. There's been a heavy landslide, enough to bury several people. But I doubt the entire camp would be inside the mound when it happened."

"Then where'd they go?" Paladin looked round, as though he expected to see the rest of the expedition suddenly pop out of the dirt.

"That question tasks me also." The old man looked quizzically at Paladin. "I am not aware of any… protection… which Thibault may have left here."

Paladin just about suppressed his smile at the Frenchman's use of words. "You mean a ravenous demon or elemental, or some kind of seraphim with a bug up its ass?"

De Molay winced. "As you so colorfully put it."

"Not Thibault's style. He was always more devious than that. He taught Machiavelli everything he knew."

"I'm sure that you are lying, there. But I'll bow to your greater experience, Grand Master."

"That was a long time ago, de Molay. Another life. You're in charge now."

They reached the base of the mound. From the ground, it could have been just another odd-shaped hill: the centuries had covered it with loose dirt, grass, and stunted bushes. Carefully, Paladin began to climb the overgrown side; time hadn't made it any less treacherous. Once at the top he paused, taking in every detail, not wanting to miss anything that might hint at what happened.

One of the walls had given way and flowed into the opened mound; as though the dirt had briefly liquefied. "Do they get earthquakes out here?"

De Molay reached his side, breathing heavily. "That I do not know. I was more concerned with how to remove the contents. Then you arrived."

The Order hasn't grown any more humane, Paladin thought. "Eldorado. Or the place that inspired the legend. Pity the Spanish spent so much time looking in the wrong place."

Movement out by the road attracted his attention. A battered Model A Ford truck was bouncing toward them. Underneath the layers of dust, he guessed it should have been black; a faded police shield was stuck across each door.

"Maybe help's on its way."

De Molay straightened up and looked at the truck as it lurched across the uneven landscape. It halted at the foot of the Temple Mound, the dust cloud catching up and drifting past. The Frenchman's face was thoughtful. "I think not."

The driver's door opened. A tall, gangly figure emerged, his faded uniform almost the same shade as the dust. He reached inside the trunk for an off-white Stetson; as he pulled it over a shock of sandy hair, he spat a stream of tobacco juice at the ground. He hitched at the gun belt holding up his pants. A moment later, the passenger door swung open and a second figure stepped out: as short and fat as the first was thin. The second guy leaned comfortably on the open door and grinned up at Paladin and de Molay from under a Stetson half the size of the county. Both radiated homespun good nature and the air of a couple of good ol' boys. Paladin wasn't fooled for a minute.

The tall one spoke first. "Morning, folks." His almost colorless eyes didn't hold still for a second. Paladin had no doubt he'd seen the deserted camp, maybe even spotted the half-hidden planes, and was already forming an opinion about the landslide. "Heard tell there'd been some trouble up here. Thought we'd come on by."

De Molay pushed both hands inside his long coat. "We are grateful, sheriff. But, as you can see, I fear we are all too late."

The sheriff nodded slowly, spat another brown stream, and spoke to his short partner. "Gage: you want to go back to town? Get them niggers and Injuns back up here; along with anyone else you can rustle up." He looked back up at de Molay. "Figure there's some heavy work ahead."

Gage, grinning even wider, got back inside the Model A, sliding into the driver's seat. Gears shrieking in protest, the truck backed up, swung in a wide arc, and headed toward the road.

The sheriff never took his pale eyes off either de Molay or Paladin. After a while his right hand slid, like it was by accident, to his holstered revolver. "Now, gents. Perhaps y'all would like to tell me how you both come to be up there."

IV

By the time de Molay had finished his interview with the sheriff, a work party had arrived from town and set to work. The old man looked around for Paladin; he was still on top of the High Temple Mound, watching as around twenty men dug into the collapse. They had erected simple wooden cranes already, dumping the re-excavated dirt a safe distance from the site. No one was working enthusiastically. De Molay assumed it was because the day was hot; a faint, humid breeze was blowing sullenly from the south, cooling nothing.

He climbed the mound, his breathing growing more labored with each yard. He resented the reminder that his youth was long gone, especially when he saw the face of the man calling himself Damian Paladin. It was not a face he could say he recognized from history: the few surviving images of Hugues de Payens were as stylized as any 12th Century painting, but he wasn't about to argue with the records of the Order.

Paladin saw him coming and waved. De Molay had to fight the urge to bow. By his own admission, the man above him was no longer Grand Master; but unthinking obedience was a well-established trait of the Order. De Molay was too old to learn new habits.

He joined Paladin on top of the mound. The younger looking man nodded toward the tent, where the sheriff had established an interrogation room. "How'd it go?"

De Molay took a moment to catch his breath before replying, surveying the rescue work as an excuse. How would the men react, he wondered, if they knew exactly what they were rescuing? "Our friend the sheriff is a shrewd man. He acted very impressed when I told him I was Guillaum, Comte de Molay. When I explained I was from the Columbus Foundation, the organization funding the dig, he grew positively servile."

"The Columbus Foundation?"

De Molay returned his attention to Paladin. "A charitable organization dedicated to preserving America's heritage."

"Based in Cuba and San Salvador, of course."

The Comte pulled a box of cigarettes from his coat. He offered a smoke to Paladin, who refused. De Molay lit one for himself. "The sheriff wishes to see you."

"Naturally. How excited did he get when you told him who I was?" Paladin started to descend.

"I don't think he has heard of you."

"Can't win them all."

De Molay watched Paladin reach the bottom and stride in a jaunty manner toward the sheriff's tent. After a few thoughtful moments, de Molay returned his attention to the mound. Most of the collapse was cleared. There was already one wrapped shape being hoisted up from the pit. As de Molay watched, another body was gently removed from the dirt, draped with a sheet, and laid to one side, ready for removal.

He took a step toward the excavation. For some reason he wanted to be down there: observe the dead as they were recovered. He almost felt responsible for the tragedy; but then his old mentor had always said de Molay had too much compassion for a Grand Master of the Order.

"I'd appreciate it if you didn't go any further."

The silky voice was so close, de Molay thought he felt its breath against his neck. His instinct was to freeze, but instead he turned. The sun blinded him; the speaker was nothing more than a silhouette. But the gun he saw: a very large, black Colt automatic, aimed steadily at his heart.

"Bonjour, monsieur le Comte. Ça va?"

"Who the hell are you?" De Molay had the impression the

figure was smiling.

"That scarcely matters for the moment, de Molay. Later, perhaps. For now, I wish us both to simply sit here, relax in the sun, and wait for the diligent serfs to expose what I almost had in my grasp."

De Molay glanced toward the distant tents, and heard his captor tutting.

"I don't think de Payens will be joining us for a while, *mon ami*. The local sheriff is diligent, I understand; not easily fooled. And if you should attempt to attract anyone's attention, even those half-breeds below us, I will shoot you like a dog. Are we clear?"

"We are." Reluctantly, de Molay lowered himself into a sitting position. Only too aware of the gun so close to his ribs, he watched the team below as it once again uncovered the stone floor, and what was hidden below it.

V

“So what is your deal?” Leigh took a sip of grape Nehi, watching Andy Raven over the bottle. He was savoring his coffee like it was the best thing he’d ever tasted. The moment she and the guy in black had stepped into the diner, stuck out couple of miles south of the end of the world, she’d been hit over the head with a sense of familiarity. Most diners looked alike, but this one… Sure, it was convenient—right next to the poky airfield where the Jenny was being refueled, but for some reason Leigh associated it with lousy coffee. Raven seemed right at home, though.

He took a couple more sips, then put his chipped mug down. “Deal?”

“Yeah. What is it between you and Damy? Or should I say, Junior?” She couldn’t help smiling at that word. *Junior*. It got her every time.

“Is there something between us?”

Leigh didn’t grace that with an answer. Instead, she just stared down the guy, trying to get a rise out of eyes that were black as coal and just as readable.

He picked up his mug again. “We could play this game all day, Amelia Earhart, and I’d win. Every time.”

That wasn’t the first time he’d called her after the aviatrix; likely because she’d changed into pants, boots and leather jacket, swapping the .38 for a Luger, before he’d returned to Chaykin

Field. It had been cute first time. "Damy doesn't have many friends; I thought I knew them all. You act like you're old pals, but he's never mentioned you. Not once." She fished in her pockets for a cigarette; by the time she'd tapped one free, he had a match ready. Once her cigarette was lit, he dropped the match in an ashtray.

"It's a family thing."

"Funny, he never mentions family, either."

"He wouldn't."

She thought about that. Her own family, both real and adopted, never came into the conversation much, either. Not if she could help it. She could appreciate Damy having his own skeletons. She emptied her soda. "Junior." This time she didn't smile. "So tell me, mister mysterious, just what kind of jam is Damy in this time?"

Raven's delicate features twitched. "By now I figure you must have seen some crazy stuff—"

"Only totally bugshit."

"—so I'm assuming your mind is, what should I say... flexible?"

Leigh mashed out her ciggy. "Like in bend or break, huh?"

"Something like that." His fingers had taken a hold of the empty Nehi bottle and slid it close to his coffee mug. He juggled both on the table top, absent-mindedly. "Your world is rich in a variety of myths and legends, and I'm betting you've discovered that even the most ridiculous fable has a basis in fact."

"And how." She thought about some of the stuff she'd seen ever since linking up with a deadbeat fly-boy calling himself Damian Paladin. At the same time she didn't miss Raven's offhand use of the phrase *your world*. Somehow, it didn't spook her like it should.

"Do you find that sometimes the reality is nothing like the myth?" He balanced his mug on the neck of the soda bottle. "That it's so far removed from expectations you can barely recognize it?"

"I guess." Raven was trying to tell her something, but he was being too obtuse. Just like Damy: wanting to tell her something without actually saying it. She sighed. Why didn't she meet up with guys who said what they meant?

"There are people in your world, sometimes not just people, who would dearly love to find certain... items. Right now they don't know where to look, or even what these… items actually are. What they look like." He caressed a side of the balanced mug with a long, pale finger.

There he went with that *your world* shtick again. Leigh wriggled in her seat, wanting another cigarette.

"The myths have grown too far from their origins. Out of necessity. Like hiding in plain sight. But if their cover gets blown—" He flicked a negligent finger at where soda bottle met coffee mug: both toppled apart and rolled across the table top. Raven caught and set them back upright.

Leigh sighed again, and took out that second cigarette she'd been itching for. She let him light it for her. "Well that was some swell explanation: I'm more in the dark than ever."

Raven grinned; she got the feeling he liked grinning. "It'll make sense eventually. Trust me." He stood, taking up his hat. "I guess it's time to fly."

Leigh almost smiled herself at his tone. It hadn't taken long to figure he'd never flown before, and wasn't taking to it quickly. He was game, though. She got to her feet, grabbing up her flying helmet. Raven walked past the counter, calling a so-long to the diner's only waitress, even using her name, although Leigh was sure she'd never introduced herself. What looked like a sawbuck appeared in his outstretched hand, as if by magic. He's one of Damy's all right, thought Leigh; wondering if that should comfort her or not.

VI

Paladin ducked inside the tent. The sheriff was sitting at a simple folding table: his boots resting on the scratched top, Stetson flung carelessly over another chair. He acknowledged Paladin with a laconic nod, motioning at a third chair. Even after the investigator had seated himself, the sheriff didn't sit up for several seconds. Eventually he dropped his feet to the ground and leaned forward, resting his elbows on the table. Paladin found himself staring straight into the pale eyes: it was the frankest scrutiny he'd received in years.

"Your French pal thinks I oughta know you." The sheriff's drawl was as lazy as his manner. "Said your name's Damian Paladin. You're some kinda big shot from up north."

"Bet he told you he was a Count, too."

"You mean he ain't?"

Paladin shrugged. "Technically, maybe."

The sheriff paused again. The pale eyes never left Paladin's. He stared back, enjoying the contest. "You're from New York, a restaurant owner. Kinda far from home, ain't you?"

"The story of my life."

"He also said you chase ghosts." For a moment, it looked like the sheriff might go nuts and break into a tight smile. "I ought to tell you I don't believe in ghosts."

Paladin shrugged again. "That's okay sheriff; long as they

don't suddenly start believing in you."

The sheriff leaned back, but fought shy of putting his feet up again. "This Count reckons he's from some historical society: that his boys put up the money for this dig. That's his angle. What's your story?"

"Just an amateur archaeologist, sheriff. Like flying planes and chasing spooks: something I do to pass the time."

"Bullshit." It was said so softly that the sheriff might have been crooning a kid's lullaby.

Paladin stared hard at a sheriff who played the rube to perfection, asking all the right questions without so much as giving away his own name. He wondered how much to tell him; how much the guy would believe. Likely, he wouldn't take it kindly if he thought Paladin was trying to make a fool of him. What the hell, he decided. Toss him the whole barrel-load; let him catch what he wanted. "You ever heard of the Knights Templar, sheriff?"

The sheriff nodded slowly. "Crusaders, weren't they? Tried snaring Jerusalem back from a bunch of Ayrabs..."

"Oh, they were much more than that. Over the years, they made so much money from looting and making loans to kings and emperors that even the Pope grew wary of them. They were accused of blasphemy, heresy, witchcraft. Enough got thrown at them so that even if only a little stuck, they were through. In 1307 the Templars in France were arrested. Eight years later the Grand Master, Jacques de Molay, was burned at the stake. That was pretty much it for the Order."

"De Molay, huh? Just like your French pal."

"Quite a coincidence, huh?"

The sheriff looked like he dearly wanted to spit. "Don't believe in coincidence, neither."

Paladin had to smile. "Why, if I didn't know better, I'd say you were a sceptic."

"Is all this taking us anywhere, Mr. Paladin? My deputy, Gage, will tell you I ain't a patient man."

"I'm getting there, sheriff. The one thing Pope and princes of Europe were after was the Templar's vast wealth. They all knew it existed, but no one ever found it. To this day. It was smuggled away before the Inquisition and all those greedy rulers got their paws on it.

"Jacques de Molay was supposed to have charged one Baron Thibault Baigent of Maloggia with the job of getting as much of the wealth out of the country as he could. In 1307, the same year the Grand Master was arrested, several ships sailed from Portugal to England, and then out across the Atlantic."

The sheriff lazily reached for his Stetson and dropped it on the table just in front of Paladin. He could see the County Sheriff badge clearly: the usual gold shield, with the words *Elmcut* stamped across the crest. Even in relief, in gold, Paladin recognized the familiar, eight-pointed cross. He sank back in his own chair with a groan.

"Should have known the Order would never leave it unprotected all this time. Is everyone in Elmcut descended from the surviving Templars?"

The sheriff nodded. "All the white folks." He paused, as though collecting his thoughts. "Only two of those ships made it across the ocean, Mr. Paladin. Both foundered in the Gulf of Mexico during a hurricane, but sixty of the Order and what was left of the treasure made it ashore. They headed inland, came across a tribe of Caddo Indians, and asked for help. They could pay anything the Redskins wanted. Well, the Caddo weren't interested in the gold, but their crops were failing. In return for food and shelter, the Order helped them. Ways they'd picked up in Egypt and such places."

Paladin leaned back himself, wondering if he'd have enough time to reach for his gun. The sheriff obviously felt confident enough not to have disarmed him already. Slowly, he reached inside one of his belt pouches, slipping a set of brass knuckles over his right hand.

"So the Caddo took them in." He kept talking, partly to distract the sheriff, partly to get in his own ten cents. "In gratitude the Order eventually enslaved them. By the time Columbus arrived in 1492, the Templars had their own colony in East Texas: all their treasures hidden inside the High Temple Mound. Of course, Columbus was married to the daughter of a Knight of Christ, which was how the Order had re-invented itself in Portugal. My guess is, he'd been sent to make sure everything was fine in the Order's bolt hole across the ocean."

For the first time, something like doubt crept across the

sheriff's face. "For an amateur, you know an awful lot, mister."

Paladin smiled back. "Ask your 'pal' the Comte about it someday—" He paused. "What is your name, by the way?"

"Debrack. Sheriff Arnold Debrack."

Paladin thought the name sounded familiar. "As in de Braque: the third Grand Master after de Molay, when the Order vanished underground?"

"Yeah. A little touch of serendipity, there."

"I ought to tell you I don't believe in serendipity. So, you and your boys arrange the little 'accident' outside?"

"What do you think?" Debrack actually did smile this time. "I wired the Count, soon as I knew what that California team was about, and kept my eye on them while I waited for him. But they got in too deep, too fast. Couldn't shoot them all out of hand, so I had Gage rig up a coupla pounds of dynamite along one side the dig. Brought half the mound in on top of them." Debrack sighed. "Course, I did have to shoot the niggers and breeds that weren't caught up in it."

"Explains why no one's eager to exhume the corpses. How many earthquakes put bullet holes in a body?"

"Oh, they got another reason, Mr. Paladin. I figure the time has come to move the mound's contents. It's taken five hundred years, but the world's catching up to us. Time the Order's heritage found someplace new to hide."

Paladin enjoyed the next four words. "You won't find it."

Debrack's smile collapsed in on itself. "Find what?"

"Everyone wants the Grail, Debrack. Hitler, Abbron, you— I guess even de Molay has some notion of flying back to San Salvador with it. But it's not there. It never was."

Debrack was on his feet with a revolver aimed at Paladin's head before he could so much as touch a holster.

"I really ought to catch more Western movies." He stared down the muzzle: it looked about as big as the hole in the High Temple Mound outside.

"On your feet, Mr. Paladin."

Paladin leapt from his seat, swinging his right fist at the sheriff's face. The brass knuckles merely skinned Debrack's chin: the man was just too fast.

Paladin didn't see the gun coming. It smashed across his

temple; fireworks filled his vision. He fell across the table, felt the sheriff hit him again: methodically, without mercy. After the third or fourth blow, he managed to lose consciousness.

VII

When he came round, the grinding agony in Paladin's head made him wish he hadn't. A troop of elephants were holidaying in his skull: stomping on his brain, shoving tusks into the backs of his eyes. He thought he'd gone blind: everything was totally black. Then a vivid flare of light swung across his vision, provoking more agony, and he guessed he was underground. The mound, most likely.

Sheriff Debrack's calm drawl came from somewhere behind the glare. "Welcome back, Mr. Paladin. Sorry I had to slug you so hard, but you were going to be ornery, I could tell."

Paladin tried raising a hand to shield his eyes, but his arms wouldn't move. "If you're thinking about someplace else to put that light, I can give you a suggestion."

Debrack chuckled dryly. "You got sand, Mr. Paladin. I'll credit you that." The light swung away. It was a large flashlight, playing across dirt walls, confirming they were inside the mound.

The elephants calmed some: contenting themselves with stamping moodily on the base of Paladin's skull. Glancing down at his belt, he noted, with no surprise, that both guns were missing. "Is this where you flood the place and leave me to drown?"

"Don't need anythin' so theatrical. Gage has sent everyone back to town with the bodies of Professor Safka and his party. Once I leave, ain't no one gonna know you're out here. By the time a follow-up team gets out here, you'll be a bag of bones."

"Got it all figured, huh?"

"I reckon."

"I think I might surprise you, sheriff."

"Oh, you've pretty much done that already, Mr. Paladin." Debrack picked out a hurricane lamp with the flashlight beam. He put a match to the lamp and placed it on a raised mound of dirt, turning off the flash. The jittery light gave the excavation a hellish look. Debrack sat himself on another pile of rubble and stared hard at Paladin.

"The Count represents our founders and he's here to protect his investment. But you… Amateur archaeologists and spook-hunters wouldn't know squat about the escape across the ocean. Too much detail, Mr. Paladin; too many names. So, who are you… exactly—?"

"You wouldn't believe him if he told you." The new voice came from the darkness beyond the hurricane lamp's glow. Both Paladin and Debrack turned in its direction, the sheriff reaching for his revolver. Two figures stepped into the light, the first holding a Colt automatic, looking huge in the thin light. The second was de Molay: his face drawn and tense.

The guy with the Colt waved it in Debrack's direction. "Hands away from the hog-leg, Wyatt Earp," His voice was smooth and confident. "I know how fast you are, but I'm pretty sure I can plug you first."

Debrack's hand was still hovering a few inches from his revolver. "And who in Hell are you?"

"Theobald." He stepped closer. As the lamplight picked out his boyish features, Paladin tried hard not to react. It wasn't easy, given that the man standing before him had died centuries ago. "Professor Theobald. I was an associate of the late Professor Safka. Too bad your little rockslide didn't catch me too."

"Quite a party we're getting down here." Debrack's eyes flickered briefly toward the darkness. "So what's your angle?"

Theobald didn't miss the sheriff's glance. "If you're expecting help from your fat deputy, I'm afraid there won't be much this side of the grave. I had to kill him: he was far too nosy." He smiled: a wide, slightly twisted grin that not only hinted at insanity, but which Paladin thought oddly familiar. He spoke up.

"I can give you his angle, sheriff. Remember Thibault Baigent, Baron of Maloggia: given the job of sneaking the Templar's wealth to safety? Well, you're looking at him." He stared at the one calling himself Theobald, sure he wasn't getting the full picture. "What d'you say, Thibault? You're looking good for a man over six hundred years old."

Theobald's expression was sour. "That's rich coming from you, Paladin. You don't mind if I call you that?"

"It's my name; don't wear it out."

Debrack was nodding. "Uh-huh. So you're Baron Thibault Baigent? You expect me to believe that?"

"Believe what you like." Theobald dumped de Molay onto the floor, he made no effort to rise. The old man had been roughed up and hands tied behind him. "You don't have to believe that the one calling himself Damian Paladin is also Hugues de Payens, creator of the Order and first Grand Master. You don't have to believe that the treasures of the Order include the Grail, the Philosopher's Stone, and a sword identified as Excalibur—"

Paladin interrupted. "You forgot God's phone number."

Theobald barely looked in his direction, more concerned by a sheriff who still hadn't moved his hand more than a thumb's breadth from his pistol's grip. "Laugh all you want, Paladin. I know that a bullet will end your life as surely as any normal man's."

"Sure. And I know the Grail isn't here. It was never in the hoard that left Portugal. Why doesn't anyone listen—?"

"No!" Theobald swung his gun in Paladin's direction. "It was there! It was loaded onto one of the surviving ships!"

Paladin shook his head. "That's what Jacques de Molay told you all. The Grail went someplace else."

Theobald lost patience. "Debrack! Take us down into the chamber!"

The sheriff looked back at the man as though he'd lost his mind. "You're not serious."

Theobald angrily cocked his automatic. "Very serious, *mon ami*. You are only one of three present who can get me inside. I'm granting you the chance to live. If I have to, I'll kill you right now and have de Molay do it."

Slowly, Debrack crouched near to Paladin's feet and, using

both hands, raised a thick steel ring. Paladin realized he was lying on a huge, bearded carving, the ring disguised among its curls. Debrack rotated it; Paladin heard the crack and groan of reluctant stonework. The surface under him tilted. He rolled to one side, ignored by both sheriff and Theobald.

Part of the carving dropped slowly away, becoming a ramp into utter blackness. Before he stood again, Debrack reached down, like he was groping for something. Paladin heard a distinct click, and the void was lit by rows of small wattage bulbs.

"Every modern convenience, eh, sheriff?"

Debrack looked sourly at him. "Didn't think we'd heard of electricity out here, huh?"

"I expected the Order to be kind of… more exotic."

Theobald was muttering to himself. He yanked an unprotesting de Molay to his feet and half-pushed, half-dragged him toward the ramp. Theobald halted just before stepping onto the slope, face thoughtful. After a moment, he shoved de Molay forward. The old man fell, rolling helplessly down the ramp. Theobald waved his heavy automatic.

"You first, sheriff, where I can see you. Paladin: on your feet and follow me."

As Debrack vanished into the gap, Paladin staggered to his feet, muttering venomously, head pounding with each movement. He staggered after Theobald, praying he wouldn't lose his balance on the uneven gradient. Only when he'd reached the bottom did he relax. The chamber was easily as big as the one above, maybe even bigger. The walls were buttressed and pillared in imitation of a Gothic church. Tapestries and icons, some of which would be familiar to the average Christian, some shockingly unexpected, lined the walls. Facing the ramp, in a position that brought to mind an altar, was a huge wooden chest. On either side, like choir stalls, were several, much smaller crates. Theobald nodded toward the largest.

"Open it."

Debrack spun about. Theobald fired twice before the sheriff's revolver had cleared its holster. Debrack pitched backwards in a slow-motion fall, hit the ground and didn't move again. The Colt's heavy roar, reverberating through the vaulted chamber, almost had Paladin screaming in agony.

"I warned him." Stepping over a sluggish de Molay, Theobald walked toward the altar box. It towered over him: almost seven feet high, black with age, carved with symbols and dog-Latin inscriptions that were mercifully indistinct in the low-wattage light. Paladin didn't like to think what might happen if someone was mug enough to start reading out loud.

Theobald stared up with reverence. "I'd forgotten how big it was."

"I'm telling you, Thibault: the Grail's not what you think it is. It's not what anyone thinks it is. And it's not there."

Theobald stared back at Paladin, his eyes crafty. "Maybe so, *Sieur* de Payens, but the Order has many artefacts. You know that. There may still be something of value. Something to point the way." He placed his gun on the ground and ran fingers over the ancient wood, probing for a hidden catch. Paladin let him: in his present state he'd cover no ground before Theobald snatched up the automatic and plugged him.

Theobald hissed; Paladin could have sworn he heard a click. Static arced momentarily across the chest. The front lurched forward, swinging down in a smooth, silent movement. There was no angelic chorus, no ghostly strings playing, just a harsh, dazzling light which overwhelmed the electric bulbs. The chest seemed depthless: a tunnel of burning silver light that went on forever.

Paladin allowed himself a moment of pride. "Boy. We sure knew how to build back then."

"Step away, Abbron." In the sepulchral hush, the calm voice cracked like a whip. For an instant, all those still able to move were frozen. Then Paladin craned his neck round. Halfway down the ramp Andy Raven was standing on guard; the ancient blackened blade of the Spear in his right hand. Immediately behind him, Leigh was watching them all with wide eyes. Why am I not surprised? Paladin thought. A bitter laugh squeezed past the lead weight that was slowly drowning his heart.

"Hail, hail, the gang's all here."

VIII

To Leigh it was like one of those old religious paintings where everyone is frozen in some kind of stiff, unnatural position. On the ground were a law officer, bleeding heavily; some old guy in a pale coat who also looked in a bad way; and Damy, not looking too pleased to see her. All the thanks she got for rescuing him. Standing next to what looked like a battered clothes chest, was a fourth guy, dressed for a safari. And everywhere was a harsh, unforgiving light.

Her eyes snapped back to that standing guy again: even though she was sure she'd never seen him before there was something familiar about him. Something that made her hackles rise—

Edmund...?

No, he was nothing like that son of a bitch. But even so...

Raven spoke again, his voice still calm and reasonable. "I won't repeat myself, Abbron."

The guy at the chest stood back, not taking his eyes away from the man in black. "You're out of your league, Raven."

"You'd be amazed how many times I've heard that. And keep away from the cannon."

The one he'd called Abbron glanced at a Colt automatic, lying in the dust. His expression betrayed around a half dozen conflicting thoughts before he settled on doing what he was asked.

"Junior—you okay?"

Damy pulled a face. “Nothing stomping on Thibault’s head a couple of times won’t fix.”

“Thibault—?”

“Baron Thibault Baigent. I’ll fill you in later.”

Raven sighed. “I miss all the fun. Miss Oswin, keep Abbron—I mean Thibault—over there covered, if you would.” Leigh drew her Luger and aimed at a point right about where the Thibault mook’s jugular should be. There was something about the guy made her pray he’d give her an excuse to drill him.

Raven walked down the ramp and kicked away the Colt. Thibault lunged for the ancient blade the man in black was holding. Raven snatched it out of reach, back-handing Thibault. The man staggered back a step as Leigh, her finger already itching to squeeze the trigger, put a slug through his neck. Without a sound, Thibault vanished into the chest’s open side, blood arcing from his throat like a rocket trail.

“Dammit!” Damy’s angry roar rose above the shot’s reverberations. “Will everyone please stop firing their goddamned guns!”

Leigh rushed to his side. Damy was struggling to free his wrists; the briefest examination told Leigh he was never going to make it. Whatever Boy Scout had cinched him up had definitely got his merit badge for knots. She reached into one of the pouches on his belt and snared a switchblade knife. The ropes parted like cobweb. She helped Damy to his feet as he first massaged his wrists, then the sides of his skull.

“Thanks, princess. But if anyone asks: I saved you, okay?”

“My hero.”

Limping slightly he joined Raven, who was already staring at the open chest, expression unreadable. Leigh made it there, expecting to see a bleeding corpse; but there was nothing. Or rather: there was a nothing which sure was… something…

The chest interior had no bottom, or top, or sides. It was like looking at the night sky, but a sky in which the stars drifted and pulsed, strung on twinkling strands of gossamer. Beams of pale mauve and brilliant orange streaked across the background; pure white halos expanded from nothing, grew and detonated, giving birth to sparks which themselves became more drifting stars. It was dizzying. Leigh felt herself lured forward.

Damy pinched the bridge of his nose. "I guess we go in after him?"

Raven nodded. "What else?"

"Nuh-huh." Leigh holstered her Luger. "If he's not dead yet, he soon will be."

Raven shook his head. "It'll take more than a simple bullet to destroy Abbron the Maimed, Miss Oswin."

She had a vague memory of Damy beheading the fake Edmund Lancaster. "Like chopping off his head?"

"At least." Raven faced Damy. "Ready Junior?"

"Nope." He took a step forward. Leigh clutched his arm.

"Hey! Not without me, you don't!"

He glared. She wasn't sure if he was scared for or angry at her. "Princess!"

"Not up for debate, fly-boy. You carrying heat?"

His hands twitched toward empty holsters.

"I do." She tapped her sheathed Luger. "Don't worry, I'll tell everyone it was you who saved me. Again."

"Better do as she says, Junior. Sounds like it'll be quicker." Raven's expression was rueful.

Damy hesitated a moment longer. "Hell!" Then he dived forward, like Weissmuller entering a pool; Raven followed as smoothly. Leigh took a deep breath, allowing the boiling madness to suck her in, and stepped into space.

The darkness flowed over her; the pulsing, drifting lights darted about her face like curious, luminous fish. She was spiraling through a shrunken universe, its galaxies no bigger than dinner plates. Or had she grown to incredible size? After drifting for a century, or just seconds, Leigh realized she was standing upright. Raven and Damy were about a yard ahead of her, their feet planted on—

"Nothing!" The word came out involuntarily. The two in front of her turned; Leigh waved an apologetic hand. *Sorry*, she mouthed. All three were suspended in space. Yet Leigh's feet were supported by something, even though she saw nothing solid beneath her. The light-shot blackness was all around them; strange patterns continued to spiral past, below, and through her.

Damy seemed to guess how she was feeling. "Just accept it, princess. Think of it like the Hall of Mirrors at the fair."

Raven pointed with the Spear's blackened blade. Leigh couldn't be sure, but was it glowing, just a little? "That way."

Damy and Leigh followed him, walking on nothing. Leigh drew her Luger; it probably wouldn't help much, but its solidity reassured her. As they moved, or the universe flowed by them, some of the drifting star-lights seemed to slow; to coalesce into ghostly columns. It was a welcome illusion: at least now she could tell herself they were moving along a corridor, no matter how unstable.

"So... this is all inside the chest?"

Damy shook his head. "Not exactly, princess. The altar box is more of a doorway."

Raven paused, his thin face was tilted, like he was sniffing the air. "The Templars had more sense than to hide their treasure in a hole that would be unearthed one day. This is an isolated Tier of the Internection: an entire universe in which they could conceal it. Barely a living soul knows how to access—" He dipped his head and frowned. "This way—" He wheeled to the left.

Leigh hadn't understood a word of that; Raven was even more maddening than Damy. "That crazy guy knew how to open it!"

Damy gave her one of his most maddening grins and fell in behind the man in black. "Exactly."

Leigh ran after them. Without any obvious effort, they seemed to be racing ahead. "Okay, be mysterious. And what in hell are Templars?"

They rushed through a maze of glittering, star-edged drapes; shimmering columns which soared to eternity both above and below. Leigh was sure happy she'd never suffered from vertigo. And that lance head Raven held before him was definitely glowing: brighter and brighter with each breathless step.

The drifting void was abruptly shattered by jagged bolts of light which flared from a lurching, silhouetted figure, directly ahead. Again, Leigh was hit by a sense of recognition, but she was pretty sure she'd never seen that bent, inhuman shape before. It was darting erratically between the columns of light, its movements crablike, like it was searching for something. It would reach for something Leigh couldn't see, lightning erupting around it. Each time it recoiled, misshapen limbs flailing. If she had to guess, she'd say it was ransacking the invisible joint.

"Abbron!" At the sound of Raven's voice the figure paused, craning itself upright. It turned a face that no longer had any claim on humanity: drooling through multiple mouths; black, multifaceted eyes sparking in the uncertain light. Its limbs bent too often, and in the wrong way.

"Raven and son." The multiple mouths twisted into a variety of grins. "Maybe I owe you an apology, Paladin. Even I have been unable to find it."

Raven edged closer to the thing, black spear point lowered. "Hidden in plain sight, Abbron."

"Isn't that always the way." The faceted eyes flickered toward Leigh, and Abbron bowed. "Miss Oswin. Good to see you again."

Her Luger raised itself almost of its own volition. That face. That voice! The nightmares she almost managed to forget every morning! She'd squeezed off three shots before Damy grabbed her wrist, pulling her close.

"Forget it, princess. Lead's no good."

Abbron twitched as each slug found its mark, the wounds smoking a little as they sealed and faded. One of his misshapen legs gave way for a moment; then he was upright, too many smiles twisting his inhuman face. "Best listen to him, Miss Oswin. Waste not, want not." He tittered.

Leigh snatched her Luger free of Damy's grasp, itching to drill those glittering, insect eyes, just to see. She held back, despite all her instincts.

"Time to go, Abbron." Raven levelled the Spear. Abbron was transfixed by its still point.

"I agree." He spun abruptly, flinging arms wide at a shimmering column of stars. The glittering curtain shattered; points of light flew in all directions: an exploding galaxy. Leigh ducked. Abbron snatched at one gleaming mote as it tumbled past him. It flashed with strange light, erupting into life as he held it aloft; engulfing them all in radiance brighter than a thousand suns. Leigh dropped her gun, clapping hands over streaming eyes. Like a fluoroscope, the awful blaze shone through her fingers. If Damy and Raven were as blinded as her, this Abbron had them cold.

IX

Paladin squinted against the blinding light. He just made out a thin silhouette stepping into the blaze, being engulfed. A moment later the light was gone, leaving Paladin blinking away the blue and purple spots filling his vision. The blackness of the pocket Tier was absolute until his eyes adjusted. “Now what?”

Raven looked annoyingly unperturbed by events. “Follow him, naturally.”

“Sure. Why didn’t I think of that? Where to?”

Raven stared at the blade of the spear as though the answer was there. “Back to the mound. That splinter of Nexus Jewel has little real power, barely enough to return him to Texas. He’ll be desperate, Junior.”

“And twice as dangerous—” Paladin checked himself. “*That* was a Nexus Jewel?”

“A sliver recovered by a forgotten knight, who had no idea what he found. Too bad it was included in the hoard smuggled out of France.” Raven held out the spear. “Take my hand, everyone; playtime’s over.”

Paladin picked up Leigh’s Luger and slipped it back in her holster. She stared in his direction, unfocussed eyes still running with tears. He placed her hand on Raven’s, squeezing it. “Hold tight, princess.”

A moment later they were back inside the mound. In the light still leaking from the altar, he saw de Molay's ragged shape slumped on the ground next to Debrack: an elegant pile of dirty laundry. Neither had moved, so far as he could tell.

"Hey, de Molay: still with us?" He bent over the old Frenchman.

"Grand Master." De Molay's voice was hoarse and breathless.

"Comte. Good of you to stay."

De Molay coughed for several seconds, a ragged and phlegmy sound. "When I saw you being dragged out of the tent by Debrack, I tried to shout a warning… Thibault didn't seem keen on announcing his presence—"

"I bet he didn't." Paladin glanced at Leigh. Her eyes seemed to be clearing so he gestured her closer. She dropped to her knees at his side.

De Molay whispered on, oblivious. "—I think he could see the sheriff had pistol-whipped you… it seemed to inspire him—" He broke off as Paladin cut through his bonds with a switchblade.

"Don't quit on me now, de Molay. We'll be out soon."

"As you say, Grand Master." The old man's voice was almost inaudible.

Paladin spoke softly into Leigh's ear. "Princess:, keep an eye on him. Do what you can."

"And where will you be?" The look she shot him left no doubt how she felt about playing nursemaid. He couldn't deny he was using it as a chance to get her out of harm's way. Even if just for a short while.

"Closing accounts." He dropped his voice another notch. "And, princess? Make sure Raven doesn't help himself to anything—" he glanced at the scintillating altar box "—down there. Okay?"

A grin displaced her frown. She winked. "Sure thing… Junior."

Paladin groaned to himself: something else he owed the man in black. He stood; Raven was already at his side, offering the Spear. "I want it back."

Paladin glanced at de Molay one last time. The Comte's eyes flickered, but the investigator couldn't be sure they actually opened. "Hang on, Comte. I'll be back soon."

"No need to… hurry on… my… account."

"You'll be fine, you old faker." He squeezed Leigh's hand one last time—she squeezed back twice as hard—before making for the exit ramp.

Outside he found Deputy Gage's body slumped over the lip of the excavation. The Comte's white Fokker D VII was in the same place, a red and gold Jenny parked alongside. There was no sign of his Curtiss Hawk. Obviously, Thibault had swiped it. He made for the D VII, scanning the air. There was the faintest cruciform shape against the clear sky. From the way the kite pitched, it didn't look as though Thibault was any better a pilot than a member of the order.

The Fokker fired up the first time, Paladin jammed two large rocks under the wheels for chocks. Kicking them aside, he stood back as the unbraked D VII taxied by. He vaulted into the cockpit and stowed the Spear blade. Clamping the stick between his knees he strapped himself in and opened the throttle. The biplane hauled into the air.

The Curtiss's top speed was twice the old D VII's, but Thibault had the kite in a steep climb. Even at that distance, Paladin could see the machine side-slipping, losing height; constantly on the edge of stalling. It was nowhere near its cruising speed or height, while Paladin had the Fokker's throttle fully open. It wouldn't be long before he overtook the Hawk, if Thibault didn't crash his kite first.

The Fokker's twin Spandau machine-guns cocked smoothly; he fired off a short burst. Paladin didn't want to start shooting up his own plane, but if Thibault wasn't going to land, he didn't see any other way of persuading him.

In minutes he was almost on top of the wildly yawing Curtiss. Thibault was too busy trying to stay in the air to notice. Paladin let the Fokker drop under the Hawk's tail: if Thibault looked back now, it was unlikely he'd spot his pursuer. If he did, and tried diving away, he'd fly straight past the twin Spandaus. Paladin winced every time the stolen biplane dropped by the wingtip and lost altitude. He compensated, keeping out of sight, not caring if Thibault did smash himself up; although he'd rather do the honors himself. Even if it meant losing one of his own kites.

Paladin cocked his machine guns again. He'd wake the son of a bitch up.

The moment he was in range, he fired. Pieces of the Curtiss were gnawed off, blasted into the slipstream. One of the wheel struts parted, the landing gear twisting half-free. Thibault finally reacted: the Hawk peeled off into a dive.

Paladin was on him instantly. He raked the Hawk with short, surgical bursts of fire; each time more pieces spun away. He had to keep Thibault on the run. Lousy pilot or not, he only needed to get lucky once. Once was all Thibault's superior firepower needed.

The Curtiss twisted in the air, almost flipping onto its side as Thibault wrenched at the stick. It turned through 360 degrees, raised its nose. Paladin felt his kite shudder as a fusillade of slugs punched though the fuselage, just a couple of feet behind him. Another burst like that, and the old biplane would be cut in half.

Paladin pushed his stick forward, sending the D VII into a tearing dive. He counted to ten before wrenching back. The Fokker climbed. At the top of the loop he jigged the stick, righting his plane in a textbook Immelmann turn. He was on the Hawk's tail again.

Paladin hesitated. He couldn't fail to shoot the other kite down from this position; but destroying his own machine, especially as Thibault would likely walk away unscratched, didn't sit right. Too bad. He dropped the D VII's nose, firing Spandaus in a continuous burst that raked the Curtiss from nose to tail. The Hawk slipped off to port again, out of control. Greasy smoke whipped from the engine; there were ragged holes in the top wing. The Hawk made its final stoop.

Paladin followed it down, more in the hope it wouldn't crash and burn. Fanned by the slipstream, the flames grew wilder; Thibault made no effort to regain control. The Curtiss ploughed into the ground, flipped onto its back and crumpled like a cheap toy. Flames engulfed it.

It wasn't the worst landing Paladin had ever made, but he couldn't remember a better one. The Fokker almost cracked up on the rough ground. He jammed a handy log in front of the wheels and made for the blazing wreck. He kept the Spear blade ready, not surprised when a figure staggered out of the flames.

Thibault was blackened and twisted by fire. He made two slow, painful steps toward Paladin, halted. White crescents gaped and puckered in the charred face; eye facets bulged and crumbled like melting honeycomb. "I would bow, Grand Master." The voice cracked. "But I seem a trifle incommoded at present."

Paladin hefted the lance tip. "Looks like you're not as

indestructible as Raven thought."

"A temporary inconvenience. I shall be able to murder you presently." He produced a shard of glittering crystal. Refracted flames danced in its facets. Thibault fumbled at it for a moment, blackened fingers splintering. Fragments of charred flesh scattered on the ground. A moment later the shard fell from his grasp. It hit the ground and shattered. A shockingly blue flame reared from the remains. A moment later it was gone, along with the crystal.

A terrible wail tore from Thibault's throat. His malformed legs collapsed and he groveled on the earth. Paladin almost felt pity for him. He stepped closer, resting the Spear's point against the back of charred thing's head.

"That's twice you've failed, Abbron. How'd you like to go back to hell with a joke?"

The head rose; crumbling eyes stared up at him in dumb query.

Paladin raised the Spear. "Both times the Grail was within touching distance…"

"*You—!*" The warped, seared head flew across the ground. Its body collapsed like a fetid balloon; moments later, the head was a stinking puddle.

X

Paladin coaxed the D VII back to Elmcut County where it glided in to land, gas tank dry as an Arizona summer. He dragged himself out of the cockpit, glancing idly at the streamers of fabric hanging off the fuselage. In places, the steel framework was visible. There was a figure waiting for him on top of the Temple Mound; it clearly wasn't de Molay.

Paladin trudged up the ancient slope. Once he'd reached the top, Andy Raven, black suit looking freshly laundered, black hat perched jauntily on his head, handed Mauser and Browning pistols to Paladin. "I think you dropped these."

Paladin wasn't feeling particularly grateful. He holstered them. "Where were you two hours ago?"

"Where's your sense of drama?" Raven's pale, not-quite-human face lit up with a smile that anyone else would have called beatific. "The Spear?"

Paladin handed it over. "How's de Molay?"

Raven pointed toward the tents below. "Miss Oswin and I made him comfortable. A few weeks rest and he'll be fine."

Paladin stared at him. After all these years, suspicion was ingrained. "You didn't put some kind of whammy on him?"

"He's tough. He didn't need any help."

"Swell." Paladin looked past Raven, into the opened mound. "I know you have something planned, otherwise you wouldn't still be here."

Raven looked hurt. "And here I thought I was rescuing you."

"Nothing's that simple with you."

The man in black seemed not to hear. He scrambled inside the mound. Reluctantly, feet dragging every step, his entire body one big bruise, Paladin followed. The ramp was still down and the lights on. All that had changed was the position of Debrack's body: propped in a sitting position against the altar box. Raven was busy wedging the Spear against the body, like Debrack was holding it.

"Did you get back the shard of Nexus Jewel?" He didn't look up from his grisly task.

"Shattered."

"Maybe that's just as well." Raven stood, dusting hands on his black pants.

"What's with the creep show? You hoping the corpse will scare off tourists?"

Raven smiled again. "He's not dead yet. Which is lucky for your friend the Comte de Molay."

"What's that supposed to mean?"

The man in black ignored the question. "Don't you think it's time this hoard was hidden for good? Your world's not getting any bigger and nothing can stay lost forever—"

"So…?"

"—So let's make sure the Order's treasures are better protected."

Paladin bobbed his head toward the sheriff's body. "Why do I feel I'm not going to like what comes next."

"Debrack will be dead soon, anyhow." Raven stood next to Paladin. He raised both hands in a curious gesture that was almost a blessing. "At least his soul can be put to good use." He added something else in a language no one on Earth had spoken for over twenty thousand years before falling silent. The anticipation was so thick Paladin could chew on it. But nothing was happening; at least, nothing he could see.

It grew darker. The low-power bulbs lining the walls gradually lost what little brightness they had. They faded to yellow, dimmed to orange, and finally red.

But he could still see Debrack. Much more clearly than he should. It was the blade: as the bulbs grew fainter, an internal, opalescent light radiated from the ancient weapon, growing stronger with each uneasy thud of Paladin's heart. "Should we be this close?"

Raven chuckled. "You're getting windy in your old age."

Radiance flooded the vault: the central point of light drifting upwards. It took Paladin a moment to realize that the Spear was actually being raised, and Debrack was doing the raising. Despite the overwhelming light, he could see the sheriff's outline, and he was dazzling. It was like trying to look at the sun. Paladin squinted, but the radiance drowned his senses. Debrack's figure shifted and writhed, billowing out like white-hot smoke.

Raven murmured softly in his ear. "Now I think we should go." Paladin didn't need telling twice.

They backed up the ramp, neither willing to take their eyes away from the nucleus of light. Paladin couldn't describe the experience. It was compelling, hypnotic, and quite deadly he was sure. Was something being born? Or released? Something created, maybe? As they made their way out of the chamber, harsh shafts of light lanced past them. Raven released the switch, the ramp rose back into place, cutting off the brilliance by degrees. When the last ray of light was quenched, Paladin felt profoundly blind. Even when he emerged into daylight, blinking away the retinal images, the sun seemed to have no more power than a full moon. "That was Debrack's soul?"

Raven spoke lightly. "Soul, essence… Whatever you want to call it."

"And you've imprisoned it down there."

"I've place a sentinel over the Order's treasure. I guarantee no one will ever be able to open the lower vault. Anyone who tries will endure a lifetime of nightmares in a few moments. They'll either run or go mad."

Paladin sighed. His head was starting to throb again. "You've condemned a soul to eternal imprisonment just to guard the Templar's relics." It would have been easier to just move everything.

"Not eternal." Raven was smiling again. A smile that could be angelic or satanic, depending on the angle you looked at it. "The Earth won't last that long."

"Why do I get the feeling you've done this before?"

"Oh, and I got you this." With an elaborate gesture, Raven handed Paladin a chunk of what appeared to be glass. He looked it over: there was something odd about it.

"I asked Leigh to stop you lifting anything!"

"Don't blame Miss Oswin. I collected it shortly after Abbron wrecked that cluster of stone and gems. It literally hung around me, when none of us were seeing too clearly. Pretty insistent. I didn't have the heart to say no."

"So what is it?" Paladin turned the item around in his fingers; light wasn't refracted the way he expected.

"I think it's the *Tzahar*. You've heard of it?"

Paladin whistled softly: the *Tzahar*? "Sure. Also called the Jerusalem Gem, although it was found in unnamed ruins during the Second or Third Crusade, miles from the city. From the moment it was dug up, everyone knew it was special, though no one could figure out how." He stared hard at Raven, trying to read past his pale, blank features. "And you're giving it to me? Why?"

The man in black shrugged. "As I said: it was insistent. In my experience, that usually means something."

"So why don't you keep it?"

"Because my gut tells me it's yours. And my gut's never wrong."

Paladin tried to think of a reason to give Raven the stone back, but as the man said: his gut was never wrong. Well, hardly ever. He slipped it into a belt pouch and started walking down the side of the mound toward the waiting, useless Fokker biplane.

"Do you need any help getting back to New York?" Raven called.

Paladin stopped and turned back. "Help?"

"Assuming you're going back, of course."

Why shouldn't I? Paladin wondered. Then it hit him: Raven was seeing himself in Paladin: always moving on, scared they'd wear out their welcome. And the hell of it was: he was right. Maybe he'd stick it out longer than Raven: years rather than days. But eventually his feet would start to itch; or some dame would begin to wonder why he wasn't getting any older as she got grayer. If he hung around too long, he'd get to watch them die…

The question which had been on his mind since that night in a New York warehouse shoved itself to the front of his mind.

Something he sure as hell didn't want to ask Raven; but he had to know. "Those visions I saw." Each word came out careful as footsteps on eggshells. "Those bits of your memories."

Raven cocked his head to one side; Paladin wanted to go back and slug him. "What about them?"

"I saw women… human women… Was one of them—?" In the end he still couldn't say it. The word was too big.

"Your mother?" Raven filled in the gap for him. "*There were giants in the earth in those days; and also after that, when the sons of God came in unto the daughters of men, and they bore children to them, the same became mighty men which were of old, men of renown.*" His smile grew wistful. "The most beautiful, the most loving… For a while there, I had it all."

"And you still walked out?"

"It's what I do. What we all do."

Paladin turned his back on Raven and resumed his descent. He'd hitch a lift with Leigh in the Jenny; the Comte could get his own machine refueled.

"Not all of us."

PART SIX:
MOONBURN

I

A scream knifed through the gaiety, for a few uncertain moments there was just crystalline silence. Then somebody laughed, it sounded like Mrs. Vandrunen, and the party rolled on, noisy and undisturbed.

Deirdre Groningen tried peering through the shifting mass of guests, spy out whoever had made that awful shriek, but she couldn't spot anyone not having a good time. The French champagne was flowing, the food top-notch, the costumes imaginative. Another memorable Halloween provided by the Herbesthals. Deirdre pushed through the crowd, making for the picture windows. The mass gave reluctantly, like cold molasses. The windows were ajar, allowing in some of the cold night air, and she inhaled thankfully. The close heat, cigarette smoke and wine fumes were making her quite dizzy.

Outside, night had fallen. To the south she made out the lights of New Rochelle, a thousand motionless fireflies. The Herbesthal grounds, acres of prime real estate, were in total darkness. Not so much as a single jack o'lantern dared puncture the blackness; any couples contemplating a midnight stroll would need a flashlight.

There was another shriek, this time choking off into a loud, unsteady giggle. Some of the guests were getting a little corked. Deirdre took her gaze away from the windows and spotted Carol Herbesthal herself: standing by a fireplace Deirdre could have parked her limo inside. The only one not masked as a witch or devil or hobgoblin, Mrs. Herbesthal was elegant in a shimmering blouse and loose, high-waisted pants. She was leaning against the mantel, holding her cigarette like a man, stern patrician profile turned on the room in general. Deirdre made toward her, circumventing the crush. She was less than three feet from her hostess when Mrs. Herbesthal saw her. She flicked on a wide, thin smile that left her gray eyes untouched.

"Are you enjoying the party, my dear?"

Deirdre raised her mostly empty glass in salute. "Another success, Carol. When does the trick or treating start?"

Mrs. Herbesthal arched an elegantly-shaped eyebrow. "I believe it may have started already, in some quarters." She took a last pull on her cigarette and threw it into the fireplace.

The penny didn't drop for a moment; the booze really was slowing Deirdre down. "Oh, the scream. Have you any idea who it was?"

Mrs. Herbesthal's expression was sour. "My husband caused it."

"I thought it sounded like a woman."

"Oh, the screamer was Helen Delemmer, but I believe I said my husband *caused* it." The tight, quick smile came and went again, so quickly Deirdre might have imagined it. "I don't know how I put up with him, really I don't."

Deirdre didn't know how to respond. Carol Herbesthal's sense of humor was too dry and brittle. The hostess swept away from the fireplace, imperiously calling for somebody to shut the windows. Deirdre didn't think it was so cold; then she caught a waft of a dreadful smell. Like something from the sewers.

"The breeze must be coming up from Eastchester again." All of the guests laughed dutifully at Mrs. Herbesthal's *bon mot*. "Besides, I think it's time for party games." There was a patter of applause which she acknowledged with a slight tilt of her head. "Now, where is that husband of mine?"

An elegant figure swept from the crowd, dressed in white tie and tails, a long opera cloak chained around his neck, purple sash sporting a huge, garish medal across his white vest. His flabby face was covered in ghastly makeup, his lips too red. Thinning hair was brilliantined flat to his skull. The guests fell back, making a small arena for him and his wife.

Carol Herbesthal commented dryly. "Why, Mr. Lugosi." Guy Herbesthal pulled a face that Deirdre imagined was designed to make him look like the actor. It didn't. However, the result was certainly more terrifying than anything she'd seen in the *Dracula* movie.

"My dear." He took his wife's hand and bent over it, faking a bite to her wrist. She pulled away.

"You'll drink wine and like it."

He straightened, looking around at his audience and hamming for all he was worth. "Sounds swell to me."

His wife turned to address her audience. "First, I think we'll play hide and go seek. The house lights will be dimmed to add atmosphere, and my elegant vampire husband will be the seeker." She pulled a small fob watch from her pants and frowned at it. "This is a large house, and some of you are quite unfamiliar with it, so I will give you… shall we say five minutes to hide?"

There was a general murmur of agreement. Not that anyone would actually dare to voice any form of dissent, Deirdre thought.

Carol Herbesthal raised a fresh cigarette. A moment later the room was plunged into almost total blackness, followed by the expected squeals. Some, Deirdre considered, more in delight at the dark than mock fear. At times like this, she wished she had somebody to bring with her.

Mrs. Herbesthal's voice sprang out the dark. "Time's wasting." There was an instant response: low murmurs, the rustle of expensive gowns, feet padding across a waxed floor. Deirdre was nudged several times by unseen guests.

Deirdre waited for the hubbub to fade before edging her own way from the dark room. She knew the Herbesthal residence well; she'd been a regular at many of Carol's *soirées* over the years, and had a clear idea of where some of the best hiding would be. But everything was so different in the dark: the room felt wider, corridors longer. She reached out with her right hand, reassured to feel the smooth panels of an internal door. One, if she was right, that led out to the main reception hall and staircase. There was a cleverly disguised maid's closet that she knew about, just under the grand staircase. If she could find it, and no one had beaten her to it, she intended to wait out this particular game.

A chill breeze stroked her cheek for a moment, and she thought she caught a whiff of that disgusting odor again. The front doors must be open, some of the guests searching for a hiding place out in the grounds. Though where that awful smell was coming from, she couldn't imagine. Maybe an animal had died out there, although she considered it unlikely the groundskeepers would have just left it to rot.

She edged her way around the reception area, back to the wall, a hand stretched out in front. She wouldn't put it past Guy Herbesthal to have deliberately placed obstacles where the unwary might crash into them.

She heard Carol call out. "Time's up!"

"Coming, my children of the night!" That was Guy, accent as lousy as his acting.

Deirdre froze. That had never been five minutes! But of course, the Herbesthals wouldn't care about shaving a few seconds off: Carol could always claim she miscounted. After all, she couldn't see her watch in the dark.

Deirdre hesitated a moment longer. Should she risk a dash across the dark reception? She was pretty confident of where she was: standing just inside the main entrance, facing the staircase. If she took off her shoes, her stockinged feet would be soundless on the polished floor. She headed in what she prayed was the right direction.

There was a cry of triumph to her left and a squeal. Guy had claimed his first victim. "The first in my army of the undead! Come, my dear!" There was another muffled squeal which sounded like Helen Delemmer again. Deirdre's outstretched hands brushed against what felt like the banister.

"Really, Guy." The darkness made Carol Herbesthal sound more glacial than ever.

Deirdre crept slowly around the staircase, hoping her memory wasn't playing her false. She slid fingertips along the smooth surface, feeling for a narrow, all but imperceptible gap. Even with senses heightened by the dark and thrill of the chase, she almost missed it. Her hand passed across the gap. Retracing, she relocated the line, feeling out the shape of the closet door.

Guy's voice came again, to her right. "Aha! Another recruit!"

"I'll come quietly." It was a male voice this time: one Deirdre couldn't place. "Let's just take the biting in the neck as read, shall we, old sport?"

Guy Herbesthal laughed, his over-hearty guffaws fading as they moved away. Deirdre waited as long as she dared before pushing against the door. There was a click sounding louder than a gunshot, and the closet was open. No one complained. She'd found her hiding place.

Deirdre slipped inside, closing the door with a chain loop that jingled far too much. Clearing a space among the mops and brooms, she sat on the floor, resting her chin on raised knees. And waited.

Time crawled to a stop. Deirdre was sure the needle of the metronome sat on the Herbesthal's grand piano would be frozen in mid-swing. There was no sound from outside; none she could be sure of, anyhow. A couple of times she thought somebody was brushing against the door and she'd been discovered. It sounded like Guy Herbesthal's long cloak. It all went silent again; she was left to wait it out in the blackness.

Her head jerked up. She'd fallen asleep, face pressed against her knees. Had that been another scream of discovery, close by? Deirdre listened carefully, but there was no other sound. She wished she knew how much time had passed; she had no watch even if she could see it. It felt like it had been hours.

Cautiously she popped open the closet door, easing it open, all too aware of the jangling chain. She stood, her joints complaining.

A sound like wild, uncontained laughter echoed, abruptly cutting off. Deirdre flinched, stumbling back into the closet, jarring items free. Something hit her foot and she winced, barely stopping herself crying out. She groped down and her fingers closed around a cold metal cylinder: a flashlight. What were the odds?

No longer caring if she was found, Deirdre snapped on the flash, sweeping the beam across the reception area. She heard a heavy thump above her, at the top of the staircase, and aimed the beam up. There was nothing.

That disgusting stench came again, so strong she gagged. The flashlight beam wavered; shadows dodged and crouched like they were trying to hide. God, she needed a drink!

There was a groan from the top of the stairs, she was sure of it. Slowly, certain it was the dumbest thing, she climbed the stairs.

Several more groans, growing louder, marked her ascent. At the top of the staircase was a short landing, with two more sets of stairs leading up beyond the flashlight beam. There were too many shadows up here: they pooled and splashed across carpet and wall.

The light beam picked out a dull, hunched shape against the banister. Another groan breathed from the shape; so faint, if the house hadn't been in absolute silence, Deirdre doubted she'd have heard. It had its own black shadows, spreading out across the landing. Shadows that glistened in the torchlight.

Deirdre stepped closer. It was a man: his Halloween mask gone. His face was terribly pale. In contrast, his shirt front and white tie glistened black as his coat.

She stepped away, almost slipping on the floor. She shook her head, denying what she was seeing. Something brushed the back of her head. She spun around, flailing the flashlight like a weapon. A length of material hung down from the gloom. A moment later, Guy Herbesthal's body unfurled: dangling upside down, cape hanging to the floor like lifeless wings. His face, already pallid with makeup, was whiter still underneath. His red mouth pouted in surprise. Where his throat should have been, a fresher, brighter mouth gulped open and shut as his body swayed gently.

Finally, the scream which had been clawing at Deirdre's throat tore itself free.

II

Damian Paladin stepped out of his Chrysler, adjusting hat brim against an early winter sun. Leigh slid gracefully from the passenger seat, touching her own broad hat delicately with a fingertip. She whistled softly.

"Damy! You never told me to expect this!"

This were palatial grounds rolling up from the coupe. Pool-table lawns, carefully planted copses, and at the summit a white, two-floor mansion in the latest Modernist style. All smooth angles and curving windows. It was deliberately impressive, an ocean-going liner of a house. Shame the half dozen or so police prowl cars hadn't been parked somewhere more discreet. They were pulled right up the house, penning it in.

"You must have heard of the Herbesthals." He slid hands into overcoat pockets and started walking up a gravel path leading arrow-straight to the house.

"Sure I've heard of them. Who hasn't?" Leigh lit a cigarette, waving it at the scenery in general. "But I didn't know they owned half the state. Look at the size of this place!"

"There have been Herbesthals long as there's been an America. Rumor has it, when the Pilgrim Fathers landed, there was a Herbesthal waiting on Plymouth Rock demanding mooring fees."

They reached an entrance blocked by two uniformed members of New York's Finest. Paladin noted the badges: not local boys. "I was told there's a Lieutenant McNamara in charge. I believe he's expecting me."

Without a word, one of the cops disappeared inside. Paladin glanced at Leigh; she was smirking. "Knock it off, princess. It sometimes pays to be polite."

She took a pull on her cigarette, saying nothing.

"So you're this ghost-hunter guy?" A figure stepped out of the house, tailed by the uniformed cop. He was tall, but somehow gave the impression of being much smaller. His gray overcoat and hat looked Sunday best.

"Lieutenant." Paladin stuck out a hand. "Damian Paladin, and this is Miss Oswin."

McNamara shook briefly; nodding at Leigh. "I know who you are. Just not sure why you're here."

"That makes two of us, lieutenant. Shall we go in?"

McNamara grunted something and stood aside, ushering them both into the lobby. "I should warn you, we're still waiting for the photographers so the place is as we found it. Better watch where you step." He glanced again at Leigh. "The lady might want to wait outside—"

"The lady might want nothing of the kind… lieutenant."

McNamara shrugged and glanced toward Paladin. "Real bearcat, that one."

Paladin laughed politely as they entered the reception room. The laugh tailed off immediately; the smell hit a close second.

He'd seen nothing like it since the days of the Great War. The area had been crudely redecorated a dark red, with human body parts as talking points. A grand staircase swept up, dividing into two smaller stairs which curved around to end at a second floor landing. A body was dangling from the landing's balustrade, its legs bent and crushed into crude retaining hooks. A second body was sprawled across the stairs, bloody and torn. Looking around, Paladin spotted several more corpses: draped over rails, steps, or sprawled like boneless sacks on what had once been a clean polished floor. Each body had a cop standing by, like somebody might want to steal it.

Beside him, Leigh breathed out noisily. "Jesus! Somebody go crazy with a machete?"

McNamara hunched further into his overcoat: a man wishing

he was a hundred miles away. "That's as good a guess as anyone's." His gloomy face looked up at Paladin. "I had two phone calls this morning, Paladin. One from my captain telling me to haul it over here, the other from the DA's office. You want to guess which one I got first?"

Paladin didn't bother answering. The only reason he was here at all was because he'd also received a call from the DA, or somebody acting for the DA, who was himself acting for somebody else. A somebody with money, leverage and a strong desire for privacy. He walked up the staircase, carefully watching where he placed each foot. "Anyone see what happened?"

"There's a Miss Groningen who found both bodies on the stairs. The medics shot her full of bye-bye juice for now. Six more were out in the grounds when we figure this happened. They were playing hide and go seek. The house was in darkness. Nobody heard or saw a thing."

"Lucky for them." Paladin stopped by the upside-down corpse. He crouched to look at the face and injuries. "Who's Count Dracula?"

"Guy Herbesthal himself. You know… Halloween."

Leigh joined Paladin. She looked at the torn body closely as he had. "Wonder if he appreciates the irony?"

"Wonder if you appreciate the lack of blood?" Paladin looked thoughtfully at the carpet immediately below Guy Herbesthal's head.

McNamara laughed. "Lack of—? Maybe you haven't noticed, pally, but we're ankle deep in the stuff!"

Paladin came back down the stairs, Leigh trailing him. He fixed his gaze on the lieutenant's face. "I'm willing to bet none of it's Herbesthal's."

"Based on what?"

"Take a look at the stair carpet."

At that moment the police photographer arrived: lugging a huge camera, tripod and flash, looking none too pleased to be out so early. He began yelling at anyone within six feet of a body. McNamara jerked his head at the doorway. "Maybe we'd better continue outside."

All three stepped out into the air, leaving the stench of old blood behind. Paladin took a deep breath to cleanse his lungs.

From indoors, he heard the fizzle and pop of flash bulbs.

McNamara dug a crumpled pack of Camels out of his overcoat and offered them around. Leigh took one. "So what's this about blood and carpet?" He struck a paper match, lighting both his and Leigh's cigarettes.

"When you get the chance, see how much blood there is on the carpet under Herbesthal's body."

"Looked an awful lot to me, Damy."

"Actually under the body, princess? The body on the stairs had bled out everywhere; same with all the other corpses. Herbesthal's throat was cut, torn out, but there was no sign of any blood escaping the wound or dripping to the floor."

McNamara took a deep drag on his cigarette, frowning. "He was killed somewhere else, then hung over the balustrade."

"Doesn't explain why there was no trace of blood on the body."

The lieutenant barked a harsh laugh. "I get it. The great Damian Paladin, ghost hunter to the rich and famous, gets called in and, surprise, he finds a ghost!"

"Ghosts don't drain bodies of blood, lieutenant."

"I don't like the way you're trying to go, Paladin—"

McNamara broke off as a huge limo pulled up next to them, its tires crunching the gravel. He glared at the car, but in a second his expression went carefully neutral. It was a Rolls Royce, probably older than both Leigh and the lieutenant, black paintwork shining brighter than patent leather. The liveried driver hopped out, opening the passenger door. A majestic woman unfolded off the back seat: tall, cadaverous, dressed in what had been high fashion around the time *The Titanic* had sailed. A broad hat shadowed her face; bright, arrogant eyes glittered from under the brim. She leaned on a long, black parasol in place of a cane. She composed herself, carefully arranging her get up.

For a moment she said nothing, favoring all three with a hard glare. When she spoke, her accent was faintly European, almost English. Paladin couldn't help thinking of Margaret Dumont: a gaunter, more autocratic version. "You will be the policeman, whilst you the physic detective, or whatever you describe yourself." She paused, staring extra hard at Leigh. "I have no idea who or what you are."

"But I know you." Leigh dropped her cigarette and ground it out on the drive. For a moment, Paladin had the crazy idea she was about to curtsey. "Mrs. Katarina Herbesthal, matriarch of the Herbesthal family and Guy's mother."

The proud gaze didn't flicker. "Indeed. But I still don't know who you are."

"Oh, I don't count—"

"That I very much doubt." She favored Leigh with an extended scrutiny before returning to Paladin and McNamara. "Gentlemen: my son, his wife and many of their friends have been brutally slain. Do you entertain any ideas as to whom may be responsible?"

The lieutenant shrugged. "At the moment, Mrs. Herbesthal, we're drawing blanks. There seems to be no motive, and—"

The old lady held up a hand, and McNamara immediately fell silent. She was that kind of lady. She flicked her gaze at Paladin. "And you: are you as at much a loss as the police?"

He paused a moment before answering. It didn't take a genius to figure out who was pulling the DA's strings. What intrigued him was why she wanted an occult detective in on what, at first glance, was nothing more than a brutal, multiple slaying. Which meant she likely knew something.

"I can make guesses, Mrs. Herbesthal, but I figure you don't want guesses. There is a question about the lack of blood in your son's body, though."

"Paladin!" McNamara looked as though he wanted to slap the investigator for speaking out of turn. Even Leigh hissed in a shocked breath. The old lady, however, stared at Paladin even more keenly.

"I think you will do, Mr. Paladin." She turned and folded herself back into the Rolls. "We will speak later. Do you have an office?"

Leigh produced a business card out of her purse and handed it through the open window. Mrs. Herbesthal glanced at it, pursing her lips as though tasting something sour.

"Manhattan." She made the place sound dirty. "I will visit you at twelve, Mr. Paladin. Be sure that your female acquaintance, who claims not to count, is there also." Rapping on the chauffeur's partition with the parasol handle, she settled back into her seat. The Rolls pulled smoothly away.

Paladin whistled softly to himself. Leigh half-laughed. “Swell! Visiting royalty, and I don’t have a thing to wear.”

III

Katarina Herbesthal arrived at the Teton Building as the clock struck midday. She swept into the apartment like a thin black sailboat, her eyes piercing every detail of the décor and furniture. She took a seat and perched stiff and upright, both hands resting on her parasol's handle; her huge hat still swamping her face.

Leigh offered coffee, which was off-handedly refused. Paladin flopped comfortably into an armchair facing the old woman. "So what did you want to tell me, Mrs. Herbesthal? Obviously something you'd rather the cops didn't hear."

"The police, Mr. Paladin, are a stolid, steadfast force whom I wish every success in solving my son's dreadful murder."

"But you don't think they will."

She paused for a moment. Her eyes fastened on a newspaper, tossed negligently across another chair. The visible headlines shouted: *HALLOWEEN SLAYING, Brutal Mass Murder in New Rochelle Mansion.* "They waste little time these days."

She shifted her attention back to Paladin. "The Herbesthals are an old family, Mr. Paladin. We can trace our lineage back in Europe for hundreds of years. Why, there were Herbesthals in the Americas as early as the 17th century."

Paladin nodded carefully. "But—?"

"Is there a but, Mr. Paladin?"

"Always."

She pursed thin lips, sucking in gaunt cheeks; for a moment she looked disconcertingly like a living skeleton. "I may very well be the last in the line. During the War, every young Herbesthal male from the European branch of the family died. Apart from the women and a few impotent old men, no one survives. My son was the only male Herbesthal in America; with him gone, we are extinct."

Leigh lit a cigarette. "But you still have the wives and daughters."

Mrs. Herbesthal glared at her. "That is not how things are done."

Paladin tapped at his chin with templed forefingers. This was getting them nowhere. "I understand, Mrs. Herbesthal, and I sympathize, but I fail to see what this has to do with me. The police think your son, his wife and everyone else were murdered by a madman—"

"You do not."

"Don't I?"

"You remarked yourself: Guy's body showed no sign of bleeding. What do you think the medical examiner will find at the autopsy?"

Paladin considered his answer. The old lady came on like a tough old bird, and probably wanted a straight answer. He guessed she already knew what he was going to say, even though might not want to believe him. "That your son's body won't have a drop of blood left."

Leigh interrupted. "You said there was no sign of him bleeding."

Paladin glanced at her. "There wasn't." She opened her mouth to say something more, frowned, and snapped it shut again.

Mrs. Herbesthal was insistent. "And your conclusion, Mr. Paladin?"

"I don't have one: not enough evidence."

"Your guess, then."

"I think you already know what that is."

"I had hoped that you would be more forthcoming."

"That works both ways, Mrs. Herbesthal." He leaned forward. "I want you to level with me. You think—no, you imagine—that all those killed in your son's house weren't slain by a madman, or a gangster or hoodlum. You're scared it was something else; something you don't want to believe in."

The old lady drew herself upright, ready to unleash a broadside of indignation, Paladin guessed. Instead, Leigh got in first. "Oh relax, lady! Save the righteous anger for the posh set up at the country club. If you're here, it's for a reason, even if it's just some crazy suspicion. I promise we won't breathe one word to *Harpers* about it."

Mrs. Herbesthal glared first at Leigh, then back at Paladin. But it was clearly mock fury. Maybe it was the only way she could mourn her son: with anger; a towering rage at a simpler, saner world which had betrayed her. Eventually she cooled; her fingers eased their bloodless grip on the parasol handle. She even sat back in her chair. "I like you, my dear. You have some of the fire that poor Carol had." Her cold eyes fluttered for a moment. "God forgive me, I believe I miss her more than my son."

Paladin gave the woman a moment before prompting her.

"As I said earlier, Mr. Paladin, we are an old family. And like all old families we have our fair share of myths and legends: superstitious baggage that has accumulated over the generations. Did you know that a Dutch ancestor of mine, a Pieter van Haardt of Noordijk, is reputed to have been a witch finder?"

Leigh was on the edge of her seat. "What happened? He come to a bad end?"

The old lady almost smiled. "Hardly. Van Haardt became a successful merchant, moving to the New World where his fortune continued to increase. Eventually he married into the Herbesthal family."

Leigh chuckled. "Sounds like my kind of guy."

Paladin continued to watch Mrs. Herbesthal carefully; she gave nothing away. "I'm a sucker for family histories, but does this van Haardt have any connection to your son's death?"

This time the old lady did smile: a hard, private rictus that had little pleasure in it. "That, Mr. Paladin, is for you to determine. I am commissioning you to investigate the events at my son's house. I am aware of your reputation, sordid and unlikely as it is, and I expect you to delve more thoroughly into the matter than the police may. I require a full explanation, Mr. Paladin; full answers. Whatever form they may take."

"You might not like the answers."

"I repeat: whatever form." She got to her feet slowly, and not just because of her dignity, Paladin thought. "You may discuss whatever remuneration is expected with my chauffeur."

"Leigh handles the finances." Paladin hooked a thumb in her direction. "He'll need to haggle with her."

Mrs. Herbesthal gave Leigh another frank look. "Why am I not surprised?"

Paladin stood, taking the old lady's free hand; it felt as insubstantial as a young bird. He raised it and bowed slightly, not quite kissing the desiccated skin. "I'm at your service, madam."

Her skeletal smile warmed just a fraction. "You are a gallant, Mr. Paladin. How refreshing." She took her hand back and turned to leave. "You need not show me out."

Paladin dropped back in his chair as she stepped out of the apartment. Leigh followed. She was back a few minutes later waving a check and grinning widely. "Look at all those zeros!" She dangled the slip of paper in front of his eyes for a second.

He tried not to look impressed. "She could add a couple more and not feel it."

Leigh flopped into the chair facing him. "I like her style." Her voice turned into an uncanny imitation of the old lady's thin rasp. "*I require full answers, Mr. Paladin. Whatever form they may take.* Classy."

"You bet. Notice she never once said what was actually on her mind."

She tore her gaze away from the check. "Which was?"

"Whatever the family legend actually is. Something to do with this Pieter van Haardt, obviously. But what?"

Leigh pointed the check toward him. "Well you, unless I know better, are thinking about vampires: all that stuff about Guy Herbesthal being drained of blood. But she said this van Haardt character was supposed to be a witch finder."

"Maybe you don't know better after all, princess. Which is why I want you to dig up the whole story."

"Me and my big mouth!" She laughed suddenly. "Dig up… I like it. And what are you going to be doing?"

"Taking another look around the Herbesthal mansion, a thorough one. Especially the grounds."

IV

By the time he'd driven back to the scene of the massacre, all of the bodies had been removed. An army of mop-wielders was doing its best to clear up. From what he could see, the blood was winning. Lieutenant McNamara was still around, flipping through his notebook, hangdog expression growing longer with each page. When he saw Paladin, his face didn't get any happier. "I guess you're working for old lady Herbesthal now."

"Your guess would be about right."

McNamara sighed deeply. "As if my job ain't hard enough, I have rich, batty old dames paying amateurs to stick their noses in." He fished out the half-crushed pack of cigarettes and took one out. Paladin refused the offer, sticking to his perennially-quenched pipe. "So what's your story?"

"I don't have one, lieutenant. Like I told Mrs. Herbesthal: I don't even have enough evidence for a decent guess. And you're wrong about her. She's not batty. Scared, sure. Very scared. And too starched to show it." He waved his pipe stem at the cold, faintly echoing lobby. "You got anything?"

McNamara stuffed the notebook into his overcoat and shrugged. "Multiple homicide by person or persons unknown. Far as we can tell the murder weapon was a blade of some kind: large, not too sharp. None of the survivors saw or heard anything; the timeframe is less than a half hour."

"Who could kill so many people in such a short time, and silently?"

The lieutenant shrugged again, his shoulders drooping like they were carrying vast weights. "Nobody could. Nobody outside the pages of some dime novel, leastways." He glanced at Paladin, somehow making it feel like he was looking up at the investigator even though they were the same height. "Which is where you come in, I guess."

"Can't help you, lieutenant. Not yet. Need to do a little snooping of my own first."

McNamara waved his arms. "Be my guest. We're done here."

Paladin stuck his pipe between his teeth. "Not indoors, lieutenant." He hooked a thumb toward the main doors. "The grounds."

"Sure. Makes sense. Over a dozen people murdered in here, so you'll be taking a walk outside. Planning on a séance?"

"Well, it would help speed things along if I could ask the victims in person." Grinning around his pipe stem he left McNamara glumly smoking at the foot of the staircase.

The day was little warmer than it had started. Despite a bright sun coating the expanse of lawns and artful copses, Paladin found himself shivering. Winter was taking hold already. He pulled his coat collar up around his ears, thinking wistfully of a huge cup of coffee.

Vampires. Herbesthal's body was drained of blood; he was dressed as some ridiculous movie idea of a blood sucker. Circumstantial evidence tied up with an ironic joke. Of course Leigh would think of a vampire. But her concept of such creatures was tempered by Stoker's lousy book, and an equally overwrought Hollywood adaptation. Neither came close to the reality. Vampires came in many types. Some drank blood, many didn't. None of them looked anything like a debonair European aristocrat. Very few were even remotely human. All were dangerous: flawed parasites that thought nothing of destroying their hosts. Assuming anything like rational thought ever went on in what was left of their minds.

He found the Herbesthal graveyard easily enough. The family had to have one somewhere on their land: they'd hardly allow their dead to mix with ordinary mortals. Encircled by a screen of willows, the last resting place of the Herbesthals was a cluster of grandiose sepulchers, Greco-Roman tombs and oversized monuments. Declaring the virtues of the living, while hiding the dead from sight.

Paladin paused in the center of the necropolis, gazing around. “Look on my works, ye Mighty, and despair…!” His laugh was cynical. Guy and Carol Herbesthal would soon be interred out here, no doubt accompanied by suitably gushing sentiments. In the fullness of time they’d be joined by Katarina Herbesthal, and that would be it. End of the line, all change. No more Herbesthal dynasty.

“Which is exactly what you want, isn’t it?” He called the words out; they echoed for a moment off the marble and alabaster. No one answered. He’d have been kind of shocked if they had.

Paladin thrust hands into coat pockets and extended his scrutiny beyond the buildings, taking in the drooping trees and the unreliable shadows cast by their branches. It was just possible to imagine somebody, or something, flitting from tree to tree, skeletal as wind-brushed twigs. He was being watched; that much he was sure of. Every nerve felt like it’d been stripped raw and coated in salt; an itch that came close to real pain.

He tilted his hat back. “I know you’re out there.” He hoped he sounded tougher than he felt. Last night Guy Herbesthal had been the prey, but it hadn’t stopped over a dozen others being torn apart in the hunt. “Just step out where I can see you.”

There was a dusty rattle from the willows. The branches and few remaining leaves hissed. Then he smelled it. Rank and poisonous; the stench of death and mold; something that had been rotting for a long, long time.

It stood by a crooked statue of an angel holding a cross. Tall, thin, blowing slow and ragged in the breeze; as black and misshapen as a dead tree. Twin sparks of red fire glowed where the eyes should be.

Paladin drew a Browning automatic from his coat pocket, cocking and aiming it in one movement. “Damn! I hate it when I’m right.”

The thing writhed, twisting like a burnt flag in the wind. In a moment it had halved the distance between them; Paladin didn’t even see it move. He fired. The next second he felt knotted claws around his throat, was suffocating in the dreadful stench. His vision was clotted by black, ragged scraps. He threw himself back, kicking out as he hit the ground. The gnarled talons tore free of his throat and he could breathe again.

Paladin rolled and sprang back to his feet; the thing was already upright: half-stooped over him. In that instant he realized the black scraps were flapping and dancing independent of the breeze; they weren't remnants of clothing. He fired again, emptying the clip into the crouched shape. It didn't flinch. The investigator had the distinct impression it was enjoying itself: laughing silently at him.

An appendage of some kind reached toward him: a bent mass of ragged black twigs that might have been an arm. It dragged sharp tips across his face, ploughing tiny furrows of pain. He heard a distant noise.

Then it was gone. The air was fresh and cold. The grounds were empty in every direction. He got to his feet, pocketing the empty automatic. Pulling out a handkerchief he dabbed at his face and throat, heading back to the mansion.

McNamara watched him curiously from the main entrance. "What happened to your face?"

"Cut myself shaving." Paladin got into his car, slamming the door and gunning the engine to life. He accelerated away, scattering gravel carelessly, thinking about that noise he thought he'd heard. It had almost sounded like words. Words spun by the wind in the trees:

Anna Roosendaal.

V

Leigh was feeling pretty buoyed as she swept into the apartment; at least until she saw Damy drying his face on a towel. His dark features were a mass of fine welts, and there were narrow bruises around his throat.

"What the hell happened?" She half-ran across the apartment, dropping her purse somewhere along the way. Pulling the stained towel away, she inspected the marks carefully.

"I ran into the Herbesthal's guilty secret."

Leigh wadded the towel back into his face, none too carefully. "If I thought you'd sent me snooping into their background as an excuse to get me out the way—!"

Damy took the towel out of her fingers and tossed it aside. "I got careless, princess. That's all."

"Careless? Doesn't sound like you." She held up a bottle of iodine, wondering just how much it would sting. Plenty, if there was any justice.

"I made a stupid assumption—" He winced as Leigh dabbed the first drops of iodine against the scratches. "Like something that kills at night wouldn't be about in daylight."

Leigh replaced the bottle and dropped into an armchair without removing either hat or coat. She located her purse and cigarettes. "So apart from almost getting yourself killed, you learn anything?"

He sat opposite her, jutting his feet out. "No. You?"

"Oh yes." She perked up, eager to tell him everything. "Old lady Herbesthal was right about her family: there are stories a-plenty. What a bunch of crooks."

"I meant anything relevant."

"Sure." She rested her cigarette on an ashtray, fished a notebook out of her purse, and leafed through it quickly. "Remember she told us the young men died during the war? Don't know about you, but I thought she meant *in* the war. Killed in action."

"I take it they weren't?"

"Nope. All five moved to the States just before the war started, getting the jump on Kaiser Bill. They took up residence in the family mansion, all full of big ideas: modernizing the place, expanding it, putting up new buildings. Bachelor pads for every man." She gazed over the notebook. "They'd all been murdered by the time we entered the war. Actually made the European papers—"

"But not over here. I don't suppose there were any details."

"How'd you guess? The Herbesthals got everything but the most basic details suppressed. There were plenty of rumors, though. The murders were supposed to be messy."

"Ripped-out throats, that kind of thing?"

She checked her notes. "Too sketchy. If you read between the lines, though—"

Paladin grunted. "Go on."

"I dug up some dope on that Pieter van Haardt, too. A real son of a bitch: ambitious, calculating; kind of guy who'd sell his grandmother for her gold teeth. Before he moved to the New World he was definitely making it big as a witch finder. It was a profitable business, way back. Most likely he made a tidy sum so as to set himself up over here."

"And the legend?"

"I'm getting to it, Damy! Patience!" She dragged on her Lucky, blowing out a streamer of smoke in his direction. He so loved to spin out his own stories; so let him wait. "No real facts this time, just a load of contradictory fairy tales." She stubbed out her cigarette, checking her notes again before continuing. "A common thread is he got the itch for some local beauty, but she wouldn't give him the time of day. Out of spite, he had her declared a witch and burned." She glanced across at Damy. "They actually *did* burn witches back then… but I guess you already knew that."

The smile he gave her was maddeningly smug. Leigh shrugged and went on. "That's where it gets vague. There's one version that says she really *was* a witch, survived the burning, and took her revenge on both van Haardt and the town of Noordijk by summoning some kind of demon. Another that she killed him, which makes no sense; and also one that *she* died, and everyone lived happily ever after. Everybody but her, anyhow. And then van Haardt sails to America, does real well for himself, finally marrying into the Herbesthal clan." She snapped the notebook shut.

Damy leaned back in his chair. Even though his eyes were still aimed in her direction, she could tell he wasn't seeing her: he had that thousand-yard stare he sometimes got. "This girl he had condemned: she have a name?"

"Oh, yeah." She opened her notebook again but before she could find the relevant jottings, he interrupted:

"Wouldn't be Anna Roosendaal, by any chance?"

Leigh checked. Annoyingly, it was. "Why do you do that: send me out looking for answers you already have?"

"Sorry, princess. Something whispered in the wind."

She didn't feel in the least mollified. "And I suppose you knew all about Pieter van Haardt, too?"

He shook his head. "Never heard of the guy until today."

"Huh!" She decided to forgive him. This once.

"One more thing: I don't suppose old lady Herbesthal's driver gave you a phone number along with that fat check?"

"Sure he did." She dug into her purse again. She took out an engraved slip of card and handed it to Damy. He took it wordlessly, stood and headed for the phone. While he was asking the operator to connect him, Leigh took the time to shrug off her coat and unpin her hat. She hung up both and smoothed down her dress. In the background, Damy was talking quietly into the phone. He was frowning, the frown growing deeper with each terse sentence.

When the call was finished, he stared at the phone like he expected it to start performing tricks. She knew that look. "Trouble?"

“She’s not at home. The maid told me she’s gone back to the New Rochelle mansion.”

“And that’s not good?”

“No. It’s real bad.” Damy’s expression was thoughtful for a moment, before hardening with decision. “Suit up, princess. Things are about to get bloody.”

VI

For the third time that day, Paladin braked his coupe to a halt on the Herbesthal mansion driveway. Stepping out, he frowned at a familiar, airship-sized Rolls Royce just ahead of them.

"She beat us to it." Leigh came round the car and stood at his side. She'd changed into her own version of Paladin's hero suit. Both were armed. Paladin's hand was already resting on the butt of his Mauser.

"Not by too much, I hope."

They hurried up to the main door. It was half-open, but this time there was no police lieutenant moping inside.

"Mrs. Herbesthal?" Paladin heard his voice resounding faintly about the mansion. It made the place sound deserted. "You check downstairs, princess. I'll do upstairs."

She drew her Luger, thumbing off the safety. "What if one of us meets the thing that gave you a love-tap?"

"Yell real loud and run like hell." He drew both of his automatics. "Good luck."

He started up the stairs, calling out to the old lady. Leigh disappeared into one of the downstairs rooms. He could hear her voice, an echo of his own. Neither of them was getting a reply.

He reached the first landing: the spot where Guy Herbesthal's body had been left dangling. There'd been an attempt to clean up, but the carpets were too deeply stained; they'd have to be burned.

The place was beginning to smell, too. Paladin pulled a face at the overly sweet, cloying stink.

He paused at the top of the staircase. The main landing looked down on the reception area, the wall behind him had three doors set in it, spaced by massive oil paintings of rural scenes. Even though there wasn't a windmill in sight, Paladin was guessing they were of Holland. From the degree of blazing sunlight and relentlessly cheerful bucolic air about them, they were pretty idealized landscapes. All had at least one willow tree sagging decorously over a pond, stream or canal. The pictures looked out of place among the clean, Modernist lines; he'd have expected a couple of Tamara de Lempickas. Had to be heirlooms.

He called the old lady's name again, this time getting an answer: faint, querulous, coming from somewhere to his right. Paladin leaned over the banister. "Princess! Up here!"

Raising his automatics, he moved toward the faint voice. Banister and landing ended against a wall in which stood a half-open doorway. Nudging the door further open with his shoulder, Paladin peered into the room beyond. It was a bedroom: a woman's, if the chintzy drapes and frilled bedclothes were any indication. Maybe it had been Carol Herbesthal's. The external wall was part of a huge, curving picture window: revealing a grand panorama of the grounds. He could just make out a stand of willows crowning a distant rise.

"Mrs. Herbesthal?"

At first he didn't spot her. She was sitting in a corner thick with shadows cast by the picture window, her black clothes perfect camouflage. Her pallid face floated in the darkness like an aging moon. "Mr. Paladin. I suppose you have come to advise me against moving back here, too. Just like that tiresome police lieutenant."

"Mrs. Herbesthal—" He took a step forward, and froze. The shadows were restless: fluttering raggedly in a non-existent breeze. Another step and he saw something like a desiccated finger gently stroking the old woman's cheek. Above her he could make out what no one would honestly call a face: a blotched skull, teeth jutting like tusks from withered gums. The twin voids where eyes should have been were the blackest of all. Deep within them something was watching him; daring him to come closer.

And the smell! Not the stench of blood-soaked carpets after all.

"Mrs. Herbesthal. I think it's time we left."

"You are very presumptuous, young man. This is my property, I have no wish to leave."

"Nevertheless, I think it'd be a good idea."

Leigh dashed into the bedroom. "Damy! Did you—? Holy Christ!" She stopped dead at his side, raising her Luger. All three guns were trained on the dark, writhing corner. "I guess you did."

"Young lady, I do not appreciate that kind of language." The old lady straightened, giving Leigh an icy stare. "And I find your apparel to be a little too … jazzy." The rearing black shape folded itself around her, dropping lower.

Leigh moved her head closer to Paladin's, whispering. "Does she—?"

"Doesn't have a clue, princess.

"And I have little time for whisperers." Any other time the old lady's hauteur might have been intimidating, now the shadowy thing running smokily ragged fingers over her in mock intimacy was far more threatening. It crouched before her, like a suitor about to declare his love.

Leigh sheathed her Luger. "I'm guessing guns won't be much use."

"You'd be right."

"So what do we do?"

Paladin holstered his own weapons. He thought quickly: mind racing through everything he knew about vampires. It didn't take long. Crucifixes, garlic and holy water were things of myth and fiction. There wasn't much could scare the dead.

He snapped a couple of incendiary grenades from his belt. "Princess, I'm about to ask you to do something really dumb."

"Need me to save the day again, huh?"

"I want you to charge into that corner—"

"You're right. That is dumb."

"—And snatch up old lady Herbesthal. Then get her the hell out of here."

She looked first at the old woman and the ragged swirl that boiled around her, then at Paladin. He couldn't bring himself to look back at her.

"Won't… *it* get mad?"

"You let me worry about that."

"You're such a comfort."

He pulled the pins on both grenades, holding the levers down. "When I say, princess. I'll give it something to think about."

Paladin tossed the first grenade, dropping it squarely onto the bed's florid quilt. Three seconds later it detonated with a thump he felt between his ears. The bed was instantly an inferno. As he'd hoped, the thing entwined round the old lady reacted just as quickly. It reared up, a towering maelstrom of seething black, trying to squeeze itself further into the corner and natural shadows.

"Now!"

Leigh sprang away from him, moving like a quarterback who'd outrun the defense. She was on the old woman in a moment, sweeping her up like she weighed no more than the shadows around her. Turning, Leigh sprinted away from the corner. The thing tried to pounce. It snatched with gnarled black claws. Leigh flinched. Paladin couldn't be sure if it had touched her.

He threw the second grenade, straight into the shadows. As Leigh sprinted by, he turned as well, looping his arm around her waist, dragging both women from the room. Out on the landing, he let go and sprang toward the door. As he tugged it shut, there was another deep thump as the incendiary grenade detonated. He wasn't sure, but he thought he heard a keening wail cutting through the explosion.

Leigh was setting Mrs. Herbesthal onto her feet; the old lady was outraged into silence. Paladin guessed it wouldn't last.

"Better call the fire department, princess, before it gets out of hand."

VII

"For once it'd be good to finish a case without burning something down." Leigh spoke distantly as she watched a fireman clambering down a turntable ladder. Apart from the bedroom, there was no real damage; nothing that fresh wallpaper and a lick of paint wouldn't fix.

Damy's brow furrowed. "How do you mean?"

"Oh, Paramount Studios… the McDonagh Estate… the *SS Margaret Heywood…*"

"Okay, okay, I get the picture. Besides, the case isn't finished yet."

Leigh sighed. "I just knew you were going to say that."

Lieutenant McNamara stomped in their direction. His Sunday best was looking as careworn as the rest of him. He swept off his hat and wiped at his brow, even though the evening was anything but warm.

"I heard about you, Paladin: your fondness for going for your guns before anything else. Thought it was just New York bulls flapping their jaws: something to talk about over coffee and sinkers. Now—" He jammed the increasingly battered hat back on his head. "Just tell me you're heading back to the city. Soon."

Damy didn't show any sign of answering, so Leigh filled in for him. "How's Mrs. Herbesthal?"

At first the lieutenant just squinted back and forth between her and Damy. He seemed to be finding her getup particularly attention-worthy. “She’s fine. A little shook up, but she’ll live. She’s one tough dame. Not too happy what you did to her house, though.”

Damy snorted. “There’s gratitude.”

Leigh jabbed his arm. “She say anything about what happened?”

“Only something about the shadows and you trying to burn her alive. Shock, I guess.”

“Guess again, lieutenant.” Damy glanced at Leigh; she knew that look. “We finish this tonight, princess. You game?”

“Always.” She looked pointedly up at the sky. “Getting kind of dark, though. Won’t the vampire be up and about, be at its most dangerous?”

McNamara snorted “Vampire!”

Damy winked at her. “You saw: it doesn’t distinguish between night and day. We’d be up against it even at noon on Midsummer’s Day.”

“Swell! And we don’t even know where this particular bruno is hidden.”

“I wouldn’t say that.” Damy walked to his car. When he returned he was carrying a gallon of gasoline, three stout lengths of wood linked by chains, two flashlights, and what looked suspiciously like four distress flares. Leigh eyed the pieces of wood curiously.

“What you intend to do, slug it to death?”

Damy smiled. With a snap of the wrist he flicked the wood. In a moment all three lengths had united, joins covered by shiny metal collars, and become a trim staff almost four feet long. One end tapered into a long, sharp point. She laughed. “You brought a stake after all!”

Damy handed the gasoline to McNamara and a flashlight to Leigh. She did her best not to bridle: why should the cop get all the fun? “What did I just say about burning stuff?”

He shrugged, balancing the long staff across his left shoulder. Thumbing on his torch he set off across the lawn. “Guess I’m just a firebug at heart.”

She fell in behind him, switching on her own flashlight. The lieutenant joined in too, though by his expression, Leigh didn’t think he was along for chuckles.

"So you're telling me we're after a vampire? An honest-to-God bloodsucker?"

"I don't know about that, lieutenant." Leigh swept her flashlight to left and right, picking out nothing but grass. "Better ask the great white hunter up front."

Damy spoke over his shoulder., "It's named Pieter van Haardt, or it was three hundred years ago."

The lieutenant grunted. "Pretend I believe you for a moment, what's the connection with the Herbesthal's?"

Leigh was glad to be able to fill in. "Family, lieutenant: Van Haardt married into the clan."

Damy raised his staff like a pointer. "But not before he'd really jazzed off a girl who'd thrown him over—"

"—Anna Roosendaal—"

"—Who was also a witch. He had her tried and convicted, and burned at the stake—"

"—But it didn't take, her being a real witch, and all—"

"—And being a witch, she cursed him. With eternal life, of a sort."

McNamara groaned. "Vampires. Witches. Baloney is what it is!"

Leigh suppressed a giggle; she felt some sympathy for the man. She hadn't believed half of what Damy told her at first, either. "We going too fast for you, lieutenant?"

"Okay." McNamara shook his head; the gasoline can glugged. "Supposing any of this horse feathers is true, why did this… van Haardt kill nearly everyone at the party? Why now?"

Damy came to an abrupt halt. He played his torch beam over what Leigh realized were a bunch of trees: drooping willows, the night breeze hissing through dying leaves.

"The five Herbesthals who fled Holland before the war wanted to build on the estate. They started to clear away these trees."

Leigh suddenly got it. "And they all died. Murdered."

"Guy Herbesthal recently began work, too. Modernization, he called it."

"Don't tell me: he started in on the trees?"

"Attagirl, princess."

McNamara was shaking his head again. "You got me all balled

up here. What the trees got to do with anything?"

"Didn't you watch the Dracula movie?" Leigh swept her torch beam across the trees; seemed to her each one was a dark, ragged figure waiting to pounce. "Vampires got to live somewhere. If live's the word."

"So this thing's been hanging around the Herbesthal's private graveyard?" The lieutenant sniggered. "Isn't that kind of corny?"

"Nope." Damy held his flashlight steady, picking out the stump of a tree which had been felled years ago. "These willows originally came from Holland, or they're descendants of the originals. Ever hear of a spirit of place, lieutenant?"

"Should I?"

"For a creature that apparently died far from the land of its birth, yet cursed to exist forever, those trees are a potent symbol. They'd draw it. Call to it, even."

McNamara put down the gas, sighed and rubbed at his face, clearly out of his depth. Leigh took pity on him. "It's living in the trees, lieutenant. The closest thing to home this side of the Atlantic. And when the Herbesthal's started cutting them down—" She left him to fill in the gaps.

"You're saying it killed them? Out of anger, or desperation, maybe even fear?"

"My guess is the family's always known about van Haardt, but kept quiet about him." Damy sounded almost wistful. "The thing he'd become never really bothered anyone, just took a little blood now and then. No one got hurt, but it's not the kind of thing you talk about in society."

"Hanging around like a bad smell?" Leigh suggested.

Damy laughed. "And how." He rested his staff point first in the grass. Swapping the torch to his left hand he raised one of the distress flares in his right. "I feel bad about this but—" Waving at the trees with the flare, he nodded to the lieutenant. "You're the man with the can."

McNamara stepped forward, uncapping the gas. Leigh watched the trees carefully, standing out like skeletons as Damy played his torch along them. The lieutenant splashed gasoline on the willow just to the left of the stump, Side-stepping, he tossed more onto a second; then a third.

"That's fine, lieutenant. Stand back, now."

McNamara backed off, re-capping the can and positioning himself behind Damy. The investigator fired the flare; it slammed into the nearest tree and spun off, landing by chance at the foot of the second. A moment later both willows caught: bright flames raced along the bark, reaching for dangling leaves and branches. The green wood resisted for a while, sap crackling and spitting, then began to burn slow and steady. Leigh watched flaring leaves drift to the ground, igniting the puddles of gas around the third tree.

They stood a while, watching the willows disappear under the flames. Eventually, Damy signaled to McNamara: the lieutenant soaked a couple of trees to the right of the stump. Not waiting for Damy to send off a flare, McNamara grabbed a fitfully burning fallen limb. He tossed it at the trees; a few moments later, with a low pop, they ignited.

Leigh folded her arms, resisting the urge to start tapping her feet. When was something going to happen? Watching the boys have a bonfire while she stood around like a fifth wheel wasn't how she'd imagined passing the evening. "So, we're just going to burn down the trees, huh? You guys sure know how to show a girl a good time."

"Patience, princess—" Damy tensed, looking expectantly to his left as though he heard something. After a few seconds he relaxed. "The show's about to start."

It happened so quickly, Leigh couldn't keep up. One moment Damy was there, silhouetted by the flames, the next he was sprawled on the ground, smothered by a huge shadow. All she could make out were red-stained highlights—a hand, part of his pants, half a face—showing through a writhing blot that reflected no light. She pointed her flashlight but the beam had no more effect than shining it down a bottomless well.

McNamara was rooted to the spot, paralyzed by confusion. His brain was probably telling him that none of this was real. Leigh snatched the gas can out of his hands and swung it at the blackness. She connected with something damp and soft, buried under layers of dried, brittle leaves. The blackness flowed aside; Damy reappeared. He got to his feet: unsteadily, like an old man.

"Back up closer to the fires!" He held up two flares like they were clubs. "It won't come through the flame."

Leigh got as close to the blazing trees as she dared; it felt like the back of her leather coat was smoldering. It occurred to her that maybe standing next to a raging fire, holding onto a half-full can of gasoline, wasn't the smartest thing she'd done all day.

"When it comes again, try and souse it with the gas." Damy never took his eyes off the darkness beyond the fire; even in shadow, Leigh could see the strain on his face.

"It's awful fast."

"Do your best, princess."

McNamara grumbled. "And just what do I do?"

Damy unhooked two incendiary grenades off his belt and handed them to the lieutenant. "How's your pitching arm?"

"Played Little League before the War."

Somehow Leigh saw it: darkness hidden within the dark. Maybe it was the hot eyes, the glint of firelight off too-long teeth, a hint of pallid, desiccated flesh; or maybe her senses were heightened by fear. There was a movement and the stench of something long dead. She tensed, raising the gasoline, and it was there, only a few feet in front of her. A shadow on the lawn cast by nothing.

Leigh hurled the gas can, feeling some splash against her skin, the pungent smell cutting through the deathly reek. There was a thick, muddy splash; a strange, arid hiss.

Damy aimed a flare. "Now, McNamara!"

The lieutenant threw a grenade just as Damy loosed the flare. Flames erupted from the lawn, lapping at the spilled gasoline. Leigh danced aside as a line of flame came straight for her. Damy fired off the second flare; McNamara tossed his second grenade. There was another, smaller explosion as the gas can itself blew up, unspilled contents igniting. Flames clawed at the stars, twisting and writhing in a thin breeze. Leigh couldn't be sure if there was something in the center of that blaze, something that writhed and squirmed even more than the flames.

"Did we get it?"

A harsh, mournful howl cut across any reply Damy might have made. Louder than a dozen locomotive whistles; a hundred times more desolate. The blaze began to move: a massive beacon swaying across the lawn, leaving a bright trail of burning scraps. All the while keening like a damned soul. Leigh's ears ached.

Damy snatched up his long staff. "Follow it! Don't let it escape."

No chance of that, thought Leigh as she fell in with Damy and McNamara. It's leaving a trail they could follow on the darkest night. Guttering patches of flame marked the thing's flight. As Leigh passed by them, the stench was unbelievable.

They tracked it through the graveyard, often stumbling over unseen monuments to the Herbesthals. The fire was dimming, but the trail of smoldering, congealed matter never let up. It ended by a drooping willow, trunk twisted and diseased, gnarled limbs clawing at the ground. There was no sign of Pieter van Haardt.

"It got away!" McNamara was wheezing hard.

Damy poked at the base of the trunk. "No, it ran home. To what it thinks is a refuge."

He dragged at the ground with a boot heel. It was dry and loose, rattling easily away as he exposed the willow's huge and ancient network of roots. Leigh shone her flashlight into the tangled hole. Huddled inside a stinking pit was van Haardt; a shadow deep within the knotted roots. It hissed; Leigh gagged at the rotting, abattoir stench.

Damy raised his long staff and drove it deep into the ball of roots. Van Haardt hissed again, trying to writhe free of a sanctuary which had become a prison. "Give me a hand!"

Both Leigh and McNamara leaned on the staff, forcing it deeper. Leigh felt it judder as van Haardt pushed back, wailing in hatred even as the staff pinned him to the earth.

"Enough." Damy stepped back; Leigh and McNamara dropped their hands. A little under half of it jutted free. The thing that had been van Haardt snatched and clawed at the wood with skeletal fingers. Its shadowy body oozed and wriggled as it tried to tear itself free.

Leigh watched in disgust. "I thought a stake would kill it."

"You can't kill something that's already dead." Damy smeared a dirty hand across his face. "The long stake's just to hold it in its grave. Or adopted home, in this case." His laugh was thin.

McNamara was wiping at a damp, pasty face with his handkerchief. "So how do we destroy it?"

Damy looked up at Leigh; his face was almost as pale as the lieutenant's. "There's another can of gas in my car. Would you fetch it, princess?"

VIII

When Leigh returned with the gasoline, Paladin poured the entire can into the labyrinth of roots. Stepping back, he lit a match and tossed it into the hole.

They waited as the trees burned. The gas blazed like a small inferno for a while, so hot none of the trio could get within ten feet of it. Once the gas was burned off, the roots continued: spitting and cracking, jerking and shifting as the sap dried. At the center of the bonfire, the creature that had once been Pieter van Haardt writhed against its imprisonment, tearing at the staff, arching its shadowy body. Howling and moaning in a voice that made even Paladin's flesh crawl. Above the wintery smell of burning wood, he could detect the vampire's stench. No one asked him why the staff didn't go up with the tree; for that at least he was grateful.

Eventually, the whole ring of willows was alight: the drooping limbs and leaves passing the fire on to its neighbors. Sometime after midnight, Paladin, Leigh, and Lieutenant McNamara were enclosed by a circle of blazing trees. The flames were bright enough for him to see the confusion on McNamara's face, the fear on Leigh's. He couldn't blame her: as he watched van Haardt continue to fight its destruction, Paladin began to wonder if he'd miscalculated. Maybe the thing couldn't be destroyed by fire, after all.

As the night wore on, the flames dampened, the willows more

ashes than timber. One by one they were reduced to piles of embers and skeletal gnarls of charcoal. The cold air began gnawing its way through the dying heat.

And still van Haardt struggled and keened.

The stars were fading under the promise of a clear November sky as the last fires guttered. In the gray dawn, Paladin looked around: the graveyard was no longer screened. Every willow was burned to the ground. Ash eddied in a chilly breeze.

Paladin felt the presence before he spotted the figure. A woman, dressed in simple clothing that, if he had to make a guess, were typically seventeenth century. Sometimes solid, sometimes as ephemeral as the smoke, she drifted closer to the guttering roots, eyes fixed on the thing which writhed and clawed at their embrace.

"Pieter..."

Paladin glanced at both Leigh and McNamara: neither reacted to that wisp of a voice. He figured they didn't see the figure, either. "Anna Roosendaal?"

The ghostly figure glanced at him for a moment: huge, beautiful eyes absorbed him, knew him in an instant. Her gaze was as cold as it was alluring. In that moment, Paladin was glad he wasn't Pieter van Haardt. Anna Roosendaal returned her attentions to the thing at her feet.

"Tijd terug te komen, Pieter." She stepped closer, losing what little corporality she had; sinking into the ball of roots alongside van Haardt. *"Verbranden wij samen."* Like dust, she settled over the struggling shape.

Van Haardt wailed one last time, broken hands wrenching at the staff. Then he fell back, the fire of his own eyes died; the endless fluttering of his shadowy form slowed and ceased. He became indistinguishable from the blackened wood and soot.

Paladin grabbed his staff and twisted it free. The polished wood bore no scar of heat or flame; the silver collars glowed in the morning light. With a practiced flick, he collapsed the staff into three chain-linked lengths of wood again, and tucked them into his belt.

McNamara and Leigh were dazed; faces pale with fatigue. His Sunday best was rumpled and streaked; her face freckled with ash, hair a mess. Paladin figured he probably didn't look so hot himself. "I think breakfast's on me."

IX

Paladin was sitting in *The Palace*, auditioning a new four-piece combo and trying not to hear what was going on in the kitchen. Leigh was letting off steam the best way she knew how, and it sounded like Franco was getting the worst of it. As usual.

Maybe they should just get married.

Paladin grinned to himself just as the band finished murdering *Don't Fence Me In*, hoping the band leader didn't misunderstand his expression. He stood, walking toward them with another, more professional smile and outstretched hand. "I'll be in touch. Thanks."

He fished his pipe out of a pocket just as he spotted Lieutenant McNamara standing on the edge of the dance floor, more ill at ease than ever. His hands were rammed deep inside a battered raincoat, an equally distressed hat pulled low across his face.

"Lieutenant. Welcome to the big city."

McNamara came closer, watching the band pack up and leave. "They were lousy."

"Thank you. I thought so."

The lieutenant pulled his right fist out of its pocket. Paladin could see there was something squeezed inside.

"Mrs. Herbesthal, the old lady, she died this morning."

"You come straight to the point, lieutenant." Paladin indicated a table and they both sat. "Around what time?"

"I think you already know that. Or can guess." McNamara raised his head; the eyes that peered out from under the hat brim had the same look Paladin a seen a hundred, two hundred times. A haunted look; stricken. The look of somebody who'd had their ordered view of the universe bent so much out of shape, they'd never sleep soundly again. Paladin wished there was something he could do to help, but you either lived with it or you didn't.

"Around the time Pieter van Haardt was destroyed?"

McNamara flinched at that word. "Quite a coincidence."

"So that's it for the Herbesthal dynasty." All gone to their rest. Except for van Haardt and Anna Roosendaal: forever united in their private hell.

The lieutenant opened his right hand and dropped something on the table. It looked like a ring, with a large stone set into it. "I had another one of those phone calls; you know the type. Asked if I could drop this off with you. Seems the old lady thought you should have it."

Paladin picked up the ring. The stone was unfamiliar, translucent, shot through with rings of blue, red and gold. Deep inside, surrounded by the opaque rings, was a vague, shadowy shape. As Paladin twisted the stone, the shape appeared to flutter and writhe. He placed it back on the table.

"Interesting. Seventeenth century, I'd say. Probably European."

"Dutch?"

"I'm no expert, lieutenant—"

"It's Dutch, and you know it." McNamara stood, rearranging his hat. "I don't want to see you again, Paladin. Not because I don't like you; I think I could get to like you a lot. You're a likeable guy. But you scare me. What you represent scares me. I go to church Sundays, but after that—" He stared around the empty restaurant before looking Paladin directly in the eye. "How do you do it? How do you stay sane? How does—?" He waved a hand in the direction of the kitchen, and Leigh's rising voice. "How does *she*?"

"Maybe I'm not sane, McNamara. And I'd say Miss Oswin is more than a little crazy right now. But she copes. We both cope. It's what we do."

McNamara shook his head. "It'll get you killed is what." He rammed his hand back into his raincoat, turned his back and left.

Paladin watched him go. The knot in the pit of his stomach, the one that was growing with each day, was a ball of nausea. He reached for the ring again, with a hand that was just steady enough, and stared at the shadowy flaw deep inside, writhing against the red, blue and gold bands that imprisoned it.

PART SEVEN:
BEYOND THE BLUE HORIZON

I

There were definitely days, Leigh thought, when it paid to stay in bed. As she crouched in snow-flecked darkness, fidgeting with her Luger, she reckoned today was a major contender. She loved the snow, she loved Vermont, she absolutely adored Vermont in the snow; but this wasn't how she'd pictured spending the holiday season.

The whooshing started up again, somewhere out in the night. It was faint, so quiet she could only just hear it above the veil of silence which falling snow draped over the forest. A soft, deep whisper of vast wings gliding through the darkness; an owl bigger than a condor.

When Damy mentioned a couple of weeks in Vermont, Leigh couldn't pack her skis fast enough. Except when they'd arrived, she found winter sports were the last thing on Damy's mind. He was chasing rumors of a huge, owl-like creature seen prowling the mountain skies. Standing ankle-deep in snow looking for giant birds wasn't the same, somehow.

She saw the huge eyes first: burning deep red, bigger than pasta dishes, swooping straight at her. She dropped to one knee, firing the Luger calmly, methodically, directly between those headlights. The gun sounded louder than a cannon against the silence. The eyes shifted, climbed, swept directly above her. She had a brief impression of wings, huge claws, and it was gone.

"Princess!"

Damy was somewhere out in the wooded darkness, sounding pretty evil. But then, for some reason he'd been acting squirrelly for weeks, and Leigh was getting pretty sore about it. "Over here!"

"And where's that, exactly?"

"Exactly where you left me, genius!" Jeez; don't blow your wig, Damy, she added silently.

He stalked into view, both automatics ready in his fists, a frosting of snow on his shoulders and black hair. The expression on his normally handsome face made Leigh wonder if she'd be better off taking her chances with whatever was flying about upstairs.

"I thought I said keep out of this!"

Leigh paused a moment, taking a deep breath. "Obviously your pal with the googly eyes wasn't listening!" She waved her Luger. "Think this scared him off, though."

Damy glowered at her a moment longer, his gaze flickering between her face and the gun. "Don't count on it."

He turned away to stare into the night. At the same time Leigh heard the rush of muffled wings. She raised her gun; Damy did the same. They stood silently, facing whatever was coming. The moment those huge red dishes appeared between the skeletal tree trunks, both started firing. The noise, even muffled by the weather, was still deafening. Leigh kept the trigger squeezed until the Luger was empty; Damy must have done the same.

And still the massive eyes zoomed closer.

Leigh braced herself, ready to dive aside. The glowing eyes dropped; continued to drop. Just as Leigh realized what was happening, the lights ploughed into the snowy ground, scant feet away from where she and Damy stood. The impact sprayed snow over them; it felt like a truck-smash. A moment later, the headlights died.

"That was easy." Leigh holstered her gun, stepping forward. Damy threw out an arm, barring her.

"When something looks too good to be true, bet your life it is." He gestured to her right, circling off to the left himself; Leigh nodded her understanding. They approached the fallen thing in a wide, cautious arc, careful not to walk into a tree in the dark. Even so, Leigh found herself stepping over the tip of an enormous wing.

There was a flash of stinging white light: Damy lighting a hand flare. It lit a patch of forest broad enough for Leigh to see what they'd brought down. Whatever they'd nailed lay on the wintery ground like a toppled cross.

Leigh couldn't make out a head, just wide, heavy wings which looked black in the harsh light, and thick birdlike legs splayed out from under them. It didn't have talons, just a pair of long, scything pincers on each foot. Even without a head, Leigh estimated the thing would stand just shy of seven feet. It could have been something prehistoric if it hadn't been covered in feathers.

"I'm guessing that isn't your mystery owl." Fishing a loaded clip off her gun belt, she swiftly reloaded her Luger.

Damy prodded it with the toe of his boot. "And I doubt it's dead. Here—" He tossed the flare over to Leigh. As she caught it, he was already checking through the pouches on his belt.

"Going to put salt on its tail?"

"Send its tail back to where it came from… If I can."

Leigh saw it move before Damy: he was too busy going through his belt pouches. One wing twitched, and then both beat heavily, powerfully. A moment later the thing was upright. The downdraft staggered Leigh, blinding her with a whirl of snow. She blinked it away, found herself looking straight into the thing's broad, bright red eyes. They blazed with a strange, malevolent intelligence, just below what would have been shoulders on a sane creature.

It boomed out a bizarre sound, although Leigh couldn't see any kind of mouth, flexing its wings again. It caught Leigh with a back-swing, pitching her into a drift. She lost consciousness for a moment; when she looked again the thing was launching itself straight up into the snow-choked sky like a winged rocket. Out of the flare's range.

Leigh began to stand; Damy was at her side in a moment, helping her up, questioning her anxiously. She shrugged his hands away: she was still pretty sore with him. "I'm not made of china, you know!"

"Sure. But for a moment there—" His voice tailed away and he backed off, the concerned look hardening again. "Fine. Let's get back to the hotel."

"What? You don't think it's coming back?" She glanced up,

half-expecting to see two bright red lamps coming at her like a crashing airplane.

Damy slipped his two automatics away. “No, I think it’s gone. For now. Things like that have a habit of disappearing… Coming back years later.”

“Uh-huh.” Oddly, though, she had to agree. She didn’t think it was coming back, either. She had a feeling it had done what it had come for; whatever that was. She tugged her collar up against the cold, although the snowfall was easing. “Damy. Next time you take a girl to Vermont for the snow, you think maybe we could concentrate on the skiing?”

II

Paladin was glad to be back to New York. It may have been only a couple of degrees warmer but it made all the difference. Leigh had been giving out with the frost all the way down, and still hadn't thawed. He didn't blame her: he'd been like a bear with a terminal migraine for weeks. And it wasn't like he could just tell her why; the time for that was long gone. He was wishing he'd had the guts months ago, but how do you tell someone maybe they'd be dead before the year was out? Especially when he was refusing to believe it himself.

He left Leigh in their Teton Building apartment, stewing silently. It was going to take a pretty special Christmas present this year.

If she made it—

Paladin slammed his Chrysler's door just a little harder than was necessary. "From my mouth to God's ears."

He yanked his overcoat collar up round his ears, rammed both hands into pockets, and strode toward Chaykin Field, breath preceding him in pale clouds. The light was dull and leaden; every plane left out on the grass was dark and anonymous. He had to get up real close to the newest additions before he could be sure they'd been rigged as he'd asked. The two Curtiss O2C Helldivers were parked gold wingtip to wingtip, fuselages a fresh dazzling red. The US Marines would never recognize them. Twin Lewis guns jutted from the Scarff rings on each rear cockpit, and brand new Browning machine guns had been refitted in their upper wing housings, two per plane. He'd had to use quite a bit of leverage to get the biplanes re-armed: like suggesting to certain Navy brass hats they wouldn't want to wake up one morning and see what had really happened to the airship *USS Macon* all over the Washington and New York newspapers. Favors he'd hoped to keep for another day, but it'd been worth it. Both Helldivers shone better than the day they first left the Curtiss factory. Gleaming like well-oiled guns. In the movies, planes like these had brought down a giant ape; now just two of them were about to take on things so much bigger; so much tougher.

"Do you honestly think you'll find him?"

Paladin didn't need to look up. He knew that voice only too well; that unplaceable accent. "I thought you'd be headed south for winter by now, Saint-Germain. And yes, as a matter of fact, I think I can."

"Interesting. And without me, at that."

Paladin straightened, brushing at his pants' knees. "I'd rather not be checking over my shoulder all the time. Watching for your knife."

The Count was dressed in pale gray overcoat and matching hat, leaning on a slender, gold-headed cane. His movie star features were hurt. He took a cigarette from his holder and lit it. "All in the past, old fellow: my callow youth. But I understand if you want to keep it in the family." He gestured at the biplanes with his walking cane. "Is the delightful Miss Oswin to pilot one of the aircraft?"

"Leigh stays out of this!"

"Indeed. Does she know?" His white smile turned predatory. "Ah, of course. The prediction: her death. And time's hand is laying heavy on us, for the year is almost out. An adventure to such a realm could easily result in the loss of more than a single life. Quite the dilemma."

Paladin's fingers were twitching; he dearly wished he had a gun in reach. See if Saint-Germain could smile away a lead slug. "She'll come around."

Saint-Germain shook his head. "How can a man live so long and remain so naïve." He raised a gloved hand, forefinger extended. "*Primus*: Miss Oswin is a remarkably strong-willed lady.

Each attempt you make to prevent her is certain to make her more determined." He extended his middle finger. "*Secundus*: if something is destined, there is nothing we can do to stop it."

"I never believed in just rolling over—"

"Indeed; you are as bull-headed as Miss Oswin. You make an ideal pair." The Count dropped his cigarette and ground it out under an immaculately-polished shoe. "But there are other ways to approach something than head on."

"I never mastered your genius in sneaking up behind."

"The universe is designed for sneaking." He raised his hat, smile bland and unthreatening again. "Give my regards to Miss Oswin and, what is he calling himself these days? Andy Raven." He replaced his hat, tapping it gently in place. "So many names, so few faces. It's quite confusing."

"Goodbye, Saint-Germain."

"Say rather, *à bien tôt*. We shall meet again, and that right soon." He turned on his heel and strolled into the leaden gloom. Paladin stared at his departing back, wondering what the self-styled count was up to.

"I'd tell you to go to Hell, but I don't think the Devil would appreciate the competition."

III

Leigh glared out of the apartment window. She should have been able to see Central Park stretched out below, already decked out for the holiday season. But all she could make out was a ghostly, floating image of the apartment, containing Damy and that strange pal of his. The one always dressed in black like the cheap hoods she remembered from her childhood. Andy Raven. They flanked her own reflection, faces serious but understanding; kind but unswerving. She hated them. She hated that they were treating her like a kid, and driving her into a tantrum. And worse, she hated herself for letting them.

Damy was speaking again, tone reasonable as all get-out. “It’s for the best, princess.”

“Sure it is. The best for you!”

“You know where we’re going isn’t just dangerous. It’s hell; literally. I can’t risk you—”

She crossed her arms, holding the fury in. “We’ve been through plenty that was dangerous, Damy. Jeez, I was there when you first went up against those things! You were happy for my help back then.”

“I wouldn’t say I was actually happy, princess.”

“Miss Oswin, Damian is sailing round the point, as usual, so allow me to be blunt.” Raven held his black hat in front of him, rotating it through both hands. “If you come with us, you will almost certainly die."

Damy's reflection glared at him. "Don't sugar-coat it any, will you!"

Leigh turned, dropping her arms. "Listen, I can just about forgive you for lying about your pal. You told me he was dead, but since you're obviously going to try and find him, he can't be. But I'm not about to forgive you for thinking you can head off without me. You know I'm a great pilot."

"You're aces, princess—"

"So what's so special about the two flyboys you've hired to man the second Helldiver?" She stared at Raven. "Aren't they just as likely to get killed?"

Damy shook his head. "They're ex-Marine pilots. Been through the War; tougher than nails. They might make it."

"Bushwa, Mr. Paladin! What's the real skinny? You let me manage *The Palace*, even allow me out to admire you kick some monster's keister every now and again, but all this time you really think I'm just another Dumb Dora. Some dame who should back in the kitchen with the pots and kids. Or am I wrong?"

Damy opened his mouth, like he was about to say something. Raven made an oh-so-tiny shake of the head and Damy clammed up immediately.

"Fine. Have it your way. Just don't expect me to be around when you get back. If you get back." Staring fixedly ahead, avoiding all eye contact, she stamped out of the apartment, slamming the door satisfyingly loud behind her.

She rode the elevator down and stepped out into the street in a kind of furious daze, feeling a little sick and dizzy. She took a couple of breaths, wondering just what in hell to do next. *The Palace* was in her name, it was a going concern. She could sell up: quit and head off someplace where Damian Paladin, Monster Hunter was nothing more than a couple of local newspaper column inches. The West Coast, maybe? Los Angeles, San Francisco? Put the money into movies—

"You look like someone in need of a cigarette."

Leigh spun toward the voice, her right hand dipping for the .38 in her coat pocket. It was another of Damy's pals: the creepy European-sounding one with the ritzy title. Count Saint-Germain. He was the picture of urbanity: pale gray homburg, long coat, cane; even spats. He doffed his hat.

"Miss Oswin."

She relaxed a little; hand coming away from the gun. "Count. You here to tell me I'm better off not going on this stag party, too."

"I would never presume." He reached into his overcoat and produced a gold cigarette case. He offered her one, fitting his own into a long ivory holder. After hers was lit, Leigh took a long pull; it tasted very expensive.

"So what do you want?"

"I admire your directness, Miss Oswin." He pointed with his cane. "Shall we take a walk in the park?"

They crossed the street and struck off along one of Central Park's winding paths.

"Are you determined to stick with Damian?"

"Like sweat-stains on a shirt."

"Colorful. Then I suggest we meet at Chaykin Field early tomorrow morning. Say, five-thirty?"

"Tomorrow? They're not ready to go for a couple of days."

"So they say. I can assure you, Miss Oswin, Damian and that meddling Raven are flying tomorrow, the moment it's light enough."

Despite her anger, Leigh couldn't help laughing a little. "Yeah, it's what I'd do, too. Sneaky little sons of bitches." She took a last drag on her cigarette and ground it out under her foot. "So what's your story, morning glory? I get the feeling you and Damy aren't the best of pals."

He smiled. It was quite a dazzling grin; Leigh wondered if he'd ever considered Hollywood. "Call it an occupational hazard: rub up against someone long enough and you're sure to generate sparks. David… Damian and I have known each other for— for a considerable number of years."

"That's no answer."

"It's the best you'll get." His grin grew wider. "The evening's still young. Would you care to take a carriage ride in the park?"

"Long as that's the only ride you're thinking of."

Saint-Germain laughed. "Miss Oswin, I really do admire your directness." He offered her an arm. "Shall we?"

IV

Chaykin Field was still in darkness. If the sun was anywhere close to rising, heavy cloud disguised it well. The two Curtiss Helldivers were prepped and ready, engines drowning out the dawn silence, exhausts occasionally flaring. All Paladin needed was something resembling daylight. He hunched into his flying coat, wishing it still had its sleeves. Andy Raven stood at his left, dressed in a leather greatcoat over what looked suspiciously like the kind of high-collared uniform worn by German pilots back in the big one. A silk scarf hung loosely from his neck. Everything was in black, naturally. He was leaning on a tall ebony shaft fitted with the ancient blade Paladin had thought left in Texas.

Raven had blown in two weeks ago, blithely carrying the Spear of Destiny on its new mounting; looking like he was born to hold it. He'd deflected every query Paladin threw at him, making the investigator feel small for even considering such dumb questions. Eventually Paladin had quit, accepting with poor grace that somehow Raven was carrying an ancient artefact which was, at the same time, buried in an East Texan mound.

"Still want to do this?"

"What do you think?" He glanced irritably toward Raven. "You ready?"

Raven laughed. "I have done this before, remember."

"Not with two airplanes, you haven't."

"Planes, horses, ships. It's all a matter of perspective."

Paladin shook his head. "Jerk." He took a look at his wristwatch. "Just going indoors."

He went into the airfield's small hut. It was noticeably warmer inside; the tiny Dutch oven holding back the cold. Paladin crossed to the cupboard, sliding the fake back away. He reached in and took out three objects: the *Tzahar*, the disturbingly organic chunk of rock also known as the Jerusalem Gem; the seventeenth century ring given him by old lady Herbesthal; and the Buck Rogers dingus from Dr. Brook's destroyed laboratory. Three totems; three objects which he hoped, along with Raven's spear, would be some use during the next couple of days. He didn't think it was a coincidence they'd come his way over the past year. He dropped them into a large burlap bag, threw the strap over his shoulder, and went back out into the pre-dawn chill.

It was growing noticeably lighter. Raven was standing alongside the plane he'd be sharing with Paladin; the crew of the second Helldiver already on board. All were staring Paladin's way, waiting for the word. He paused a moment, wondering if it was worth saying a prayer to any gods who might be listening. Shrugging the bag into a more comfortable position, he strode toward the planes, holding up his right hand and circling the forefinger. Time to roll.

Paladin jumped into his cockpit, watching the eastern sky. Blackness was slowly giving way to a leaden gray; the horizon clearing. Behind him, Raven struggled into the observer-gunner cockpit, not helped any by the long spear shaft. He stashed it on the floor and gave a thumbs up. Paladin waved back. "Here goes."

He raised his right arm, looking back at the second plane with an exaggerated wave. Both Helldivers' engines roared as they were opened to full throttle. They bounced across the airfield, tails lifting. Paladin pulled back on the stick, and they were airborne. He checked on the second plane: it was in the air right on his tail, perfectly synchronized.

Leigh couldn't have done it better—

He rammed down that thought. Leigh was better off where she was. Safer. He banked his plane to the left, heading north.

They hit the low cloud in minutes. Visibility was slashed to a few feet; it grew darker still, the air on the cusp of freezing. The rainclouds' internal air currents rattled Paladin's biplane like a toy, pressing down one moment, throwing it high the next. It was all he could do to keep the Helldiver on a level course. He clamped his teeth against the bone-deep chill as much as the vibration, squeezing the stick in a choke-hold, checking the instruments to be certain they were climbing.

Eventually they lurched free, bobbing into a brighter sky. High above there was another layer of thin gray cloud. The eastern sky was stained a pallid yellow with the promise of dawn.

Paladin felt a tap on his shoulder; he half turned. Raven was glaring at him, face ashen. "Is it always like this?"

Paladin just heard him above the engine and rush of air. He laughed and shook his head. "No! Sometimes it can get kind of rough!"

Raven pulled a sour face and huddled back in his seat. Paladin checked the second plane was still with him. It had fallen back some, lost its heading in the clouds, but was matching him for altitude. So far, so good, then.

Correcting his course by compass, Paladin climbed a couple of thousand feet more, levelling off at a shade over ten thousand, sandwiched between the cloud layers. Providence was an hour away, might as well stick with the clear air and enjoy the flight.

But once he no longer had to concentrate on flying, the thoughts came back. The doubts. He'd taken months to equip the expedition, refitting the two planes with weapons and extra fuel. Raven was along to provide his own special skills: if anyone could reopen a gateway to the parallel world which had swallowed Jim Stanley, he was the guy. Paladin had done everything he could to prepare for the foreseeable, but what about the unforeseeable? What would this place be like? How easily would they find Jim, assuming they could find him? And what kind of life might they encounter? He and Leigh had already experienced something of what to expect; maybe they'd just been small-fry?

He knew Raven would enjoy the dive straight into the unknown: feet first, eyes open. But he was an Eternal, harder to kill than a cockroach. Paladin wasn't so lucky. He'd seen humanity pull itself up from its primitive beginnings, been hated and worshipped by a thousand cultures, loved and lost countless friends, but he couldn't laugh off a lead slug.

“Penny for them?” Raven’s voice pulled him up out of his dark thoughts.

He shook his head. “I’d be overcharging.”

“She’ll be fine. You did the right thing.”

It took Paladin a moment to catch on. He meant Leigh, of course. And sure he’d done the right thing. She’d be fine. Less than a month to go before the New Year. Piece of cake.

But Saint-Germain was also correct: you can’t cheat Fate. Paladin had been concentrating on keeping her out of trouble, but what was to stop her getting hit by a bus, or gunned down by some punk with a gun. Leigh was a tough cookie; even so—

No, he couldn’t think that. No one could. Go down that road and you’d never get out of bed in the morning. He’d be back in New York in a couple of days, by then she’d have cooled down and they could go back to looking out for each other.

“Sure. Everything’ll be just fine.”

So why did he feel like the universe was about to end?

V

"Guess it's time."

Paladin double-checked their position. Neither cloud layer had thinned, instruments were all he had to go on. That and gut-feeling. He twisted in his seat to check on Raven: he looked half-asleep. Seemed like he'd gotten over his fear of flying. Paladin reached back and tapped the other on his nodding head. "Reveille, fly boy!"

Raven twitched, jerking awake, hands raised in a curious gesture before relaxing. He pushed up his goggles and glared. "Don't ever do that again!"

Paladin grinned back nastily. "Never had you down as a jitterbug. Relax. Take a deep breath. You're on."

Raven eased goggles back into place, still giving Paladin the evil eye, and stared up into the leaden sky. The sun was up. Although wintry, it was dazzling in the cold, clear air. He unbuckled his harness and stood up in his cockpit. "You keep this machine steady, now."

"As a rock." Paladin faced front even though he wanted to watch Raven; see exactly what he was going to do. Instead he gripped the stick. The air was pretty calm, but with the rising sun, you never knew how that might change. He thought he heard the man in black chanting something that was masked by the rhythm of the prop and engine. For what felt like hours he kept the plane level, scanning the skies for changes that didn't happen. To come so far and then screw up—

A blast of thunder ripped through the air; clear above the engine noise. A second, and a third: the pounding of a titanic bell. Like an invisible giant was battering the firmament, trying to smash its way through. Paladin looked wildly about, seeking the source. A fourth rumble rolled across the sky, he clearly heard it pass above the plane, and this time something followed. A rip in the air: an ugly black rent which trailed behind the thunder as though caused by it.

The rent grew, expanded. In seconds it spread across over eighty degrees of arc, threatening to tear the sky ahead in two. A bloody light poured through. Paladin felt a rap on the head, and heard Raven's delighted laugh.

"Yeah, yeah. I see it."

He signaled to the second plane; though the pilot would have to have both eyes tight shut not to see the gateway Raven had opened. Pulling back on the stick, he put his Helldiver into a climb, heading straight for the blood-red breach. As they drew near, Paladin could see how the edges of the rent boiled and churned: tendrils writhing into the normal air like vast plumes of sickly-pink smoke. The entire gateway yawned and puckered, threatening to close at any moment.

The planes flew closer: gnats engulfed by the raw, smacking mouth of a leviathan. One moment they were bathed by the wintry sun of earth, the next the air was crimson and maroon, bilious green and livid purple, shot through with stringy clots of black. Huge threads which coiled and writhed in a resemblance of life. As the planes flew deeper, the threads coalesced into shapes; the sickly hues adding subtle shades, filling out the gaps, giving depth. Gargantuan faces stared down at the fly-past, expressions enigmatic and sardonic. Paladin couldn't shake the feeling he recognized some of them. From somewhere came a keening: the dirge of an entire universe in mourning.

Paladin felt Raven's breath on his cheek. "For the next few minutes, things might get a little strange."

"You figure?"

Raven chuckled and drew away. "You have no idea, my boy."

Paladin did his best to ignore him, concentrating instead on his instruments. He could no longer tell which was up or down; just prayed the altimeter and compass still worked in wherever the hell they were.

The scenes around him grew more real, if that was the word. They were beyond weird: no longer outlines, movies projected against the ghastly sky; moving pictures beyond the imagination of the most drug-addled Hollywood hack. He saw something like a three-faced Siamese temple statue, huge, and living. As it strode across the sky it became a figure of gold, at once both more and less human. For a while something like a transparent boat, its hull a pale green crystal, sailed parallel to the airplanes, floating on the sky as an ocean flowed above it. A vast, multi-limbed figure paced through crumbling ruins, life and a recreated city springing up in its wake. Five ragged islands rose from a fuming sea, becoming a clenched hand…

Whatever the images were, Paladin knew where they sprang from: Raven. The man in black was forcing his will on the universe, gouging a path between the worlds. The link was so intimate that his own memories took on a brief, blood-tinted life. It was something so outside Paladin's experience that he was grasped by helpless terror. He was so small, so insignificant; how in hell did he expect to find one man in a whole world? It would be like trying to find a single specific grain of sand in the Sahara. He realized he was trembling. Frigid sweat oozed down his face. God help him … how did Raven do it? How did he stay sane?

Lieutenant McNamara's face flashed across his memory for a moment, asking the same question. In that instant, Paladin sympathized.

Another giant, filling the sky ahead; pure black, its angular frame apparently cut from planet-sized chunks of obsidian, reached for the two biplanes. A flaming maw split its faceted head, and they were sucked into the inferno—

"Easy boy. We made it."

Paladin's eyes were squeezed shut. Not the best way to be flying a plane. He opened them, shivering in an icy sweat. The images had gone; the blood-red firmament had gone. Instead they flew below a sky the color of scoured bronze; below them stretched a rolling landscape of black and pale blue. Two suns, small and weak, hung in the dark sky.

"Jesus—"

"Like you said, sometimes it can get kind of rough." Raven clapped him on the back. "You did fine, Junior. For a beginner."

Paladin looked around the brazen sky. It was empty, no sign of anything like the huge shapes which had invaded the skies over Rhode Island. Opening a belt pouch he pulled out one of the corpse-white buds. Raising it by its short, soft stem, he watched as it stirred into life. The stem straightened, reaching for the bizarre suns; the bud cracked and opened, flowering into a glistening eye-like blossom. "Looks like we're in the right place."

Raven huffed. "I'm hurt you doubted me."

Paladin dropped the alien blossom over the side, watching as it spiraled to the black ground. "I think we ought to land for a while; take our bearings."

"You're the boss."

Paladin twisted in his seat, waving at the second plane. He gestured toward the ground; the pilot waggled the Helldiver's wings in acknowledgement. Returning his attention to the ground, Paladin thought: Now all we need's a flat stretch to get down on.

"Looks like rain ahead!"

Paladin glanced up at Raven's call. Sure enough, about a mile or so in the distance there was a dark, brooding mass that back home would have signaled rainclouds. There was even a faint, misty curtain hanging down. Paladin hoped they could find some place to set down before it hit, but it was moving fast, and toward them. "I'm not so sure that is rain."

He searched the ground with renewed urgency. It didn't look promising: everywhere the terrain rose and twisted; hills or small mountains serrated the surface; blotched growths which might have been a madman's idea of forest crawled along every surface. Well, he'd never kidded himself it was going to be easy.

He sneaked a quick glance at the approaching storm: it had gotten close far too fast. And it was bigger than he'd first thought: the cloudy mass appeared to be several miles deep; spread across half the sky.

Nothing for it. Paladin put his Helldiver into a shallow dive: get below whatever the storm was; skim the landscape, ready for the first sight of a suitable landing-site. A quick check confirmed the second plane was doing the same.

They dropped to what Paladin estimated was a couple of hundred feet above the crazily-undulating ground, following the extreme contours. If they couldn't maintain their altitude, a buffer zone between the airplanes and hard ground, it wouldn't be flying, just attempted suicide. At the peak of yet another climb, Paladin glanced up to the dark mass. It was directly above, blotting out both suns and the bronze sky. No rain was falling, or anything vaguely liquid.

He was wondering what the misty curtain was, and if he'd overreacted, when a thin black tendril speared out of the air, right in front of his plane. He slammed the stick to the right, hoping Raven was belted in, banking the Helldiver in a steep turn which had it slipping out of the sky. They dodged the tendril by a finger's breadth. As they passed, Paladin could just make out its knotted, twisted length, thicker than a man's torso, a curved, glistening hook on the end. A moment later it jerked, retracting back toward the dark mass.

"Fishing lines!" Raven sounded amused by the idea. Paladin didn't think it was so funny. He looked back: the second plane was banking left and right as a succession of hooked tendrils dropped around it, snapping back up each time the Helldiver twisted free.

They needed to fly even lower: into the suicide zone.

Dropping his plane's nose, Paladin was thankful that of all aircraft, he'd bought along dive bombers. Or was that another coincidence? They were certainly stacking up.

He banked wildly as another tendril writhed down, jerking back even as the starboard wingtips grazed it. Two more fell down to his left, and he jinked the plane to the right. Straightening up barely fifty feet above the erratic terrain, he realized there was nowhere for them to go: ahead, tendrils snatched and jerked at the ground, and a black and purple cliff reared almost to the cloud's base. They were either going to smash headlong, or be hooked, gaffed and landed by the mass overhead. "I could sure use some help right now!"

Raven yelled back. "What do you think I've been doing all this time? I can't affect those fishing lines, and to work on the angler I'd need to get a lot closer!"

"You might just get your wish!" Paladin turned the biplane away from the cliff, sending them straight toward a forest of bobbing tendrils.

With one hand on the stick, he pulled the burlap bag onto his lap and fumbled inside it. After a second's blind groping his fingers located something and pulled it free. The *Tzahar*: found in nameless ruins and stored in the fabled Templar Hoard since the days of the Crusades. As he raised the disturbingly asymmetric rock to eye level, he felt Raven behind him, leaning in close.

"You know what you're doing with that bauble, Junior?"

"Any bright ideas?"

"Beats me. Good luck!"

As Raven slumped back in his cockpit, Paladin peered at the opaque stone, looked at it, through it. Seen through a broken lens, he made out the writhing curtain of tendrils ahead, colors oddly shifted, drawing close far too quickly. He let his mind reach out, gazing mentally through the rock. For an instant there was nothing, just the object's cold, crystalline structure. Then he felt it: hiding from his perception, like it was standing just behind him, at the periphery of his vision. The *Tzahar* was alive, in a sense; or it was the home of … something. The shell of a weird, unearthly hermit crab.

The plane was almost in the midst of the forest of tendrils. Whatever he was going to do, Paladin had to do it now.

He threw the stone up as hard as he could, at the same time drawing his Mauser. Not even aiming, just trusting in his senses, he snapped off a shot. The slug hit the tumbling stone squarely, shattering it. There was a deafening retort, far too loud for an exploding rock. Bright streamers of nameless color splayed across the air. The tendrils recoiled as one, drawing swiftly up toward the dark, billowy mass. Something snatched for them, a something Paladin could see only in the corners of his eyes: a shifting, roiling shape which consisted of endless tentacles or thrashing arachnoid legs. It soared into the brazen sky, growing bigger and less tangible. By the time it reached the drifting, nebulous angler, it was more absence than presence, as vast as the dark cloud.

Paladin turned his plane, climbing; gazing up as he tried to make out what was happening far above him, but his brain refused to make sense of it. The dark mass was shredding, torn apart by something invisible, or so strange his mind blanked it out. He had an impression of thrashing, swirling, slithering, then the sky was clear of both vast cloudy fishing things, and whatever had hatched from the *Tzahar*.

Behind him, Raven was smiling, thumb and forefinger ringed in an *OK* gesture. "Impressive." Paladin was more concerned with the second plane. After a moment he spotted it: a half mile or so away, looking in good shape. So far, so good.

They were flying above the cliff face. Beyond it the ground was smooth and flat, stretched level. Paladin couldn't help but smile; it was like a game: they'd passed the first obstacle, so they were rewarded. Waggling the Helldiver's wings, he descended.

It wasn't so flat as it appeared from the air: scored by ruts which made the ground look like stretched taffy. Paladin's landing was bumpy, punctuated by Raven's endless complaints, but the landing gear held. Once they were down, Paladin vaulted from his cockpit and waited anxiously for the second plane to land. It stuttered. For a moment the tail reared, looking like the Helldiver was about to nose-first into the rocky, blue-black surface. It held, drawing to a halt a few feet from Paladin's own machine. The crew got down, dragging off flying helmets and goggles. Even as it occurred to Paladin that the pilot was far too short for a Marine, the clumsy coveralls both wore faded, drifting off in ectoplasmic smoke.

His world flipped, stomach taking a dive down a bottomless shaft. The short pilot was dressed in a pale brown, fitted flying jacket, tight riding pants and boots. The other was draped in a dove gray, ground brushing overcoat with a thick gold astrakhan collar and matching buttons. It was Leigh. Somehow, it was Leigh. And to make the day complete, her observer-gunner was Saint-Germain.

VI

Leigh braced herself for the eruption. It never came. Instead of verbally tearing her a new one or pulling one of his bean shooters and plugging Saint-Germain, Damy just deflated. His normally dark features paled and she could have sworn his eyes dulled: not the black, irrepressible blinkers she was used to.

This wasn't bad; it was a whole lot worse.

He turned away, muttering something to Andy Raven; sharing a look that meant nothing to her. She was in the soup, all right, just not in the way she'd figured. Behind her, the self-styled count cleared his throat.

"Not exactly the happy reunion I'd anticipated."

Damy stared at Saint-Germain, an ugly emotion back on his face. "If we didn't need four for this job, I'd drop you right now and leave you to whatever passes for tigers in this jungle. But when we get back to New York, you'd better start running. And fast!"

"Charming to the last." Saint-Germain stepped in front of Leigh, raising his cane. He brought it up to his face like a fencer saluting his opponent. After a moment he flicked it down and away, bowing in Raven's direction. "It's been too long, sir."

Raven gave a strained, half smile. "And still not long enough, Leo. I thought the last time we parted I promised to kill you on sight."

The count shrugged. "I was a foolish boy, my lord, with the arrogance of youth."

"Maybe so." Raven brushed at the lapels of his long black coat. "But keep it in mind, just in case Junior misses."

Saint-Germain turned to Leigh, grinning insolently. "Such gratitude."

She ignored him, feeling in her jacket pockets for a pack of Luckies. She lit up. It felt reassuring: a familiar gesture in this bizarre landscape. "Listen, mister, I don't care what game you're playing—" She glanced at Damy and Raven, including them. "Any of you. But as I understand it, we're here to rescue some guy from a fate worse than death. So if you'll can the pissing contest, maybe we can get on with it?"

Raven clapped Damy on the shoulder. "She's all right, Junior. Damned if I don't think we'll make it after all."

Damy continued to glower at both Saint-Germain and Leigh, but when he spoke his tone was lighter. "You mean you didn't earlier?"

The man in black waved a hand. "I had a couple of doubts."

Damy shook his head, glancing up at the weird sky. "So now we are here, you think maybe you could locate Jim?"

Raven laughed. "Hell, no. I'm here just to make up the numbers. Just give me a moment." He strode off in the direction of the planes.

Damy stood in front of Leigh. She tensed herself, but he cupped her face in his hands. The haunted look in his eyes made her ache all over. "I'm not happy you're here, princess." He dropped his hands, catching her round the waist, pulling her close. "Maybe it's better this way: looking out for each other. It's what we do best, huh?"

"You got it, big guy— But now you're scaring me."

"Plenty to be scared of." He released her and turned away. "Raven! You ready yet?"

"You know what they say about patience, Junior— Ah! Ready."

Leigh watched Raven jump down from the plane. As he came toward them, long black coat flaring out like a cloak, she shivered involuntarily. He looked far too much at home in this nightmarish world. More than he ever had back in Manhattan. Despite his ready grin and careless manner, he gave her the heebie-jeebies.

They gathered round Raven. He held a bundle in an upturned palm: a simple leather bag, cinched around the neck with strips of rawhide. Raven cleared his throat in a theatrical manner, tugging at a sleeve with his free hand. "Now pay attention, kiddies. At no time do my wrists leave my arms."

Leigh found it hard not to be amused by Damy's pained expression. Behind her, the count muttered a phrase she hadn't heard in years.

Raven deftly untied the rawhide strips and opened the bag, each gesture as exaggerated as a two-bit stage performer. Spreading the pouch flat across his palm, he exposed three small items. They looked like a tiny kettle, a bowl, and a juicer. Toys, Leigh thought, from a kid's dollhouse.

Saint-Germain muttered over her shoulder. "Splendid. We're about to take a picnic."

"Cork it, Leo!" Raven picked the kettle up between thumb and forefinger and handed it to Leigh. "Hold tight, your grace; things will get strange in a moment or two."

Your grace? She hadn't heard that one since she'd been out of diapers. She tried to catch Raven's eye, but he was too busy handing out the remaining toys: the bowl to Damy, juicer to the count.

"Are we ready?" No one spoke. He made an odd flourish, Leigh felt the kettle twitch. A moment later it was weighing against her palms: it was growing, getting heavier. Within seconds it wasn't a doll's kettle anymore, but full-sized. She had to adjust her grip real fast; otherwise she'd have dropped it. Glancing up, she could see the bowl and juicer had gotten big, too.

"Oh, murder!"

Raven looked pleased with her reaction; Damy pulled a sour face. "He's showing off, princess. We could have packed the full-sized stuff just as easily."

"Don't spoil it, Junior. Let the audience have their fun."

"Just the audience?"

Raven didn't reply, but his dark eyes twinkled. Taking the bowl he placed it on the scoured ground, three-quarters filling it with water from the kettle. Then he picked up the juicer and removed something from a coat pocket. Leigh thought it was a lime, up to the moment it tried to squirm free of Raven's hand. Before it could escape, the man in black pushed it down onto the juicer, twisting and wringing until the shape stopped moving and a thin, clear gray fluid trickled out of it.

"Jeez…!" Try as she might, Leigh couldn't help feeling a little nauseous. What in hell was that thing?

Raven tossed the crushed shape onto the ground and carefully poured gray fluid into the bowl in a slow corkscrew pattern. The liquids didn't mix, staying separate as oil and water.

"Anyone got a light?"

Wordlessly, her hand shaking not so much, Leigh handed over a book of matches. Raven struck one, dropping it into the bowl as it flared. Leigh thought it had gone out. A moment later there was a dull pop, and thick smoke curled slowly up from the bowl. Leigh gagged: the stench was unbelievable.

The smoke twisted and roiled, bending around itself like it was alive, becoming a gray, oily, upward wriggling spiral. For a moment it reared, swayed and twitched like a snake scenting the air; then it arched across the bronze sky, skimmed the top wings of the landed airplanes. Counting off the seconds from a heart which felt like it was about to fill her throat, Leigh knew half a minute passed as the column of smoke writhed into the air and away, drawing an almost perfectly straight line across the sky. Then the slow writhing stopped, the line collapsed into foul-smelling, coarse dust.

Raven folded his arms and gazed off in the direction the smoke had indicated. "If this was back in New York, I'd say Jim was only around twenty miles away."

VII

Airborne, they covered the twenty miles in minutes. The only problem: the terrain looked impossible to land on. Beyond the scoured plain, the land rose up in ragged black peaks which looked needle sharp from the air. Once they were circling the spot where Raven assured Paladin that Jim Stanley would be found there was nothing but tall, sheer peaks which raked the air like the teeth of a colossal shark. It was starting to look as though they'd have to turn back and walk.

Then Paladin saw the scar: cutting through the black peaks in a straight line; heading in exactly the direction they wanted. Anywhere else, he'd have said it looked man-made. He dropped his plane, circling down toward the slice through the mountains. Up close it resembled a canyon, scoured out of the black rock. There were even long, parallel grooves in the surface like a team of vast steam-shovels had gnawed their way through the terrain, scooping out the bed for a new highway.

The second Helldiver was circling a hundred feet above him. He pointed toward the canyon with an exaggerated swoop of his arm, before going in for a landing. The ruts grew deeper, too deep, waiting to catch at the landing gear and snap off wheel struts. He took his kite down as gently as he could. Even so it bounced and lurched across the hard, uneven ground, threatening to tip. He dropped the tail and brought the plane to a quick stop, watching anxiously as Leigh repeated the maneuver. Her two-seater hit the ground so hard he couldn't believe the landing gear didn't shatter. The tail slewed to the left, the whole plane spinning. She got it under control, cutting the engine and allowing the plane to coast to a shaky halt. Paladin started breathing again.

He climbed out of his cockpit, Raven half-stumbling from his own. Leigh and Saint-Germain were already out of their plane and walking gingerly toward him, the count carrying what looked like an oversized rifle. Leigh's pale face was glistening with perspiration.

From behind him, Paladin heard Raven snort. "An elephant gun, Leo? Rather pedestrian for you, isn't it?"

Saint-Germain rested the massive gun on the ground. Typically, it was gold plated and inlaid with pearl. "A Mauser 13 mm anti-tank rifle, actually. Think of it when a blimp-sized creature is bearing down on you and you can't get the wording right." He levelled the cannon at Raven's head. "Bang."

Paladin fetched the burlap bag from his plane. As he looped the strap across a shoulder he gave the small expedition the once-over: four against a world. They really were insane. "Anything you can think of, grab it now. Food, water, and whatever might make good weapons. We leave in five minutes." He gave the sky a quick scan: it looked clear. No cloudy thing trailing living hooks, no vast tentacled monstrosity. But for the bizarre colors and needle-sharp mountains all around, they could be about to going hiking among the hoodoos of Utah or Wyoming.

He didn't see Leigh until she prodded his arm. "You see any giant apes, don't start getting any ideas."

"Yes, Miss Wray—" With a stab of alarm, he realized what she'd used to poke him with. "Where in hell did you get the Chicago Typewriter?"

She shouldered the Tommy Gun, wide grin on her face. "'S the matter? Counts as a weapon, don't it?" She was also carrying a large bag over the other shoulder; the way it clattered, Paladin guessed it was chock full of spare 50-round drums for the submachine gun.

"You can take the girl outta the gangs—" He checked on Raven and Saint-Germain. "We hot to trot?" Raven was absently balancing the Spear over one shoulder. Saint-Germain, cradling his

Mauser, was staring at it like a starving man in an abattoir. Both nodded.

Leigh brought him up short. “What about the planes? We can’t just leave them; something might, I dunno, chew them up, or something.”

“Oh, yes, almost forgot.”

At the sound of Raven’s voice, Paladin turned. Too late: the two Helldivers were already gone.

Leigh stared at the empty stretch of rutted ground, and back at Paladin. “Hey! Where’d they go?”

Paladin stared at Raven in irritation; why did he have to showboat all the time? “He made them vanish.”

“As in invisible?”

Raven looked hurt. “Vanish? Invisible?”

Saint-Germain snorted. “You see, my dear, if they were simply invisible it’s possible one or more of the things living here might detect them: different senses, you know. Raven, with typical grandstanding, has moved them… sideways, a touch. They’re still there, and at the same time, not.”

Leigh groaned softly, glancing at Paladin. “Sorry I asked.”

Paladin touched her arm lightly. “C’mon. I don’t want to be still here when whatever passes for night falls.” He set off; the rest fell in behind.

Saint-Germain called after him. “Regarding that, nightfall, I mean, have you been watching the two suns?”

Paladin paused to glance up at the blue stars glowing sullenly overhead. It took a moment before he caught on. “The biggest one hasn’t shifted.”

“Exactly. Whilst the smaller has moved through around thirty degrees. I might suggest this world never has a night.”

“That might be no bad thing.”

“You reckon?” Raven didn’t sound convinced. “Eternal daylight might mean nothing ever sleeps.”

Saint-Germain chuckled. “Intriguing concept: an entire realm driven half-mad through sleep-deprivation.”

“If I’d known the kids were going to keep arguing, I’d have left them back home.” Leigh’s *sotto voce* comment almost made Paladin laugh out loud. He bit his lip.

The quality of the light grew oppressive, the blue suns casting an unsettling deep-water gloom over the landscape. Though it wasn't particularly warm, Paladin felt hot and clammy. For a place with no obvious open water, it was strangely humid.

"You know any hiking songs?" Leigh's voice was loud and startling in the quiet.

"Getting to you too, huh?"

"What about Krazy Kat and Ignatz back there?"

"If they do, it'd be like nothing you ever heard."

"Afraid you were gonna say that." A moment later Paladin heard her whistling softly to herself: a muted but defiant sound. He smiled, despite the pang the hushed tune gave him. Attagirl.

The smaller sun was close to setting, exaggerating the underwater feel. It may never get dark, but Paladin could tell the lighting was going to vary considerably. As it sank toward the horizon, the blue sun cast blood-tinted shadows off spear-pointed peaks. Automatically, Paladin drew his Mauser, thumbing off the safety. Who knew what might be hidden by those shadows, drawn out by sunset and partial twilight. Life back home responded to changes in the Sun and Moon; why should it to be so different here?

He called a brief halt. On either side of the canyon, spears of black rock towered above them: the spires and minarets of a nightmare cathedral. Paladin pulled a canteen out of his bag and restricted himself to a couple of swallows even though his mouth was drier than any desert. Leigh drank some of her own ration; Raven passed a dark flask to Saint-Germain, who sucked on it greedily. The count produced cigarettes. As he, Leigh and Raven smoked, the smaller sun disappeared, leaving them in a bloody, oppressive gloom.

Paladin heard a dry rattle to his right, off in the mountains. He glanced up, raising his Mauser. There was another rattle, a stone jarred loose. The eerie silence returned.

Leigh leaned in close to whisper. "Mountain lions?"

"If we're lucky." Paladin dropped his canteen back in the bag. "Okay, coffee break's over."

They moved slower now: in the poor light it would be too easy to slip on the rutted surface, turn an ankle. Leigh fell in beside Paladin, swinging her machine gun in one hand. "I got to say you sure know how to treat a lady."

"I thought you girls went ape for a walk in the moonlight."

She glanced at him. He couldn't make out her expression. "You really think your pal is still okay?"

"You mean not dead? No, I'm pretty sure he's still alive." Though he might not be sane any longer. Even Raven would have gotten the willies after thirty or forty years spent in a place like this. "Would I have gone to all this trouble otherwise?"

She stared at Paladin for so long he stared to get twitchy. "Yes. Because you'd never allow yourself to believe anything else. It's a kind of faith. I've never known anyone have so much faith as you… Except maybe that Andy Raven bird."

Paladin blinked heavily; the damned place was dusty as hell. "Yeah, well… You've heard of the faith of angels?"

"No."

"Guess you wouldn't. Think I just made it up."

"Don't get me wrong, you can still be a real jerk. Like not wanting me to come on this caper."

"Yeah, about that… How'd you persuade Saint-Germain to bring you along?"

"I didn't. He offered."

Paladin froze. He grabbed her shoulder, turning her to face him. "Just out the kindness of his heart, huh? He say anything else? Like why I didn't want you along in the first place?"

Leigh's face set in stubborn lines. "He said you had your reasons."

He dropped his hand, sighing. "I do. And you can be sure he's got his own reasons, too. Don't trust him, princess."

"Who says I do? And when you get down to it, I'm not sure I trust Andy Raven too much, either. Don't care what he is to you."

Paladin tried on his hardest glare but couldn't keep it up. His face relaxed despite himself. "You're learning."

After a while, she smiled back. "In case you hadn't noticed, it's getting light again."

She was right. A quick check of the sky showed Paladin the smaller sun was rising. "Well that night sure flew by."

Saint-Germain pointed with his artillery piece. "Now what do you suppose that is?"

Ahead was a sheer cliff of what at first glance looked like ice: opaque, shot through with blues and pinks, surface sparkling in the strange dawn. It was too smooth for ice, too round; bulging near the ground like Jell-O. And there were things moving inside it: small, black, wriggling sluggishly.

They moved nearer: Paladin aiming his Mauser, Leigh leveling her Tommy Gun. Up close, the cliff was obviously quivering faintly, vibrating. It was attached to the upward-spearing black rocks on either side of the canyon, hanging from thick, gelid ropes of goo. Paladin touched a palm to the surface: it twitched, as if alive. And it was warm; he could feel it even through the leather glove.

Something wriggled in the depths of the gel, dark and shadowy. Paladin had the impression he was watching some dimly-seen predator rising out of the ocean's depths. He took a backward step just as a glistening tentacle spat from the ooze, lashing the air where, a moment earlier, his face had been. "Natives none too friendly."

"They just want to invite you in for breakfast." Raven had caught them up, though Saint-Germain was still lagging. The man in black pointed at something in the gel, around a yard or so above Paladin's head. It looked the size and shape of a football. Whatever it was, it didn't seem to be moving much.

Paladin rubbed at his face. "I had been thinking frogspawn; now I'm not so sure. A trap of some kind?"

"Frogspawn?" Leigh's eyes were scanning the quivering surface. "I wouldn't want to meet the frog that laid that. Five bucks says it'll have tentacles!"

Raven prodded at the surface with his forefinger. A dark shape flowed to the surface; a glistening tendril whipped out of the goo. Somehow Raven dodged the squirming limb, catching it instead with both hands. "Somebody give me a hand!"

Leigh jumped forward before Paladin could stop her. As Raven hauled, she grabbed at whatever he was trying to land. Paladin swore quietly, holstering his pistol, and joined in.

The thing was strong; black, multi-jointed body hard and chitinous. It was like trying to hang onto something the size of a dog which could tie itself in knots, was covered in feelers and squirming tentacles, and coated in thick, slippery jelly. Even with three of them hanging on it almost slimed free. Eventually they hauled it out and dumped it, writhing, slashing and snapping, on the scoured ground. As he watched it flailing a variety of limbs and stretching what looked like rudimentary wings, Paladin felt a touch of recognition. Leigh caught on first. “It looks like those flying things I shot down over Rhode Island!”

She was right. It did resemble those flying tentacles which had come through the rift. Simpler in form, maybe. You might even say embryonic.

“A larval form.” Raven crouched beside the thing, gingerly prodding it. “Maybe the things you fought weren’t fully mature, either, Miss Oswin.”

“Jeez.” Her face wrinkled with disgust. “Don’t like the thought of killing babies.”

A harsh, metallic buzzing scoured the air besides Paladin’s head. He leapt aside, going for his Mauser again. It was a bug, a big one; but it didn’t seem to have any interest in him or the others. For a moment it hovered clumsily above the gel’s twitching surface before settling. Paladin found himself eyeballing something like a football-sized, flying wood louse, its segmented body splashed by a scintillation of rainbow colors. Another buzzed past and landed on the surface, followed by three more, then a dozen. In seconds, the whole surface was darkened by a swarm of huge bugs. If he had to guess, Paladin would have said they were eating the stuff.

Heavy wheezing announced Saint-Germain’s arrival. “I thought we were here to rescue someone!” He sounded tetchy as he did breathless. “Not admire the wildlife!”

Raven clapped him on the shoulder, smiling. “Relax, Leo, I’ve a hunch you’ll enjoy the next bit.”

Paladin took a couple more steps back. The thing on the ground spat out a long tendril, trying to snare his ankle. He stamped down, hard.

There was an eruption in the squirming layer of bugs. A thrashing, fleshy limb spat from the goo and coiled around one of the giant insects, dragging it down. More tendrils lashed out, each one fixing on a bug. For a minute or more, the surface was alive with wriggling limbs, a vast, ciliated single-celled organism. Then everything quietened: the flailing limbs vanished. The carpet of bugs gradually dissipated, leaving the opaque gel dotted with newly ingested footballs. Most were still moving.

"Well, that was pleasant." Leigh pouted with disgust.

"I think you'll find there are parallels in your world." Saint-Germain seemed to have recovered his morbid wit along with his breath. He fitted a cigarette in his holder and lit it, inhaling with relish. Leigh snapped her fingers at him.

"Hey, Nelly, butt me!" The count lit a cigarette and handed it to her.

Raven was staring at the towering cliff of ooze. "I guess we'll have to go around."

Paladin shrugged. "They've had lunch. We should be—" A loud rasp cut through his words. He spun around. "What in hell?"

There were a couple more rattles, louder than gunshots: the sound of something big and jagged dragging against the black rock. It set Paladin's teeth on edge. He drew both automatics. "I don't think we're out of it yet."

Harsh and staccato, the sounds rattled on all sides. The four spread out in a rough semicircle, the wall of ooze at their backs. Paladin, the count and Leigh held their guns ready; Raven stood tense and alert, leaning on the Spear.

Something out of nightmare lurched over the spears of rock. Big as a truck, it could have been a giant lobster, or scorpion, except claws and barbed stings projected from every jointed, armored limb. Its exoskeleton looked as jagged as the rocks, shot through with the yellow and purple of a day-old bruise. It crawled down onto the flat surface, a scattering of eyes across its head flashing in the blue light. The way the thing watched and moved, Paladin couldn't help thinking there was a more than rudimentary intelligence at work inside the vast, misshapen body.

Another of the things appeared to his left, and a second. Three more loomed over the crags to Paladin's right. Two scuttled out of cover, either side of the gel cliff and level with the top. They skittered along rocky peaks, legs clashing against the keen edges, flanking the humans below as they made straight for the opaque wall. Paladin trained his Mauser on the one nearest him. "Watch out!"

Raven raised a hand. "I don't think it's us they're after."

A moment later, both creatures bulldozed the top of the ooze. Claws churning like shovels, they hacked into the gel, carving away dripping clods of the stuff, tunneling slowly but inexorably.

Dead bugs were snatched free and dropped into mandibles whirring like buzz saws. Anything still alive was impaled by whipping stingers before suffering the same fate. A dirty froth bubbled from churning mouth parts. Ragged strips of flesh hung in ribbons from claws and stingers.

Paladin divided his attention between the two feeding and the six on the ground: so far, none of them had made a move. Almost as if they were waiting.

Leigh flicked her cigarette away. "Looks like it's just the tadpoles they're after. We could just step aside while they chow down."

Paladin wasn't so sure. A moment later, Raven put his thoughts into words. "If I'm not mistaken, that ooze is pretty resistant to things from outside. Those super-scorpions look like they're having a tough time getting in."

Saint-Germain dropped his cigarette stub, collapsed the holder and slipped it carefully into a pocket. "And you're suggesting they might find us a little easier as prey?"

"Something like that."

"Oh, murder!" Leigh levelled her machine gun, aiming it in the general direction of the six super-scorpions. "Any one of those so much as gnashes its teeth, I'm opening up!"

"Maybe we ought to just try and step aside first, princess." Paladin began to shuffle to the right side of the canyon, not taking his eyes off the unmoving creatures. "Standing between them and dinner's making me kind of nervous."

"*You're* nervous!" But she stepped away, attention and gun fixed on the giant arachnids.

The four of them split evenly: Paladin and Leigh on the right, Raven and the count to the left. If nothing else, it gave them good crossfire. The creatures still didn't move. If their multiple eyes had been capable of swiveling, Paladin reckoned they would have been like gunfighters in the final showdown: motionless except for the eyes.

He risked a glance up: the other two monsters were deep into the ooze now: slow-moving silhouettes; swimmers in a sea of cold molasses. Was there meant to be some kind of signal? Would the other six only move when the vanguard reached a specific point in the ooze? Or was he giving them too much credit?

In the end they caught him by surprise. From total stillness to freight train speed, all six leapt forward together, not making for the wall of ooze, but his party. Three and three, split evenly; claws raised, stingers whipping.

Leigh opened up without prompting. Her Tommy Gun clattered in brief, sporadic bursts; the shells bouncing off the creatures' armor. Paladin took a more clinical approach, snapping off 9 mm shells at anything which looked like a target: joints, eyes, mouth. The things twitched in irritation and kept on coming.

"Back up!"

Paladin wasn't sure who yelled the order, but it seemed like a smart idea. All four of them retreated into the needle-sharp, rocky forest beyond the scoured canyon. They could at least take some shelter amongst the towering black spires. He ducked as one of the things crawled over the rocks, blotting out the sun. Emptying his Mauser and Browning into the exposed underbelly just made it mad. Claws and stingers raked between the peaks, straining for him. Dodging and ducking, he reloaded rapidly. A stinger knifed the air inches from his face; firing at point-blank range, a Mauser slug shattered it. Thick, foul-smelling fluid splashed the rocks, etching ruts in it.

"Princess! How you doing?"

"Oh, real swell!" She threw aside an empty drum magazine, snapped in a fresh one, and blazed away at the head of a scorpion which was trying to ram itself into her sheltering channel.

"Watch the blood! It's like acid!"

"Now he tells me!" She scrambled back, still firing. The thing pursuing her jerked and squealed, small pieces of it spinning away. Pools of foul blood smoked on the ground.

"Raven!" He doubted the man in black could hear above the gunfire and was surprised when he heard a reply: calm and clear above the clamor.

"No need to shout, Junior..." He was using some trick, of course; literally throwing his voice.

"How's it with you...?"

"Peachy, as Miss Oswin would say. Leo's about to try out his oversized pop gun—"

The deafening roar actually drowned him out. Paladin risked a glance between the black spires: one of the creatures was rearing up on the far side of the canyon, blood pouring from a splintery hole in its armored body. Several sharp spires of rock were slowly dissolving.

"I'll be damned. He brought something useful."

There was a flash of black light, and another mammoth scorpion fell back, two legs and part of the head sheared cleanly through. Raven's work: putting the Spear of Destiny to good use. Two out of three, Paladin thought: they were doing better than him and Leigh. "I'll leave you boys to your fun."

"Actually, Junior—we're in a bit of a spot. Leo's howitzer doesn't work so well in tight spaces, and neither of us has anything else to hand."

And there was one left. "Jeez…!"

"What's up?" Leigh slid in beside him, twisting to throw more lead at a creature which was combing between peaks with its forelimbs. It backed off, hissing. Paladin had the feeling they were learning.

"We got two magicians and no spells."

"Of course we do—"

They both blazed away at a creature as it scuttled above them, multiple legs balancing on the needle points. One of its limbs split, leaking acid blood, and it skipped away.

"So I guess it's up to me." He swung his burlap bag in front on him; reaching inside, reaching out with his senses. Reaching for—

It was like an electric shock; he snatched his hand out. Nestled between his fingers was the bizarre chunk of Buck Rogers paraphernalia from Doctor Brook's lab: the thing Marie had given to Leigh. Well that was useful; he didn't even know what it was for.

"Princess, I'm going need you to watch my back for a while."

"Just like normal, huh."

Paladin crawled to a chunk of rock which had a deep hollow in the base: somewhere that protected him on nearly three sides, safe from ambush. The rest was up to Leigh. Tucking himself into the niche he slowly blotted out all external distractions: the chop of Leigh's machine gun, the squeal of the creatures, the occasional roar of Saint-Germain's cannon, the splashes of corrosive blood landing scarily close.

He sank into the piece of machinery, drifted along the wiring, stretched across the relays and switches; probed and quested. Eventually—

My, my...

He snapped back, the noise of battle deafening after the profound silence. He glanced around, momentarily confused. Then he spotted Leigh, standing between two black peaks, drilling a purple and yellow nightmare which snapped foaming mandibles a yard from her head. An unstoppable Amazon. The magazine emptied; she unclipped it, spun it straight into the thing's eyes, pulled a fresh one from her bag and reloaded. The scorpion lunged, taking advantage of the lull in fire, jaws gaping. Paladin leapt to his feet, snatching a grenade from a belt pouch and pitched it.

"Princess! Duck!"

She dropped to the ground. The grenade sailed overhead, landing underneath the scorpion, and detonated. Shrapnel tore through the joints in the thing's armor. It shrieked, trying to scrabble up and away, but it was too crippled. Paladin lobbed two more grenades at the thrashing shape. The blasts cracked it like a Maine lobster. It stilled, hanging from a tangle of limbs, too big to fall to the ground, blood dissolving a pit below it.

Leigh got back on her feet, glancing briefly at the dripping ruin. She turned a wide grin on Paladin, making an OK sign with her right hand.

"Why don't they just give up, princess?" Quickly he checked the loads in his two automatics. "Digging tadpoles out of thick goo's easier than this."

"I think they're just burned."

Paladin looked around. Far as he could tell, there were just three of the giant arachnids left, plus the two which had buried themselves in the goo. Maybe he'd get away with it at that.

"Princess!" He held up Doctor Brooks' gadget. "I'm going to finish this. In a couple of minutes it's going to get pretty crazy round here."

"Get?"

He blew her a kiss and vaulted an outcrop of black rock. Weaving through the crystalline forest, he called out to Raven. "How you guys doing?"

"Swell. Leo's now out of ammo..." It was just like the man in black was beside him.

"And you?"

"Just ideas."

Paladin laughed softly. "That I lived to see it—" He was out of the rocky shelter now, out in the open, sprinting for the wall of goo. "Hold tight, the cavalry's coming!"

"Should I be reassured?"

Paladin ignored the tone, skidding to a halt right up against the quivering wall. He placed Brook's dingus on the ground, flicking a couple of switches, hoping he was guessing right. A green light lit. Encouraging.

He turned, pulling off a glove. Sticking thumb and a finger between his lips he blew a long, blistering whistle. "Hey, uglies!"

Three arachnids—one to his left, two on his right—paused, turning in his direction. They waved a variety of damaged and dripping limbs, tensing.

He knelt, reaching for the gadget, placing his right forefinger over a plain button. He could feel the device gently vibrating; he was sure it was whining softly. The moment they made their charge—

But they continued to wait: poised, wary. "Well? What you waiting for?"

He had his answer seconds later as over a dozen more of the things scuttled into the canyon.

VIII

Leigh was on her feet the moment she spotted the new bunch of super-scorpions. Slinging machine gun over her shoulder, she climbed the nearest spire of black rock, ignoring the rips in her clothing, each stinging cut. Reaching the jagged peak she saw Damy far below: crouching by the wall of jelly, watching both the original trio of monsters and the newcomers swarming toward him.

She unslung her chopper, aiming at the scuttling mass. At this range it'd be as much use as a pea shooter, but by God she wasn't leaving him alone down there. She squeezed the trigger. Bullets sprayed into the advancing hoard; they didn't so much as twitch. Even the three standing guard ignored her.

"If I had a couple of Damy's pineapples I'd get your attention!"

She clipped in a fresh drum, emptying it into the nearest of the things. She could smell hot metal, knew the machine gun was overheating. She didn't care.

The swarm in the canyon was almost on Damy. Leigh screamed, her fear and anger beyond words. He was going to get torn to bits right in front of her, and she was so goddamned helpless.

The world turned inside out—

It was as though ripples spread out from Damy's kneeling figure, distorting the forest of black rock into waves of pulsing black light. The swarm of scorpions was drowned by the dark sea. Moments later Leigh could see nothing. She heard the roaring of vast breakers. The flood smashed into her, she staggered under the impact. It washed through her mind; thoughts torn out by their roots. She felt it scour every atom. She was a kid's sandcastle hit by high tide; in seconds there'd be no sign she'd ever existed.

Then it was gone. The flood subsided, leaving her bruised, battered, alive. She blinked; with each squeeze of her eyelids the world grew a little clearer. More in focus. She raised her head: she was still standing on the black peak; she hadn't been dashed to the spikes below, ripped and impaled to death. It just felt like it.

She was terrified to look down into the canyon. But Damy was there: him and nothing else. The scorpions had gone, and so had the towering wall of jelly. No, that wasn't right; shreds of gloop still clung to jagged outcrops, slowly puddling on the ground. And the floor of the canyon was littered by what could have been chunks of giant bug.

Leigh took in an unsteady breath. "Pharaoh's army got drowned; O Mary don't you mourn…" Her limbs shaky as her breathing, she descended the black spire.

IX

Paladin flicked his left hand, trying to shake off the thick goo stuck to it. The stuff didn't budge, just hung in oozing strands from his fingers. There was a clot of it hanging from his nose too. Classy.

"Let me know when you plan something like that again, Junior. It's given me quite the headache." Raven and Saint-Germain were stepping out of their concealment, both dusting at their long coats as if they were the ones dripping with disgusting gel. The count spared a glance for the twisted, blackened chunk of metal Paladin was holding in his right hand.

"Would you mind telling me where you found that toy?"

Paladin took a last look at the ruined dingus before dropping it. "Off a crazy man back in New York. He had a real bee in his bonnet about the human soul."

Saint-Germain nodded thoughtfully. "Doctor Brook. I thought I recognized the workmanship."

"Of course you'd have known him." Paladin had another try at flicking off the goo, but it seemed to be growing thicker.

"Our paths crossed occasionally."

Raven prodded at the mangled device with the heel of his spear. "Interesting gizmo. It's had a profound effect on anything in range not possessed of a human soul." He glanced at the destruction around them.

"So how did it blow up that wall of Jell-O?" Leigh picked at the stuff glued to Paladin: it stuck like fresh gum.

Saint-Germain chuckled. "It was filled with soulless creatures, my dear. Like so many cherry bombs." He clicked his fingers. "Poof!"

"At least it cleared us a way." Paladin was relieved to discover the drying gel was starting to peel away in ragged sheets, leaving clean patches on his dusty leather coat.

"Not exactly." The count pointed with his now useless gun. In the distance there was another wall of glistening jelly, if anything bigger than the one Paladin had just brought down.

Raven was looking at the brazen sky. "Not only that, but I think the sun's about to go down again."

Paladin glanced at Leigh; she was the only one not taking peculiar pleasure in the situation. "Swell."

She shouldered her Tommy Gun carelessly. "C'mon. Didn't they tell you nothing was easy back in hero school?"

"I must have cut that class."

They stepped carefully through shards of giant scorpion and chunks of drying gel. The stuff was hardening rapidly, shriveling and wrinkling into gnarled shapes. And it was starting to smell. As the smaller sun plunged out of sight and the bloody gloom descended again, the unnatural twilight was thickened by a growing stench. Leigh gagged. "Smells worse than the East River."

Paladin sniffed unobtrusively at his flying coat, not entirely sure he wasn't carrying some of that stench around with him.

There were exploded remains of bugs mixed in with the hardening gel, black ribbons of matter, torn and shattered by whatever Dr. Brook's gizmo had done to them. Paladin was sure he could make out other corpses, out on the edges of the canyon, hanging off spears of rock, so torn up it was impossible to even guess how they'd looked alive. The only sound Paladin heard in the half-night was the rattle of chitinous remains falling to the ground.

Brook had missed his true calling: the government could have used a man with such a genius for destruction.

They'd pretty much halved the distance to the next blockade when the smaller sun sprang above the horizon again. Paladin halted, looking at his wristwatch. "Must be midsummer. That was even shorter than the last time."

“Oh it’s better than that.” Raven was looking over Paladin’s shoulder, his expression that of a man who’d found lost treasure. “That sun has just risen from the exact point it set.”

Paladin produced his canteen and took a careful sip of tepid water. “Long as those giant bugs don’t spontaneously reassemble themselves, I really don’t care.”

Leigh spun around, leveling her machine gun, and glared back the way they’d come. After a second she faced front again, lowering her gun and looking sheepish. “Just checking.”

Saint-Germain shrugged and took out his cigarette case, offering smokes all around. “Nothing would surprise me here.”

They continued in silence, the smell of the count’s expensive tobacco drowning out the decaying gel. The wall ahead loomed taller, appearing to glow with its own azure light. It was definitely larger than the first: a Boulder Dam formed out of heavy, slow-moving gel. Gentle waves crisscrossed its surface, taking minutes to lap from one corner to another. Small dark shapes oozed deep inside; smoky forms moving with a leisurely, dreamlike ease. Stopping around twenty feet from the base, Paladin gazed up at the opalescent monolith. “Here we go again.”

Leigh joined him. “Guess you don’t have any more of those soul bombs handy?”

Both Raven and Saint-Germain were glancing around uneasily; the man in black’s hands twitching on his spear’s shaft. Paladin wondered what they were both looking for. “Something on your mind?”

The count ignored him, but Raven’s coal-black eyes flickered in Paladin’s direction. “The last dawn, or whatever you want to call it, things got interesting.”

Leigh raised her gun, suddenly as jittery as the two men. “Feeding time, huh?”

“Everything has to eat.” Saint-Germain kept his attention on the skies. “Sun-up’s as good a time as any.”

Paladin left them to it: with three pairs of anxious eyes scanning the terrain he didn’t think they were likely to get bushwhacked. He kept his concentration on the wall of thick goo. They were going to have to get past it somehow; blowing it into stinking chunks wasn’t an option any more. So if they couldn’t go through or around it, that left—

He dug into a couple of belt pouches, slipping out two large jack-knives. He flicked open their blades, both nearly five inches long, and wickedly sharp. Leigh spotted what he was doing.

"You figure on carving your way through?"

"Nuh-huh." Stepping up to the wall, he stabbed one knife in and leaned on it. The gel seemed dense enough to take the weight. He stretched up and stuck in the second knife, pulling himself up. Then he slid out the first—it resisted more than when it entered—reached high and knifed himself another hand-hold. He heard Raven laugh appreciatively.

"Good job, Junior. Think you make the top without getting eaten?"

Leaving both knives embedded in the goo, Paladin unholstered his automatics. "That's where you come in." He handed the Mauser to Raven and the Browning to Saint-Germain. "Try not to hit me."

Saint-Germain's face lit with understanding. "I will do my best to keep the hands steady, old sport."

"You'd better." He nodded at Leigh's machine gun. "Princess, switch that Chicago Typewriter to single shot."

"Will do, coach."

He gave them all a brave smile he didn't feel and faced the wall again. "Then here goes man's first attempt on the North Face of the Jell-O Horn."

He started to scale the gently undulating wall, carving his way slowly and painfully up the opaque goo. He found he could kick the toes of his boots into the muck easily enough, and the footholds bore his weight; it was dragging them free of the sucking gel which took time. After five minutes, sweat was running down his face and soaking his undershirt. He understood how the mammoths stuck in the La Brea tar pits must have felt.

A black shadow grew out of the opalescent gel in front of him, growing sharper as it neared: its multiple limbs needle-edged and many-jointed. For an instant he was staring at it face to … whatever. He heard a strange, muffled kind of thud and the thing twitched. It flowed back into the ooze, sinking by tiny degrees. Paladin watched in fascination as it grew indistinct; flinching as something else swam past and snatched the sinking shape away.

"Close enough for you?" Saint-Germain's laconic tones floated up to him. "I'd hate for you to end your days preserved in aspic."

Paladin blinked. He knew the wall had reminded him of something; now he couldn't get that image out of his head. "Gee, thanks a million, Leo."

He started up climbing again. It didn't get easier: each foothold felt like an anvil was tied at his ankle, each knife-blade like it was embedded in concrete. His clothing was heavy with sweat, rubbing his limbs raw. His hair flopped in eyes burning with salt. He wondered why in hell he had to be the hero; couldn't Raven have made the climb? Just floated up to the top with that spear resting over a shoulder? Or Saint-Germain? He tried swearing out his frustration but didn't have the breath. He had to be content with a mental stream of bad language running continually in the background: a broken record.

He paused a moment, dragging in lungfuls of air. Risking a glance down he saw all three staring back up at him: kids' dolls, their expressions too small to be readable. He looked ahead, trying to figure out how far he had still to go. It was impossible.

There was a distant clatter of gunfire, the dead sound of slugs hitting the wall. To his right the goo twitched and quivered; slow ripples undulated against his body. He hadn't seen whatever it was; only too happy those on the ground had.

"*Per adua ad astra!*" The motto was a harsh whisper in his throat. Shaking sweat from his eyes, he set off again.

He was only too aware that he was slowing. Legs and arms were starting to shake. His heart was a trip-hammer, out of control, about to break free of his chest. The burlap bag across his shoulder grew heavier. In the translucent wall, dark shapes welled and sank, never rising close enough for him to see them clearly. Small mercies. There seemed to be more: life in this thick, gelid ocean was more abundant in the shallows. He felt himself smiling at the thought, not that it was all that damned funny.

He was at the top before he realized. Stabbing out with a jack knife he impaled air instead of goo. Blinking to clear sore, blurred eyes, he looked above him: the wall ended only a couple of feet from his head. He stabbed both knives into the peak, hauling himself up with palsied arms. Slowly, he crawled onto a flat surface. He flopped onto his back, a spent, landed fish, and stared blindly at the bronze sky, willing away the shakes. Gradually his heart slowed, his breathing approached normal. Knuckling his eyes, he dashed away most of the sweat and he could see again.

It was like being on the empty deck of a Navy flat-top. The gel spread out for hundreds of yards, almost perfectly smooth, coming to an abrupt end where the black sides of the valley closed in. The surface reflected the sky, making it a plain of polished brass. In its own way, it was beautiful.

"Made it!" Paladin wasn't sure his cracked voice carried too far. He crawled to the edge, looked down at the three tiny figures far below and waved. He thought they may have waved back. He backed away from the edge, not wanting to risk vertigo, and found himself staring down into the pale, wide-eyed face of Professor James Morton Stanley. No more than a foot away, embedded in the ooze.

Paladin froze: this wasn't at all what he'd expected. Then action took over. He slapped the palms of both hands against the opaque surface. It barely gave, merely resonating with all the clarity of a cracked bell. Stanley's pallid face didn't react in any way.

"Jim!" Paladin leaned his mouth so close up to the quivering stuff he could almost taste it. "*Jim!*"

Nothing.

"I'm guessing that's you making all the ruckus." Raven's light, ironic tones hovered in the air just behind Paladin's right ear. *"Is everything okay?"*

"I've found Jim—"

"Well of course you have. Didn't I tell you?" The tone altered, growing serious. *"How is he?"*

"Can't tell. He's stuck in the gloop, a couple of feet down. He's not moving, though. Almost like—"

"Don't go jumping to conclusions, Junior. Come back to the edge: I'm going to throw something up."

"Throw some—?" Paladin bit off his response, slithering back to where the ooze fell away. Below he made out action among the dwarfed group, something moving. Seconds later he saw the Spear of Destiny arrowing straight for him. He rolled aside as the shaft arced past, flopping onto the horizontal surface. There was a rope attached.

"Anchor it, Junior. We're on our way."

Paladin was speechless for a moment. He glared back down the vertical face and yelled furiously. "If you could do that, why in hell did I have to climb?"

"Don't be foolish. Sending it up the wall is one thing, being sure it's anchored quite another. Now: ram it in deeply. We've all seen how reluctant the muck is to letting go. It should be quite firm."

Paladin stared a moment longer, then turned away. What was the use? Before he could take another step, he felt the ooze under his feet vibrate. A sound too deep for him to hear ground at his guts. He looked wildly around. What he saw rearing up over the distant neck of the valley chilled the sweat still soaking his body.

"Better make it fast. We got company!"

X

Raven tugged on the rope. He gave Leigh an encouraging smile. “Ladies first.”

She stared at the thin line. “This too late to admit I’m no great shakes at climbing?” And she already had one hand occupied with her machine gun.

Saint-Germain flicked at an invisible speck on his overcoat. “I wasn’t going to say anything, but I’m not so hot myself.”

Raven chuckled. “Have none of you seen the so-called Indian Rope Trick. Observe.” He grabbed the line with a hand, looping it about his wrist. He did the same with a foot, the line snug around his ankle. With his free hand he gestured up: the rope began to ascend, carrying him along with it.

Saint-Germain leaned close to Leigh and whispered: “Showboating again. Is it in the blood, I wonder?”

For a moment, she didn’t catch his meaning; then she thought: Damy. “Guess so.”

Raven descended, unhooking himself from the rope and gesturing for Leigh to try. She secured both left wrist and ankle, right hand clinging firmly onto her chopper. “Ready when you are, Houdini.”

Raven gestured and the line jerked to life, hauling Leigh slowly off the ground. It wasn’t too uncomfortable. She’d risen around ten feet up when the line paused for Saint-Germain to rope himself on;

Leigh smiled privately at the expression on the count's prim face. They rose another ten feet before Raven added himself.

"I'll pause when you get to the top, Miss Oswin: give you chance to unlimber yourself."

"Too kind, Mr. Raven—"

The rope ascended swiftly. As she rose past the strange cliff-face, Leigh watched carefully for signs of local wildlife. Many shadowy, indistinct shapes drifted by, and several somethings burst from their thick environment: claws and tendrils lashing. Each time Leigh sent them packing with a faceful of lead. From the sporadic gunfire below she guessed that Raven and the count were having fun, too. Maybe because all three were dangling like bait, Leigh thought there was a whole lot more activity than when Damy was climbing, and he'd been slower. There was something frantic about the things; panicky, almost.

The ascent slowed, stopped. Leigh realized she was almost there: just above her head the line had sliced a rut into the clifftop. She threw her gun over the lip, reaching out with her free hand. Something wrapped around her fingers; she almost yelped.

"I got you, princess. Up you come."

Trusting her weight to Damy, she unwound the rope from her ankles, not easy with the combined weight of Raven and Saint-Germain holding it taut. She hauled herself up and over before freeing her left hand. Damy helped her to her feet. As she glanced over his shoulder she saw it: looking higher than the Empire State Building, moving with all the unstoppable force of an avalanche. "What in hell—?"

"Like I said: company." He bent down to pull a complaining Saint-Germain up onto the plain. The count's endless bitching trailed off when he saw it, too.

A towering mass of slowly weaving limbs, it was oozing over the distant black crags: grinding them away like a fast moving glacier. In its wake was a type of flattened, furrowed valley they'd seen before. Something about its countless undulating limbs struck a chord with Leigh, too. By the time Raven had joined them, she knew what it was: each waving limb ended in an appendage that was uncannily like the owl-thing Damy and she had met up with in Vermont.

The monstrous thing had reached the edge of the gelatinous

plain. Not pausing, it plowed on, carving its way through the ooze like it was water. The bizarre, winged branches on its limb-tips dipped down, trawling through the gel. Even at this distance Leigh could see scores of creatures scooped from the gel with each pass, enfolded in the wing-like appendages.

Raven plucked the Spear free, hefting it like a harpooner confronting a whale. "Feeding."

Saint-Germain handed the Browning automatic back to Damy. "Now we know what made the valleys."

Damy nodded, holstering the gun. He pointed at a spot in the smooth plain. "Jim's there, entombed in the crap. I figure—" He glanced at the slowly advancing behemoth. "—I figure we got no more than fifteen minutes to get him out."

The count pursed his lips. "And how do you propose we do that?"

Damy held up both hands. "How do you think?" To Raven he added: "And that outsized toothpick will be handy, too."

The man in black looked affronted. "You mean I should use the Spear of Destiny as an entrenching tool?"

"You got a better idea?" He snatched the weapon from Raven. Reversing it, he drove the tip into the gel, carving it. Leigh was surprised to see how easily the muck fell away from the point, almost as if it was melting.

After a moment, Raven shrugged. "Very well, I'll take it from here."

"Nuh-huh." Damy shook his head. "You're going back to the planes with Leigh—"

Leigh bridled immediately. "Getting me out of the danger zone already?"

Damy leaned on the spear-shaft as he stared at her. "Once we dig Jim out, we need my plane to load him into. Raven can't fly; you can't find the planes on your own."

Leigh opened her mouth to say something, realized she had nothing to say. Instead she shrugged. "Okay." Then something did occur to her. "Say: where do I land?"

Damy gestured at the plain of solid ooze. "Think you can make it?"

She laughed at the sheer craziness of it. "Why not?"

"Then go!" He went back to hewing with the Spear. Raven

took Leigh's arm.

"Close your eyes, your grace. I'm told this can be disconcerting first time."

"Wha—?" The world vanished before she could finish.

XI

"Fifteen minutes might be a little optimistic, don't you think?" Saint-Germain was casually lighting a cigarette, ignoring Paladin as he hacked away at the stuff around James Stanley's body. Paladin paused, glanced at the approaching thing, and went back to work.

"We have time. Just get your hands dirty. For once."

"I fancy my hands are dirtier than yours, old sport."

"I meant literally. Dig!"

Paladin cut slabs of quivering gel out of the plain, grateful it parted so easily at the Spear's touch. The count removed his overcoat and topcoat, folding them neatly, and then rolled back his sleeves.

"Time's a-wasting, Leo!"

Saint-Germain shot him a filthy look before throwing away his cigarette, collapsing the ivory holder and slipping it into a pocket of his dove gray vest. He dropped onto his knees. "This isn't why I came on this jaunt, you know." He levered up a chunk of loose gel and tossed it away.

"Then why did you?"

"Oh… Ennui. Curiosity. Miss Oswin's sake."

Paladin halted, glaring down at Saint-Germain. "Leigh would've been just fine left back in New York—!"

"You'd bet her life on that, would you?"

Paladin bit down on his reply and went back to work.

"For the scion of an Illuminated One you have a very strange perception of how the universe works."

Paladin's breath labored as he forced himself harder and harder. He slashed at the gel like he held a grudge. "Meaning?"

"What you learned back in May has, in some respects already happened." Saint-Germain scooped carefully at a handful of collapsing gel: James Stanley's head was almost exposed. "Only the how of it is open. You can influence that as much as Miss Oswin."

"So did you in bringing her here!"

"In this place she has all of us to watch out for her. Death is not always the end; you know that."

Paladin threw down the Spear. He twisted the count's immaculate necktie. "It's too soon! Leigh shouldn't have to go so young!"

"That's not for you to say." Even though his face was congesting with blood, Saint-Germain spoke diffidently. "Besides, you've overlooked something."

"What?"

The man in gray glanced over Paladin's shoulder. "Ah: they've returned"

Suspecting a trick, Paladin didn't release his choke-hold on Saint-Germain's throat as he turned. Skimming toward them was a Helldiver, wings waggling in celebration. Raven had obviously given the plane a little nudge. Paladin straightened, letting go of the count. He waved back as the Curtiss roared overhead, heading straight for the towering nightmare.

"What is she—?" He realized the moment the words were out: the wind was blowing toward the monstrosity. Leigh was going to have to skim by it to land upwind. And even then it would tricky: how easily could she brake the plane on this surface?

The Helldiver banked steeply; to Paladin it looked like the wingtips almost brushed the face of the towering thing. The colossus ploughed on, oblivious to the gnat buzzing it, even though many of the flailing limbs strained in the dive-bomber's direction. The biplane came straight for Paladin and the count, dropping out of the sky as Leigh cut the engine. It glided onto the plain, bounced three times as it impacted clumsily on the gel and then coasted.

Paladin ran forward to catch a wingtip, grateful the count had thought to do the same. They turned the airplane within feet of the drop. Leigh hopped lightly out of her cockpit, the engine gently idling for a quick getaway. She left Raven to struggle clumsily in the rear.

"How we doing?" She glanced anxiously at the advancing behemoth.

"Time to spare." Paladin wished he actually felt that confident. He strode back to the excavation and starting cutting without another word. Jim's head was clear now, he slid the blade gently around his shoulders. Leigh dropped to her knees and helped the count clear the accumulating debris. Raven leaned in to inspect the professor's pale features. He flicked gel from around Jim's mouth and nose, putting an ear against his nostrils.

Paladin tried not to sound desperate. "How is he?"

Raven's expression was thoughtful. "Can't hear any breathing, but that's hardly surprising." He joined in the dig, raking ooze away with his gloved hands. Slowly the pit grew deeper and wider; Stanley's shoulders were free, then his waist, his knees.

Paladin grew aware of a deep thrashing sound. He risked a look up: the thing was moments away, its arms beating the air. It towered above them, filling half the sky. "It's going to be close."

The look Raven gave him was eloquent: it was going to be more than close.

They doubled their efforts. Stanley's ankles were free; then his feet. They hauled his unresponsive body out of the pit and laid him on the flat surface. Another glance told Paladin they only had seconds left. "We have to stop it."

All of them were incredulous. Saint-Germain shook his head. "With what?"

"We have to lift off!" Paladin was thinking hard. "Leave it any longer and there won't be enough runway!"

"I'm open to suggestions, Junior." Raven looked uncertain.

It hit Paladin: why hadn't he thought of it earlier? He felt in his burlap bag, drawing out the ring old lady Herbesthal had given him. Like it had jumped into his hand. He stared at its concentric rings of blue, red and gold deep it contained, and the vague, shadowy shape writhing deep in the stone's core. Imprisoned by the circles.

His Browning still had a couple of shells left. On sheer impulse he hurled the ring high in the air, drew the automatic and snapped off a shot. The stone shattered, exploding as though something far more potent than a bullet had ripped through it. Paladin staggered as a hurricane scoured the plain. He looked up into a sky which had turned almost totally black, the darkness somehow solid. The two blue suns had vanished. Something huge had risen above the horizon, blotting out the heavens.

The approaching leviathan paused. All of its limbs ceased harvesting the ooze and aimed themselves at the inky sky. The wingtip appendages twitched; red eye-spots glowed, wing-like extensions spread wide, pincered arms and legs spread. Like it was sensing the changes, Paladin thought. Sniffing the air.

He yelled above a wind which showed no signs of dropping. "Princess! This time I *am* getting you out of here! Raven: get back to the second plane. Wait there!"

Leigh forced her face in close to his. "That's what you think, mister! I'm not quitting!"

"Who said you were? Only three can take off in that Helldiver and only two of us can fly it!" He turned away, ignoring the rest of her protests. The howling wind helped some. "Raven! Give us a half hour! If we don't show before then, we're not coming!"

The man in black waited long enough to give Paladin a frank look: he knew the odds. He seized a struggling Leigh around her waist, rapped the Spear once on the plain, and was gone.

Paladin spun to face Saint-Germain. "Help me get Jim into the plane!"

"How—?"

"Just do it!"

Saint-Germain grabbed the unconscious man's legs as Paladin took the shoulders. Off-balance, they staggered against the wind, shuffling awkwardly toward the dive-bomber. Lowering Stanley to the ground, Paladin flicked at catches on the rear fuselage. A panel dropped, revealing a plywood-lined space just large enough for a man. Lifting the professor once more, they slid him inside. Paladin tightened a couple of safety-harnesses around the unconscious form, and then snapped the panel back in place.

"Uncomfortably like a coffin." The count's words were scattered by the rising wind. Paladin checked the sky again: the darkness was growing thicker, congealing. It didn't take much imagination to picture a colossal form, dwarfing even the massive multi-limbed thing paused in the gel, shaping itself out of that utter blackness.

He pointed at the Helldiver's tail section. "We're going to have to drag it!"

"To where?"

"Up close to that thing! We need as much runway as we can get!"

"I always knew you were insane, Paladin!"

"I always thought you had guts, Leo!"

Saint-Germain laughed bitterly as they lifted the tail and started to haul. Two men could normally walk the Helldiver, but in the spiteful wind it bucked and kicked like a kid's kite. Twice the starboard wings lifted and Paladin thought the whole machine was going to flip.

They approached to within fifty yards of the behemoth, well inside the reach of its huge limbs, but it was still distracted by whatever was approaching. Not taking his eyes off the thing rearing from the ooze, Paladin ordered Saint-Germain into the rear cockpit, ignoring pleas concerning the coat and overcoat left back at the cliff-edge. As Paladin vaulted into the pilot seat, the whole gelid plain shuddered; the airplane skidded sideways, the nose turning a little to the right. Paladin looked over his shoulder: the congealed blackness reached out for the multi-limbed behemoth. There was a suggestion of talons; of jagged teeth, brimstone eyes.

"We've overstayed our welcome!" Paladin opened up the Helldiver's throttle. The dive-bomber jittered and skated over the smooth, heaving surface. The cliff-edge raced up to meet them. At the last moment, Paladin hauled back on the stick, embedding it in his guts. The plane spilled over the edge.

It plunged for the scoured valley below. Paladin kept the stick back, screaming encouragement as though sheer willpower could get the machine level. Too late, it seemed, the nose began to lift. The engine roared, about to tear itself free. Then they were level, rising. Paladin thought he heard the landing gear scraping the ground. But they were up. They were flying.

Safely in the air, he risked a look back. It was a scene from a Doré painting. A suffocating, thick blackness, shot through with blood-red light, stooped over the thing in the ooze. A multitude of limbs thrashed and gouged at the darkness, ripping away shreds which boiled like filthy smoke. It became impossible to distinguish where one thing ended and another began. The plain of ooze and the cliff face were crushed under a writhing, tearing mass of glistening, fiery black.

Paladin's words were almost a prayer. "Thank you Anna Roosendaal. And thank you old lady Herbesthal—"

He turned the Helldiver toward the rendezvous with Leigh and Raven.

XII

Leigh watched Damy's plane land ungracefully. Her first reaction was to rush up, pull him from the seat, and hug him. Her second was to haul him out of the same seat and kick him nine ways come Saturday. In the end, relief won out.

She reached the Helldiver just as he was hopping to the ground. He gave her a tired ghost of a smile, but took more interest in removing a panel in the fuselage of his plane. Saint-Germain, looking distinctly undressed in vest and shirt-sleeves, helped in unstrapping and removing the motionless body of James Stanley: laying him carefully on the rough ground. Leigh dropped to her knees. The man was still staring blindly at nothing, apparently lifeless. "Is he going to be okay?"

Damy sighed. "I hope so, princess. Raven?"

The man in black knelt at Damy's side, removed a glove, and ran his fingers over Stanley's waxen features. He reached inside a shirt stiff with drying gel, feeling for the heart. He sat back on his heels. "He appears to be in a form of self-induced, catalytic state. Most likely a Dhuranghur Trance."

Saint-Germain shook his head. "That would only sustain him for a day. Two at the most…"

Raven nodded. "Leading us to one conclusion—"

"Can you get him out of it?" Damy seemed impatient.

"Of course, Junior. The work of a moment. But he'll be pretty disorientated when he comes to. Be prepared." He removed his second glove, rubbed his palms together, and placed them on Stanley's temples. Leigh couldn't make out what he was muttering, but it didn't sound English. It didn't sound like too much of anything. Raven leaned forward and seemed to whisper intimately in Stanley's left ear. A moment later the fixed stare relaxed. Stanley's eyelids fluttered; he blinked. He drew in a deep, hoarse breath—

—And jerked upright with a shriek that made Leigh's scalp crawl.

Raven held him gently by the shoulders, talking softly and reassuringly. Damy leaned forward, his face gaunt with worry. "Jim? Jim, are you okay? It's me. Dami— Dexter. Dexter Phillips."

Stanley's wild eyes focused on Damy, softened. He grinned; suddenly very handsome. "Dex? Is that you, old man? That was damned quick!"

Paladin grabbed Stanley's right hand in his own, throwing his left arm around his shoulder. "Quick? It's been thirty years!"

"The Dhuranghur Trance, remember: no more than two days." Raven stood, dusting at the knees of his pants. "Time obviously travels at a different rate, here."

Stanley came unsteadily to his feet, aided by Damy. He looked around at the faces of his rescuers, dazed and unfocussed. Leigh was sure his broad, handsome smile grew broader when he spotted her. "So what year is this?"

"Back in New York it's 1935." Leigh reached out a hand, ignoring the smell of decaying gel wafting off the professor. "I'm Leigh Oswin. Guess you know everyone else?"

Stanley wiped his palms on his pants before taking her hand. He kissed the back of it. "Enchanted, Miss Oswin. It *is* Miss, I hope?" After a moment he released his grip. "And yes, I am familiar with the rest of your party."

Damy and Raven helped Professor Stanley back into the hole in the fuselage. Leigh warmed up the engines on the second Helldiver. She watched as they secured the side panel. "Is he going to be all right in there?"

Damy gave her a pallid smile. "Compared to what he's been through already, it'll be a cakewalk."

Raven briefly rested a hand on her shoulder. "He'll sleep, Miss Oswin. Believe it or not, that's just what he needs right now." He walked up to Leigh's plane and hauled himself clumsily on board.

Damy took Leigh's hands; she wondered what in hell he was about to say. "Take the lead, princess. Raven will do his voodoo again and I'll be right behind. Don't stop until we're back at Chaykin Field."

She stared at him, hard, trying to figure what he wasn't saying. The last step would be a walk in the park, surely? "What about this time difference your pal mentioned?"

"That's a smart question, princess." He frowned. "I'm sure he's thought about it. I hope…"

"Attaboy—keep making it up as you go. Next stop: New York."

He looked like he wanted say something more, but pinched his mouth tight, gave her another pat on the arm and climbed on board. As Saint-Germain pulled himself into the rear seat, Damy waved her back.

"Fine. Let's dangle." Leigh hurried to the second plane, got herself strapped in and comfortable. She yelled at Raven above the engine noise. "You all set?"

"Not really."

She grinned to herself and gunned the engine. The Helldiver lurched forward, jolting over the uneven ground. They made it into the air without breaking anything. Checking over her shoulder, Leigh watched as Damy's Curtiss lifted off safely. Everything was copacetic. She opened up the throttle, easing back on the stick. The Helldiver rose eagerly. From behind, she was sure she heard Raven's heartfelt groan.

She spotted the thick, cloudy something ahead, recognizing it immediately. The floating mass with barbed fish-hooks they'd had to dodge on arrival. That or its twin. Leigh turned her head a little, raising her voice.

"You about ready to get us home, Mandrake?"

Raven leaned his head close to hers. "We're not in position yet! We need to get as close to the original incursion point as possible!"

"And how will I know?"

"I'll tell you!"

"Swell." The mass of cloud was spread across half the sky.

Going round would waste time and gas. Same as before: they'd go under.

She waved an arm to get Damy's attention, pointing to the black ground with an exaggerated gesture. The other plane waggled its wings. Leigh dropped her plane's nose, ignoring Raven's complaints. He could take it up with her later. She took the diver-bomber to within feet of the jagged surface, imagining the tires almost brushing the razor edges. She had to fly by the seat of her pants: banking, climbing, twisting the plane out of trouble. It was like skimming a forest canopy back home, except these trees could slice the Helldiver in half.

They were under the churning, cloudy mass. If she strained her eyes real hard, Leigh imagined she could just see the fine threads of the hooked lines dangling above her: spread out in an all but invisible curtain. They moved of their own accord, dipping and snatching, but she was pretty sure she was out of range.

Something like a barbed eagle's talon tore across her plane's upper wing, ripping through wood like old tissue. Leigh jinked the plane to the right, and then the left.

"What the hell?" Raven sounded outraged.

Leigh yelled back. "Sorry. That thing's got a longer reach than I thought!" Less cocky, she divided her time between ground and sky: checking if any more of those deadly hooks were close. She spotted several and threw the Helldiver crazily about, somehow dodging them without cracking up on the needle-sharp ground.

Something flashed blindingly white above and behind her. And again. Raven, she realized: using that fancy javelin of his to hack away at anything coming too close. Well fine; if nothing else it took his mind off his flight-sickness.

Around a dozen snares twitched and snatched at the air in front of them: a final gauntlet to run. Leigh opened up her guns even though there was little chance of hitting such fine threads. She dodged and wove across the suddenly crowded sky, forgetting all about the ground. Lines and their deadly hooks were all that concerned her.

Jagged rents appeared in the top wing, trailing splinters; so fast she didn't even see what caused them. Too late to dodge, she just piled on the revs and prayed.

And they were free.

Leigh risked a glance back: the cloud-like thing was behind them. They'd made it. Damy's plane, skidding through the air like its pilot was insane, less than a hundred yards behind. She looked at Raven's pale, relieved face, and grinned like a loon. She raised a thumb.

"We made it—!"

At first there was no pain: just a punch like she'd been clobbered by a freight train. She glanced down and saw it protruding from her stomach, dark with her blood: a huge, wickedly-barbed talon.

XIII

Paladin saw Leigh was in trouble. Even though her plane had to be free of the cloud-creature's hooks and snares, it was wallowing like a drunken whale. Raven was half-standing in the rear cockpit, thrashing with the Spear. It spat violet lightning; drizzled white sparks.

Paladin opened up the throttle, racing the leading plane. Even though it was going full-out, its erratic flight lost it headway. Leigh's Helldiver rose and fell: a ship foundering on vast, invisible waves. Paladin pulled alongside, wingtips almost touching, putting himself in as much danger as Leigh. A sudden side-slip and her kite would plough straight into his. He could see her slumped in the cockpit, head bobbing with the plane's motion. Raven had unbuckled himself and was leaning forward, checking on her.

Paladin yelled her name out loud, even though he knew she couldn't hear him.

"I'm sorry." Raven's voice rang clear and level in Paladin's head. *"One of those barbed hooks— Neither of us saw it—"*

"How is she?" Even though he feared the worst, Paladin had to ask.

"Not good. She's conscious; even flying the plane, somehow." Raven's figure straightened; he seemed to be looking for something. *"I'm going to start the translation. We're close enough."*

"Can she survive?" There was no reply; Paladin yelled the question again.

"Do we have a choice?" Raven's tone was unequivocal.

A pallid glow oozed around the frame of Leigh's biplane. Balls of strange light guttered at wingtips and flickered around its tires. The plane began to rise: slowly and clumsily at first; gradually accelerating as it soared up from the beckoning ground and into the comparative safety of a clear sky. Paladin climbed his own biplane to keep pace.

"Is— Is Leigh—?"

"She's fading. I'm pulling the machine up as far as I can, but once I start on the translation I'll have to let go. We'll be gliding—"

"Crashing!"

"Gliding, Junior. Have faith."

A glowing crucifix, Leigh's Curtiss rose higher in the bizarre atmosphere. Paladin divided his attention between her kite and his altimeter. It was reading close on 10,000 feet when the glow around Leigh's plane snapped off. If the nose dipped at all, Paladin couldn't tell. Matching course and height, his own plane remained steady.

The sky ahead began to twist and fragment. Brutal tears ripped through the growing vortex, throbbing with nameless color. Raven stood in the observer's cockpit, Spear aloft. He was bathed in a writhing spectrum of colors that didn't belong in a sane universe. They spread, engulfing first Leigh's plane and then Paladin's. Both machines appeared to shatter, then re-assemble; in their wake they left a staccato trail of identical airplanes: flickering and burning, gradually fading.

Both aircraft fell into the vortex.

Paladin knew that vast imagery and symbolism was projected against a bruised background, just like before; but he had eyes only for Leigh's sagging shape. "C'mon, princess. Hold it together." He knew he was repeating the words: a desperate mantra.

Despite the violence swirling all around them, sounds were muted. Even the engines were muffled: coming from a thousand miles away. Paladin was aware of Saint-Germain's own silence, and he was more than grateful. If the count had said one word, Paladin was pretty sure he'd have tossed him overboard.

When the light changed, Paladin was concentrating so hard on Leigh that it took him a second to notice. He glanced up at a brooding purple sky already lightening to the east. Before them was the island of Manhattan. Dawn was breaking. They'd made it.

Leigh's machine was slowly losing height: nose slightly down in a flat dive. It was gentle at the moment; Paladin had no idea how long that would last. A quick check showed him Leigh's head was slumped forward, motionless. In the rear cockpit Raven had collapsed, no doubt on the brink of exhaustion. No help there. They were heading away from Chaykin Field. Even if Leigh's plane did manage to glide safely down, where could they land?

Abruptly, her plane tipped to the right, port wings caught in an up-current. The nose dropped and the Curtiss began to spin lazily, corkscrewing toward the ground. Paladin dived after it, though there was nothing he could do. The only ideas he had were insane, suicidal; he'd wind up killing all of them.

"Raven!" He'd never been so desperate in his life; never needed his father's help so badly. "Raven!"

"Please don't yell, Junior. I have a terrific headache!"

"You're crashing! Can't you do anything?"

"Sure. I'll just learn to fly in the next couple of minutes—"

"Raven!" How could the man be so infuriating?

"Sorry, Junior. Bad habit." The pallid glow spread around the Helldiver again: fainter, flickering; Raven still in a semi-collapse. The biplane's nose came up. It turned out of the spin, no longer plummeting.

"I'd appreciate a little quiet now, I have to concentrate."

Paladin forced himself to relax. It was in Raven's hands now, just how the man in black liked it. A hand fell on Paladin's shoulder. He jerked, heart lurching. It was Saint-Germain in the rear cockpit, offering some kind of solace. "You know he can do it."

Paladin steeled himself against the attempted comfort: he wanted nothing from the count. "For your sake, he'd better!"

Leigh's plane dropped confidently, almost as if she was piloting it. Occasionally the sickly glow faltered, the nose or a wingtip would dip; but after a moment the corona flared back, and the Curtiss stabilized. Manhattan grew wider, larger; its streets and avenues clearer. Purple shadows stretched westwards along the streets, bisecting the avenues.

From behind, Paladin heard Saint-Germain draw in a hard breath. He didn't want to know, whatever it was. All his attention was on the plane ahead: homing in on one of the world's busiest metropolises. They weren't losing height any more: New York's high-rises and brownstones were swooping up to meet them. He had a flashback to the place they'd just left, and the black forest of deadly-sharp rocks.

The glow around Leigh's plane sputtered out; the Helldiver dipped its right wings, turning clumsily. It was heading due east before the spectral light flickered back on and Paladin breathed again. The plane had also lined itself up perfectly with one of the city's east-west streets. If traffic was light … maybe.

Raven must have thought the same. Somehow he slowed the biplane, bringing it down in what looked like a textbook landing. Paladin stayed back, circling a couple of hundred feet up, watching. Luckily there was no early-morning traffic, and only a few baffled pedestrians on the sidewalks. The landing plane glided toward a brick and concrete canyon, catching up to its shadow.

"Easy." Paladin craned from his cockpit, chewing his lip. "Easy."

Within fifty feet on the street, the glow enfolding the plane took once last flicker, and died. Paladin told himself it was fine: it would glide in from there. But the nose dropped; the tail flicked high. It fell toward the street, scattering gawkers. Smacking into the asphalt, the Helldiver bounced, lurched to one side. A streetlight tore through the left wings, spinning the whole airplane round. It smashed across the sidewalk, impacted against a shop-front, losing the tail section. With a final shudder, it collapsed to a stop.

Paladin dived straight down. He dropped his kite onto the street with a force that should have shattered the landing gear. He cut the engine and had his straps undone before the plane had come to a halt, vaulting from his seat. When he reached Leigh's cracked-up machine there was already a small crowd gathered, helping Raven from his seat. Leigh was laid out on the sidewalk: still and white. A scimitar-tip talon reared out of blood-stained clothing.

Paladin dropped to his knees and cradled her head. "Princess—!" She was cold; her limbs flopped like a rag doll's.

"Junior."

Paladin glanced up, blinking. Raven was limping toward him: clothes ripped and dusty, face ashen. But he'd be fine; he always was. "I'm sorry."

"Yeah—"

"Gentlemen, are we going to kneel in the dust in self-pity? Or do you intend to save this girl's life?"

Paladin squinted into the rising sun: it was framed perfectly by the street's buildings, shining directly east to west. "What?"

A silhouette shifted out of the orange glare: Saint-Germain. He was holding something in a hand. "It's December 5th: an auspicious date for this city. At sunrise it mimics a megalithic observatory, like England's Stonehenge. By accident, I'm told." He knelt by Leigh's lifeless form. "Heralding a new beginning. New birth."

"Go to hell—" Paladin bent over Leigh, his vision blurring again.

Saint-Germain shoved his hand under Paladin's nose. Two shapes cradled in his palm: two ugly figurines. "Remember that night in The Bowery? She walked the Tangential Gate; defied the *genius termini*. From that moment her life was changed, made special. She has straddled two worlds; still has a foot in each."

"What are you saying?" He didn't want to look at the ugly carvings, but he couldn't drag his eyes away.

Saint-Germain sighed in irritation. "Raven: explain it to him."

Paladin felt his father crouching at his side. "I knew there was something about her first time we met, Junior. If Leo's right, we can still save her."

"How?" Paladin was hardly listening.

"She needs to pass through the Gate again. Be brought back."

Paladin swallowed and stared Raven full in the face. "If you're lying. If either of you—!"

"Trust me, Junior. And trust Leo, for once." Raven got to his feet and stepped away. Paladin looked down again at Leigh's waxen features. He gulped a breath, before scooping her limp body in his arms. He lurched to his feet, grateful for Raven's steadying touch. The street still framed the rising sun perfectly. Saint-Germain was kneeling on the opposite sidewalk, placing a figurine on the curb. The first was already in place, just a few feet away from where Paladin stood.

Raven walked toward the closest figurine, the Spear in his hand. He waited for the count to step away from the second before dipping the ancient lance, brushing the ugly carving with its tip. Then he crossed the street, and touched the second carving. Stepping back, he turned to Paladin and nodded.

Paladin stepped off the sidewalk. As he faced the sun its rays reflected off the tiny figures, flaring to an eye-watering brilliance. Sprays of light fountained off the sidewalks, arching across the street, forming a Tangential Gate. The archway was flooded by an opalescent light, tinged by the rising sun. He heard a distant roar: the sound of planets grinding against the matter of space. He took a step toward it.

The orange light swirled; reached out eagerly for his burden. Glowing tendrils enfolded him, wrapped themselves intimately around Leigh, tugging at her. He staggered at the embrace, almost falling to one knee, but kept his balance and stepped through the Gate.

Sparks flared; lava poured over them both; gales frigid as Hell tore at him. Voices from throats a thousand miles high deafened him. Leigh seemed to grow lighter, like she was being raised from his grasp, even as he grew heavier. Another step. He looked down at Leigh: the strange light gave her face an illusionary flush; its flickering imparted movement where he knew there was none. And another, harder step. Leigh felt insubstantial as mist. Paladin weighed a ton. From where it was embedded in her torso, the blood-caked talon glowed white-hot, then flashed away like rice paper in a candle flame. Yet another step. He could barely lift his feet: the whole world was anchored around his ankle. Leigh was a ghost, no heavier than a memory. One more step—

—And he was standing in a deserted street, a pale yellow winter sun now far above the horizon. He felt its thin warmth.

In his arms, Leigh shifted.

Paladin stared. Though her clothing was shredded and bloody, the hole ripped by the talon was little more than a puckered, pink scar. After a moment, even that faded. She groaned and opened her eyes. "Damy?"

He almost dropped her. "Princess! I thought—!" He lowered her to her feet. She looked around, dazed, fingering her ruined leather coat.

"What in hell happened? I thought—" She shook her head, coming out of a dream. Paladin said nothing, enjoying the moment. He didn't know how he could explain it, anyway. Raven led Leigh away; past a small group of people who were staring as though they'd witnessed the second coming.

"Did I miss something?" James Stanley was awake and yawning, stretching thin arms. He scrubbed at matted hair and looked around, baffled. Paladin stifled an urge to giggle.

"Here." Saint-Germain dropped two charred lumps into Paladin's hands. "Completely futzed, I'm afraid." He glanced at Stanley and tapped a finger to his forehead. "Professor." He took a step before reconsidering. "Miss Oswin is a lucky woman, Paladin. And unique. I'm not sure what we've done here; what we've made. But I'll be sure to come back and check." He walked away, fussing at his awry collar and flapping shirt-sleeves, the sun on his back.

Stanley clapped Paladin on the back. "I think there's one hell of a story here, Dex old man. And one day I'll let you tell me. But meanwhile— "He took Paladin's hand and squeezed it. "Thanks for coming back for me."

Paladin was watching Leigh: someone had rustled up coffee, handing cups to both her and Raven. A couple of kids were playing around the wrecked Helldiver, laughing. He could hear sirens in the distance.

"It's good to have you back." He scrubbed at his face with filthy gauntlets. "Both of you."

ABOUT THE AUTHOR

Mike Chinn lives in Birmingham, UK, with his wife Caroline and their tribe of guinea pigs. In 2012 he took early retirement so he could spend more time writing. Over the years he has published over sixty short stories, as well as editing three volumes of THE ALCHEMY PRESS BOOK OF PULP HEROES, and SWORDS AGAINST THE MILLENNIUM, also for The Alchemy Press. His own contribution to the Pulp Adventure genre, THE PALADIN MANDATES garnered two nominations for the British Fantasy Award in 1999. In 2015, his Sherlock Holmes steampunk mash-up, VALLIS TIMORIS (Fringeworks), sent the famous detective to the Moon. He has two collections of short stories in print: GIVE ME THESE MOMENTS BACK (2015 The Alchemy Press) and RADIX OMNIUM MALUM (2017 Parallel Universe Publications).

47811325R00168

Made in the USA
Middletown, DE
02 September 2017